Unhallowed Graves

By

Nuzo Onoh

D1556410

CSP

Unhallowed Graves

First published by Canaan-Star Publishing, United Kingdom. www.canaan-star.co.uk

This book is a work of fiction. Names and characters are the product of the author's imagination. Any resemblance to actual persons living or dead is entirely coincidental.

A Catalogue record for this book is available from the British Library.

ISBN: 978-1-909484-85-6

Book cover by Eugene Rijn R. Saratorio Printed and bound in United Kingdom by Lightning Source, (UK) Ltd.

Dedication

This book is dedicated to the tragic souls *of Igbo Landing* situated at Dumber Creek in St Simon's Island, USA, who made the ultimate sacrifice in May, 1803, opting for mass suicide by drowning rather than be taken into slavery.

Kinsmen, your bones shall rise again....one day.

About The Author

Nuzo Cambridge Onoh is a British writer of African heritage. Born in Enugu, in the Eastern part of Nigeria (formerly known as The Republic of Biafra), she lived through the civil war between Biafra and Nigeria (1967 – 1970), an experience that left a strong impact on her and continues to influence her writing to date.

She attended Queen's school, Enugu, Nigeria, before proceeding to the Quaker boarding school, The Mount School, York, (England) and finally, St Andrew's Tutorial college, Cambridge, (England) from where she obtained her A' levels. Nuzo holds both a Law degree and a Masters Degree in Writing from Warwick University, (England).

Her book, *The Reluctant Dead* (2014), introduced modern African Horror into mainstream Horror genre. She sometimes writes under the pseudonym, Alex Stranger-Onoh. Nuzo has two daughters, Candice and Jija, plus her cat, Tinkerbell, and lives in Coventry, England.

Acknowledgment

To my great friend, editor, critic, motivator, advisor and all-round literary partner, Edward (Ted) Dunphy, whose hard work has given this book its final polish. *Irish,* I truly thank you.

To my wonderful cousin, Ike Onoh (Ogbodo-Efungwu), who taught me the lore, superstitions, beliefs and practices of our people and gave me the material to work with. Ike, you are the best. I'm honoured to call you "family". Thank you.

To my dear friend, Peter Stephenson (OBE), who gave me both the idea and the lore behind *Night Market* and has always advised, encouraged and supported my writing. Peter, this story is as much yours as it's mine. I owe you a drink…and much, much more. Thank you.

And to Robert (Bob) & Anne Morritt, the best Canadians on God's earth. Guys, you've encouraged me to write and to take better care of myself in mind and body. Your positive words and zany jokes have cheered me no end. Anne, your critique was amazing. I thank you, dear friends…and not forgetting THE CATS.

Contents

The Unclean

"There is nothing the eyes will see that will cause them to shed blood-tears" – Igbo Proverb

Unhallowed Graves

Ukari Forest - 9pm

My husband's corpse lies on the raffia mat, spread underneath the giant Iroko tree that towers over the thick vegetation of Ukari Forest. The Iroko tree is legendary in the ten clans of Ukari and even beyond. Its broad branches reach up to the skies, fighting for airspace with the eagles and the kites. Its circumference covers at least eight arms-length of marriage-age men. Its roots are so swollen they escape the depths of the earth, projecting barked talons that crawl across the forest, staking its territory and frightening the rest of the vegetation to a cowering distance. The other trees in the forest hug themselves tight, stealing the sunlight from the skies while bowing their leafy obeisance to the Iroko tree, paying homage to their great lord, just as the humans of Ukari village kneel to it.

All is still. Nothing breaks the grave-like silence of the vast forest. Apart from the occasional snake or lizard, no other creature stirs in the perennial gloom of this accursed forest. From my kneeling position by my late husband's body, I force my bloodied eyes to look upon his reviled face, coal-dusted by death and decay. His features, swarthy and harsh, have not yielded their cruelty to death. The white cloth shrouding his bloated body is stained with the death fluids seeping from his fast decomposing body.

In the two nights I've spent in the forest with my husband's corpse, I have been unable to keep my eyes from his face....and IT. *I feel its malignancy, the threat in its unnatural turgidity. I live in terror of what* IT *would do to me should I take my gaze away from its terrible erectness.*

I look away, return my gaze to his face. My body shudders yet again, expecting those swollen lids to lift, his cold eyes promising harsh retribution for sins I can never recollect. Yet, I cannot escape. I am rooted to my husband's side by limb-freezing terror. My heart leaps into my mouth, filling it with bile and panic each time the trees stir, the dry leaves rustle or an owl hoots his midnight vigil from a distant tree. Had I slept, my dreams would have been dreams of escape, freedom - and peace. But I am forbidden that relief, chained as I am to my husband's corpse by the witch-doctors' powerful incantations and the customs of our land.

I am a prisoner in a jail without bars. I am the condemned, convicted before her trial. I am the accused, facing her judgement at the one-man jury in the court of the great Iroko tree, known to the villagers as The Tree of Truth. The Tree of Truth is the final arbiter in every dispute in the village, the righteous judge and jury that condemns and sentences with ruthless efficiency. It is said that none who is guilty ever escapes its merciless justice. Its roots are swollen with the blood and cries of its victims, men, women and even children, accused of crimes ranging from witchcraft to night-flying.

And I, Desdemona, first daughter of Ukah, wife of Agu of Onori Clan, have joined that wretched fraternity of The Tree. I am a condemned criminal awaiting my fate beneath the unforgiving leaves of The Tree of Truth.

As I prepare to endure my third and final night by the side of the putrid body of my late husband, I know with a feeling of total despair that my ordeal is far from over. Even if by some unbelievable stroke of fortune The Tree of Truth rejects my blood; if by some divine intervention my husband's vengeful spirit fails to strike me dead by dawn as is widely expected in our village, I could yet be dispatched to my own ancestors' hell by a myriad of foes, too strong, too powerful, for a mere widow to resist.

For, I am the most accursed of widows. I am a widow without offspring, cursed with the womb of a man, my belly filled with soured eggs that will never again yield the precious fruit of a child. Even worse, I am a widow without a son,

11

left without protection like a day-old baby abandoned in the middle of an African thunderstorm, exposed to the flings and thumps of the merciless force of nature.

For my failure to provide my husband with an heir and name-protector; for my desperate and foolish attempts to produce that precious gift; for my own mad folly and ignorance, I will pay with my life when the cock crows in the dawn and his relatives came to extract the life from beneath my chest - my coward's heart, my foolish heart.

*****

I married Agu a few months after I turned seventeen, just one year past the age of female wisdom. It was a time of great changes in our country. More of our men wore suits and ties like the white masters. We had more black doctors and teachers than ever before. It was a time when people said the white men would give us back our land and they would return to their own. I remember that day as if it were burnt into my skin like the dark birthmark on Mama's stomach. The calendar in our parlour had the year, 1953, stamped on it. It also had pictures of our new ruler, Queen Elizabeth 11, on all its twelve pages. There used to be pictures of the king. But the king was dead and the queen now owned our lands and calendars.

Agu arrived at our house one rainy day, as we made to prepare Papa's lunch of *yam fufu* and bush-meat soup. From the corrugated zinc roofing of our bungalow, I could hear the steady roar of the sudden mid-day storm, which made me crave for my bed and a novel in the solitude of the bedroom I shared with my sister, Gono. Instead, I was stuck in the smoke-clouded kitchen, attempting to keep the kerosene stove going, while wiping the onion-induced tears from my eyes.

The kitchen door flew open and my little brother, Ibe, rushed in, all excitement and glee, knocking over Mama's wooden stool in his haste.

'Desee, Papa wants you now,' his eyes were wide with what seemed like awe, his voice pitched like a girl's. I wondered what had given the sudden animation to his customary indolent disposition. Ibe took his role as the only son very seriously. And both Papa and Mama made sure we, the daughters, recognised and respected his privileged status as "heir," regardless of our superiority in both age and intellect. I had already passed out of senior school with grades that were good enough to secure me a teaching apprenticeship at the village primary school. My sister, Gono, also seemed certain to follow in my footsteps.

But Ibe, despite the attention and praise lavished on him by our parents and family at large, never succeeded in producing a report card that could make any teacher or parent proud. Yet, Papa would insist on giving him the chair of honour in the family living room, right next to grandfather's stone grave, while Mama would chant her "hero song" whenever he sneezed, coughed or even farted, her face glowing with a mixture of pride, determination and a sad kind of martyrdom that left one wondering why she'd even bothered giving birth to her precious son in the first place.

"Jealous people, leave my tiger alone,
Envious people, look at my prize,
Evil people, turn your eyes from my son,
My hero, my solace, my king."

And well might she praise the little sod, since without his timely appearance, Papa would have replaced her with a second wife to produce the much-wanted heir and "name-protector." As Papa was fond of telling my sister and me, a woman has no name, no religion, no country, no custom and no honour except that given her by a man, a husband. Ibe's name said it all - clansmen,

14

brothers! Ibe was the only one amongst us given an Igbo name, showing how valued he was. We, the girls, had been left to the mercy of poor Mama when it came time for name selection. She in turn had turned to her "learncd" brother, uncle Silas, who had promptly lumbered us with the most high-faluting names imaginable, courtesy of one Mr Shakespeare of England. Everyone knew me as Day-see-mona (Desee, for short), except my schoolteachers, who had struggled in my student years to read out *Desdemona* in the class register every morning. My younger sister was known as Gono to everyone, but diligently wrote her full name in her textbooks - *Goneril.*

'Desee, hurry up or Papa will get angry with you,' Ibe was almost hopping by the open kitchen door. I heard a grunt and turned to look at Gono, who had stopped pounding the *yam fufu* in the wooden mortar as soon as Ibe made his announcement. Her brows dipped in a frown of displeasure. I was unsure who her anger was directed against - Ibe or Papa, both of whom she loathed with equal intensity.

'What does he want with Desee?' Gono barked at Ibe. 'Can't he see we're busy preparing lunch for you two bigheads?' she shot Ibe a look that dripped with contempt, her body, wiry and small, as tense as a featherweight boxer's in a

15

boxing ring. Aggression emitted from every pore in her body as she stood clutching the long wooden pestle. She looked as if she intended to bash in someone's head with it.

Ibe looked at her and quickly averted his eyes. 'I don't know,' he mumbled, slinking out of the kitchen, but not before I caught a shifty look in his eyes that convinced me he was lying - as usual. That boy would lie to God Himself if he ever made it to St Peter's gates. Gono was the only one amongst us - Papa included - who inspired some form of fear in the lout. Gono's temper was notorious in the five clans and many had already predicted she would remain a spinster with her harridan's temperament - a fact that pleased rather than dismayed her. Even Papa avoided sending her on errands, at least, as much as he could without appearing weak. Gono was the only one of his children that never cried when he took the birch to her.

I entered the sitting room, hard on Ibe's heels, to see two strangers, both men, seated on the whitewashed wooden benches that circled our sitting room. Each of the strangers, including Papa, cradled a ceramic mug of palm-wine in their hands, while a brimming cup of the brew was placed atop my grandfather's raised grave positioned in the centre of the parlour. Papa never drank palm wine without offering some to my grandfather. I did a small curtesy to the seated strangers and a deeper one to my grandfather's grave.

'Aahh! Desee, come sit down my daughter,' Papa patted the chair of honour, the seat next to his own and nearest to the elevated rectangular grave, Ibe's special chair! Papa's face beamed with a benevolence I'd only ever witnessed when he addressed Ibe. More worryingly, he had called me Desee, instead of his habitual "*Agbogho*" - girl. Something was clearly wrong. My heart was thudding as I took the proffered seat, ignoring Ibe's displeased frown as he settled for the little stool by the snuff table.

'These gentlemen are from Ukari,' Papa said, with a nod at the strangers. I glanced up quickly and lowered my eyelids just as rapidly, to preserve my modesty. 'They've come a long way indeed to see us, or should I say, to see you, my daughter.' Papa chuckled in a manner that could have been interpreted as coy had he been a woman. I wanted to hide my face beneath the thin fabric of my yellow cotton dress; such was my discomfiture.

'Yes indeed. We have travelled a six-hour journey to come and view your famed beauty,' I heard one of the men say, the old grey one. The oily quality to his voice repelled me. I felt the heat of embarrassment on my face, at the same time feeling a sudden prick of apprehension at the back of my neck.

'Our son here is Agu, son of Onori of the Onori clan,' the old man continued. His hair was sprinkled with ash, as were his bushy brows and thick beard, giving him the look of a grey-dappled hyena. But despite the whites in his hair, I could tell he wasn't an old man, merely prematurely grey, as happens on occasion with certain reincarnations. I felt my soul reject his at first sight, a clear sign we had been antagonists in a previous incarnation. Something in his ferocious gaze wilted my spirit and I kept my eyes downcast.

'Agu is a prosperous trader and travels as far as *Ugwu-Hausa*, the Moslem northern territories, to buy and sell various foodstuff,' continued grey hyena, nodding at the young man next to him. 'In fact, Agu owns the only storey building in our village and a Mercedes Benz, which you can see parked outside your father's compound.' His voice was oiled with pride. Instinctively, I glanced out of the open curtainless window, as did Ibe, to see a white car - a large silver-wheeled car - getting washed by the pouring rain outside our compound. Papa feigned

18

disinterest, though I could read a gleam in his eyes that indicated otherwise to me. But he was a proud man and I guess he deserved his dignity. A bicycle, even an almost new British Raleigh that had cost him a handsome sum, could never compete with a Benz.

'As we were telling your good father before you came in, we'd heard of the famed beauty of the white chicken he housed beneath his roof. So, we decided to rush in and express our interest in purchasing that white chicken before others, less worthy, beat us to the market,' the grey one smiled at me, a front tooth missing. I quickly averted my gaze and glued my eyes to my hands, which had suddenly started trembling as if I'd been struck down with malaria. 'Your father has been very kind in indicating his willingness to sell us his precious chicken. So we thought it was a good time for you to meet your future husband, Agu, before we begin formal negotiations for the marriage rites. After all, a girl must be allowed some choice in these matters even though the ultimate decision rests with her esteemed father - and rightly so,' Grey Hyena gave a small chuckle, which was echoed by Papa and even that little idiot, Ibe.

I felt the racing of my heart. *Some choice indeed!* It was as I had feared. Papa was marrying me off to a complete stranger. And just as I was about to complete my apprenticeship and progress to full teacher status. I felt the sting of tears in my eyes as my palms broke out in hot sweat. I wanted to get up and run out of that crowded room with the stuffy odour of strange bodies and palm-wine. But fear of Papa's wrath and a cramp of embarrassment kept me glued onto Ibe's special seat. I forced my eyes up and took my first proper look at my future husband, Agu.

What I saw was a man, short of stature and lacking in bulk. Age-wise, he was in the peak of his manhood, somewhere between thirty and forty years. It was difficult to tell his exact age because of his small size. He was dressed in an *Agbada*, a loose native garb covered in an assortment of animal prints. His hair was trimmed close to his skull, giving him an almost bald look. Sat next to his older relative on our wooden bench, his head barely reached Grey Hyena's shoulders. Yet, there was a carriage to his head, an arrogance of bearing that marked him as the leader despite his puny size. He was dark, very black-skinned, like the Enugu coal miners at the end of their work shift beneath the bowels of the earth. His eyes were small, closely set. There was an expression in them that reminded me of the eyes of the frozen fish heads we used in cooking Papa's chilli pepper-soup. Their black depths betrayed little emotion as they settled on my person; just the detached assessment of a trader inspecting some ware before making final purchase. Even when he smiled at me as our eyes briefly met for the first time, there was no gentling in his pupils or his lips - thin, fleshless lips - unusual in a native of our country. Something about him frightened me, placed a cold hand over my heart, a silent terror that didn't subside even after I got up and noticed how I towered over him by at least three fingers' length.

Instinctively, I hunched my shoulders, feeling ashamed of my tall slenderness, emphasised into giant proportions by his small stature. I caught the strangers' nod of satisfaction as I returned to Papa's side and knew with a tight feeling in my stomach that my fate was sealed. Despite knowing - always having known - that my duty as a daughter was to reward Papa's sacrifices with a good bride price, it still rankled that I was denied the choice of deciding who should pay the price on my head. I had secretly hoped it would be Chudi, one of the teachers in the primary school where I did my apprenticeship - tall, handsome and intelligent Chudi, with the gentle smile and soft voice of a deep thinker. Instead,

Papa had effectively sold me to the illiterate trader with the cold eyes and thin lips.

I did not doubt that I would fetch a handsome bride price as a result of my light skin and secondary school education. I was after all, the reincarnation of my great-grandmother, who had been famed in her lifetime for her amazing fairness and beauty. The children she reincarnated in within the family, including Mama, had a special black circle on their stomachs. All except me. But I had something more visible than that special birthmark. I had great-grandmother's hair; hair so long and fine that people often wondered if there was a secret white ancestry somewhere in our bloodline. Others, with malicious blood in their veins, would say I was lucky to have escaped being an albino, those unfortunate people cursed with skin that must forever hide from the sun.

I went through my days more concerned with my books and my ambition for a successful teaching career than my purported beauty. My command of the spoken English language was second to none in the entire village and people would often ask me to draft letters for them, a fact that pleased Papa no end. When in a good mood, he would call me *"Onye-nkuzi"* – teacher, with a teasing gleam in his eyes, secretly proud of my achievement and literary prowess. Otherwise, he constantly berated me for the precious time I wasted with my incessant reading, reminding me of the reason for my education.

'I don't want you to forget that I only allowed you an education to ensure you command a good bride price and hopefully, marry one of the new lawyers or doctors that are on the lookout for educated wives. Keep that in mind and don't go wasting your time with those useless books.'

My sister, Gono, on the other hand, with skin as dark as our father's, even if smoother to the touch and glossier to the sight, was not burdened with any such great expectations. I once heard one of our elderly auntie say that Gono's beauty would outlast my own because she wasn't a morning flower like me, the light-skinned daughter. She wouldn't bloom early and fade away early like I would.

I don't think Papa or Gono bought into her theory. Papa said that Gono's only hope of bagging a respectable bride price lay in acquiring an exceptional education, but only if her stubbornness allowed her to complete secondary school without getting expelled. But we knew we would be lucky if Gono deigned to give any man her hand in marriage for a bride price, respectable or otherwise. I pitied my sister because I feared she might never know the joys of marriage, as was the right of every woman as nature intended; a situation I suddenly found myself now facing without any feeling of joy.

Later that night, after our guests had gone, I cried as I had never cried in my seventeen years of growing up in Iburu village. I cried for the impending loss of my home, my family, my freedom, my career, my burgeoning affection for Chudi. In particular, I cried for the man, Agu, that cold stranger, who was soon to become my husband and my master.

*****

Ukari Forest – 11.45pm

The cold night wears on in the dreadful forest, as I feel the bile rise in my mouth for the umpteenth time. I turn away from my husband's corpse and retch into the wet grass, already stinking with my urine and vomit. The pain in my stomach is unbearable. It feels as if the imps of Satan have taken residence in my belly, wrenching my innards for their sport. The thirst burns my throat and my body shivers and trembles with cold and hunger. I cast eyes, made blurry by tears and bruises, at the water jug that stands on the mat next to my husband's body. I

*stretch out a trembling hand in its direction. Then
I stop, pull back my hand as if stung by a
scorpion, as remembrance floods my memory,
dulled by four days of starvation and sleep
deprivation.*

*The water in the jug is corpse water, the
water used in bathing the decomposing body of
my husband; the water I had been forced to drink
in the presence of all the clan as punishment for
my crime. In the aftermath of Agu's death, I was
held down by cruel hands, my nose squeezed shut,
as endless cups of corpse water were forced into
my open mouth in relentless succession.*

*I cannot begin to describe the taste of that
hideous fluid, the sour salty tang, the cloying
milkiness of pus, the lingering bitterness of
decayed flesh. The more I retched the more I was
fed the cloudy corpse water, with punches, slaps
and curses to compound my humiliation.*

*And now, even as I crouch beside my late
husband's corpse, I can still feel the swelling on
my face from the beatings. My ears still ring with
the invectives heaped on them – Murderer!
Husband killer! Child murderer! Mermaid witch!
Evil stranger! Wicked sorceress! Ogbanje! Man-
woman!*

*And much more... much worse. And all
because of my desperation, my bad* Chi *my*

foolishness, a desperate need that has now brought me to this wretched state.

As I listen to the painful growling of my stomach, draw in my knees to keep within the salt-lined boundary set by the three witchdoctors on the hard soil of the forest, I turn my eyes to the dry-barked trunk of The Tree of Truth. The tree hulks over us, its branches stretching into black infinity. Its massive trunk is scarred with ridges of dry gum, flaky barks and aborted stumps of unborn branches...and blood; a red-wash of blood. There is an ancient power within its unfathomable depths that shrouds it with wisdom and terror. Within its all-knowing roots lie my salvation.

I bare my body and my soul to the towering guardian of justice. I plead for its vindication, its protection, its forgiveness. And when finally my wailing voice grows hoarse, whimpers into a whisper, I bury my head in my hands as I allow my mind to travel back into the terrible events that has led to my present sorry predicament and could yet lead to my ultimate demise.

*****

26

From the day I entered Agu's house as his bride, I ceased expecting anything good. I had always believed that I was amongst the fortunate people born with a good *Chi,* favoured by good fortune due to my good deeds in my previous life. Even my Igbo name, *Chioma*, good personal god, reinforced my belief. My marriage shattered that conception.

As the weeks merged into months and the swollen moon brought in numerous years, I gradually became immune to the bad things that befell me in my matrimonial hell. Queen Ill-fortune sent her minions to me with the regularity of mosquito bites – broken glasses, stolen wrappers off the wash-line, burnt *Egusi* soup pots, punches from my husband and his three fat sisters, a crushed finger from the grinding stone. They were all small and regular irritants, harmless like most mosquito bites but malaria-deadly when the big one struck – Queen Ill-fortune herself, the all-powerful and all-knowing ruler of my destiny, the controller of my bad *Chi.*

She visited me with the regularity of my monthly curse, usually on the last day of the full moon, when the hidden madness in men's souls are raised from their dormant sleep to wreak violence and evil on womankind. Queen Ill-fortune's visits always left my soul as bloodied as the woman's curse that plagued my soured groin.

As I observed the birth of each new moon, my heart felt like a bare bottom sat on a heaving ant-hill. My eyes would seek out its thin curves as I pounded my husband's *Akpu* cassava meal in the hollow of my wooden mortar. Every sundown, as I brought in the washing from the lines or ushered in the goats into their pen, I would feel the slow terror build in my heart as the moon began to swell, fed on its diet of rain and clouds….and malice.

Soon, it would be a perfect melon of doom, ready to burst its calamity on my braided head. Queen Ill-fortune rides the full moon as every child and adult knows. Together, they invoke evil, awake the dead and spread devastation along their route, as they journey through mankind's lands and lives. Everyone cursed with a bad *chi* knows to dread the arrival of the full moon.

Initially, I was blissfully ignorant of the unholy union of these two deities, a malevolent partnership that brought nothing but misery to my life in my matrimonial home. I started keeping score after the loss of my sanity on that accursed day, the eve of the New Yam festival.

Married life had never been a life of songs and dances for me because I was a learned wife from a different village. Things took a turn for the worse when four years went by and I failed to produce the desired heir for my husband. Worse, I was blessed neither with a miscarriage or a stillbirth. Despite Father O'Keefe's novenas on my behalf, nothing stirred in my womb. It remained as fruitless as a man's stomach.

One day, Agu's eldest and fattest sister, Uzo, took matters into her hands and dragged me to their witchdoctor to find a solution to my barrenness. We arrived at the thatch-roofed mud house of the witchdoctor before the cock crow and waited our turn outside the small compound populated by other troubled souls. The sun was on high-noon by the time we were ushered into the feather-littered shrine of the witchdoctor by a small skewed-eyed boy, bare of feet and dressed in torn undersized trousers.

The man was seated crossed-legged on a hard, cement floor with strange drawings and herbs strewn around him. Blood still dripped from the neck of a freshly butchered chicken hung above the witchdoctor's head. The red fluid soaked his unshaven head, crawling around his face and neck like bloated worms. The sight caused my empty gut to heave. It clawed at my pounding heart till I felt it would burst. I forced my eyes to study the thin veins on my folded hands instead. I felt his eyes on me, burning, probing. My shoulders folded in on themselves in a hunched pose of shame. I felt the sudden trembling of my hands. *What sinful thoughts would he read in my mind? Holy Mary! Please help me! What will he read in my future?*

Suddenly, the decrepit man-demon screamed, pointing a gnarled finger in my direction.

'*Ogbanje!* Water sorceress! Be gone!' he shrieked. Turning glaring eyes at my sister-in-law, he shouted, 'Why have you brought me this accursed daughter of the river Niger?' Still pointing that filthy forefinger at me, his thin arm weighted by multiple charmed amulets, he demanded, 'Why do you bring upon my old head the wrath of the powerful mermaid? Go! Take her away! No one can help her. She belongs to the water. She is not your brother's wife. She is no mortal man's wife. Her womb will never yield fruit to your brother. Go! Depart from my presence and never return! Go!'

We scurried away, my heart pounding in terror. My sister-in-law abandoned me at the dust-road, leaving me to make my own way back to the house. I dreaded what awaited me at Agu's house

when he discovered my curse. *I am an Ogbanje…
a cursed spawn of the evil mermaid and I never
knew! Holy Mary save my soul!* I wandered the
dusty paths, the bushes, even the asphalted main
road, thinking, wringing my hands, tugging my
braided hair, walking - just walking - with no
destination in mind…anything to delay my return
to Agu's house.

Within hours of Uzo's return, the entire
village had heard of my stigma and my shame. As
I made my way back to Agu's compound, people
gathered in groups, staring at me, pointing at me,
laughing, cursing, spitting as I walked by, my
head lowered into my chest. My throat hurt from
the salty water I fought to keep behind my eyes. I
lost my erect tallness, made suddenly clumsy by
the jellying of my legs.

'We should have known she's an *Ogbanj*e
mermaid,' the fat sisters snapped out the demon
over their heads with outstretched arms as I
walked by. 'Have you ever seen anyone so light-
skinned unless they're albinos? Or with hair so
long it stretches like a mermaid's? But this one is
clearly not albino, just water-bleached by her real
mother, the evil *Mami-water* mermaid. Agu
should have listened to us when we warned him
of the perils of marrying an outsider. One can

31

never tell the curses that follow such people. Oh! Our poor brother!'

By the time Agu returned to the house, a great crowd of relatives had gathered inside his parlour, waiting to fill his ears with the news of my curse. Even before I heard the great roar of his rage rumble past the stairs and into my bedroom, I knew my fate was sealed. I prepared myself to be sent back to my village in shame, a reject of both husband and God.

I was standing by my bed when Agu crashed into my room, the whites of his eyes red-streaked, his pupils as coal, burning with a hate that had hitherto been absent in the four years of our marriage. I barely had the time to mutter the obligatory *"onye-ishi"* master, when he grabbed my hair, forcing my knees to the floor and dragging me into his room with a strength that defied his puny size and my considerable height. Once inside his room, he descended on my body with every arsenal at his disposal, venting his fury with his fists, his belt, his birch whips, his walking sick and even the twisted metal cloth-hangers that harboured his array of clothing.

My screams fell on deaf consciences. Everyone in that over-populated household heard my howls of pain but no one dared or even wanted to venture into the master's bedroom to halt my thrashing. I pled for mercy, seeking his forgiveness for my barrenness, for the bride-price money he had wasted on the defective good I had now become.

Agu's hands continued to descend on my head, pulling clumps off my scalp. His feet shot home countless goals on my body. Soon, my screams turned to whimpers and my voice grew hoarse in my throat. When eventually his arms grew weary and his breathing laboured from exhaustion, Agu dropped his belt on the floor and matched out of the room in the same death-silence with which he had carried out the prolonged attack on my person.

As for myself, I was at the gates of mental darkness and mortal hell, my vision hazy from dizziness and pain. Choking back the countless hiccups that threatened to kill my breathing, I crawled my way back to my room, bright blood stains marking the white linoleum floor of the corridor. I stumbled my way to the wall mirror, fearful, yet desperate to see the damage to my person. The scream that escaped my lips at the image the mirror returned to me was louder than any I had made while the damage was wreaked on it. I shut my eyes tight, fighting to blank out the swellings, the open cuts, the blood dripping from every opening in my face. But I couldn't shut out the agonising throbbing in my body, the shame and the fury. Most of all, I couldn't shut out the sudden hate that burnt in my heart like a bush fire gone wild.

That night, and many more nights over the course of several months, Agu vented his fury and frustration on my body with his fists and everything he could lay his stumpy hands on. His three obese sisters who shared the house with us, took equal liberties on my person, till my loathed light skin was repainted with a collage of blues, reds and blacks. On numerous occasions, I was kept locked up in my room, guarded by the mammoth sisters and numerous house-helps. The only times they were let off guard duty were on the nights my husband came to claim his conjugal rights on my body, a brutal ritual carried out in silence and darkness, leaving me with a feeling of defilement and shame.

Eventually, I could bear the abuse no longer. One day when Agu left for his monthly trade trips to the Moslem north, I made my escape back to my father's village. I caught the mammy-wagon bus that ferried traders to *Onitsha Market* once a week, usually on a Friday morning. I hunched in my seat, head bowed, as the rickety bus rumbled along the potholed road, spewing black smoke into the air, its horn blaring out with nerve-wracking regularity as if to say "look at me, I can talk, I can shriek!" Its manic racket fed the emotions that burned in my heart like a *Harmattan* bush-fire. A mounting rage engulfed my body, fury at what that horrid midget and his vile sisters had done to me. *Just wait till I tell Papa,* I thought over and over again as the bus rumbled its bumpy way to my village. I pulled my headscarf almost to my nose like a Moslem woman, desperate to hide my latest bruises from the other passengers. I did not want anyone to see my shame… save my family. For them, there would be no pride, no humiliation. For my family, I would bare my very soul.

*****

I arrived at my father's village a few hours later and walked the short distance to his compound, my eyes fixed to the ground to avoid recognition. As I walked through the low metal gate of our compound, I saw Papa's Raleigh bicycle perched against the whitewashed wall of our L-shaped bungalow. The sight of that bicycle flooded my mind with memories, bitter-sweet nostalgia that stung my eyes with salty water. I felt my feet grow sudden wings as I raced the last few yards to our front door. I pulled my scarf from my head, wincing in pain as the cloth connected with my bruises, dislodging fresh scabs. I heard the sound of approaching footsteps and felt the sudden tears spill down my cheeks, tears of self-pity, relief, pain and anger all mixed into one loud bawl.

My sister, Gono, opened the door. She took one look at my battered, tear-streaked face and started howling. She just stood at the open door, her hands pressed tightly against her ears, staring at me with wide streaming eyes, her bare feet stamping on the floor like the frenzied dance of the *Adamma* masquerade. Except her dance wasn't one of joy or excitement, but rage and pain; a pain I knew was as biting as mine because of the great love she bore for me. Behind her, I saw my brother, Ibe, craning his neck, trying to see what the ruckus was all about. His eyes widened as he took in my bruises before hurrying away without a word to me. Mama rushed out, Ibe fast on her heels, his eyes gleaming with sly excitement.

"What's all this foolishness about? Don't you know your father is having his afternoon siesta?' Mama scolded, pushing Gono away from me. Then, just like Gono, her eyes widened as she too took in my battered face. She threw her arms wide into the air, her eyes raised to the low ceiling in an attitude of supplication. 'Jesu!' she shouted, making a quick sign of the cross before leading me by the arm into Papa's presence, her breathing hard and fast.

'Papa Ibe! Papa Ibe, wake up,' she shook Papa's shoulder with urgent hands. I felt the slight irritation of old stir in my heart at the usurpation of my right. I was the first born and prior to Ibe's arrival, Papa had been known as "Papa Desee" by everyone. But with Ibe's birth, him being a son and all, that coveted status had been taken from me and given to the wretched sod.

As Papa slowly awakened, Mama went over to her armless chair, folding her arms over her bosom. She had the look of a guard dog awaiting the "attack" order from its master. It was a look that filled my heart with a warm glow. I felt like a child whose big brother was going to thrash the school bully for picking on him. Papa forced his eyes apart, his movements sluggish, confused. A look of annoyance clouded his face as he kissed his teeth in an angry hiss.

'Can't a man get any rest in his own house?' he grumbled, stretching his hand for his snuffbox by his side table. His mood didn't lighten any when his eyes settled on me. I could see the dark brown tobacco stain at the tip of his nostrils, just above his lips. I felt a strong urge to

37

wipe it with a cloth… a hankie… something. *Anything.* For some incomprehensible reason, I couldn't bear the sight of that dark tobacco stain under Papa's nose. I had more pressing problems, yet, that unsightly dot overshadowed everything else to such an extent that I even forgot to curtsy to my grandfather's grave in the centre of the living room as was customary. In fact, for several confused seconds, I couldn't recall why Mama had brought me into the parlour till I heard her discreet cough beside me. I tore my gaze from Papa's dirty nostrils and dragged my mind back to my troubles. Mama nodded at me to speak.

Once again, I could not hold back my tears as I told Papa my tale, showing him the wreck Agu had made of my body. I was angry, shouting, as I recounted the litany of abuse Agu and his people had inflicted on my person. It was as if my voice, long buried, had been given a new life; as if my pride, long murdered in Ukari, had been re-animated within the safety of my father's house. I wanted vengeance. Someone had to pay for what I had suffered. Someone needed to feel the pain I had felt. That someone was Agu, my so-called husband and his three fat sisters. I wanted Papa to round up a band of youths from the masquerade age group, those muscle-chested boy-men, who could beat the hard-skinned drums from dusk to dawn without tiring. They were our village braves, self-appointed guardians of the community, who made it their duty to ensure no crimes occurred on their watch or went unavenged when committed. I wanted Papa to take those tough boys to Ukari and trash the skin off that midget trader and his obese sisters. I wanted Agu and his family to cry as I had cried, to feel the burning of birch, the pounding of fists, the cutting of flesh, just as I had done. I wanted them to be so familiar with the tangy taste of blood and snot, which no food, no matter how sweet, would ever wash from their taste buds for eternity. But most of all, I wanted my old room back; that small book-choked room I'd shared with my sister once upon a blissful time, before I was driven from its womb-like warmth to the cold soulless Hades of Agu's house.

Papa listened to me in total silence, his dark face inscrutable, unyielding. He kept piling tobacco powder into his nostrils all the while I spoke, his eyes boring into mine as I talked. The hard blackness of his eyes told me that he would not save me from my matrimonial hell.

I was not mistaken. Papa looked at Ibe as if to say, "Take good heed of this crucial lesson for when you have troublesome daughters of your own", before turning back to me. A deep frown creased his forehead as he piled his nostrils with yet more tobacco powder.

'You are your husband's chattel now,' Papa said, fixing me with a fierce look that would brook no arguments. 'Nobody can come between a man and his wife. Whatever food they dish out to you should be eaten with endurance and gratitude. It is bad enough that you have shamed this family with your barrenness without adding the dishonour of a divorce. Where do you expect me to find the money to refund him the dowry he paid on your head should you return, eh? Do you want me to sell my *Ogodo*, loincloth, to raise your dowry refund? Go, return to your husband and cease your whinging and childish behaviour. Kindly remember that you're the *Ada,* my first daughter. Your sister looks to you to set a good example. Do not let her down.'

My father waved me away from his presence. I cast a wild look at my mother, unable to comprehend, to accept what my ears had heard. Surely, Mama would not stand by and let this happen to me. Surely, she would talk to my father, convince him that I must never return to Ukari under any circumstance. I was even prepared to forego revenge, to let Agu get away with his crime if I was certain I would never see him again.

But my mother shrugged and looked away. My mother would not meet my eyes.

The guard-dog look left her face and instead, I saw her lips curl down in that familiar manner I remembered from childhood, that silent message that said, "Your father knows best. You have to do as he says". But this was no longer some petty quarrel between siblings, some childish ploy for attention. This was a matter of life and death… *my life, her daughter's death!* Surely, she would not fold her hands and watch me die. She was a married woman like myself. My father had never treated her as Agu treated me. She had to do something, say something to change his mind. She was my mother, *my mother!*

'Mama!' my cry bore the weight of my pain, my terror. It forced itself from the depths of my soul, insisting to be heard. But my mother remained silent, a silent partner to her husband's crime. For in my mind, what they were doing was criminal, heartless, even evil. How could two people who conceived and gave life to me calmly hand me over to my killer for thirty pieces of dowry silver?' They were no better than Judas Iscariot. In fact, they were worse that Emeka, that childless village drunk, whom rumour had it sold his own daughter to the slave traders in his previous incarnation, resulting in his present

41

curse. Five wives down the line and Emeka was still childless. His last wife finally ran off with a mami-wagon driver and promptly had a child by her lover. I could finally empathise with that wretched man as I had never done in my ignorant youth.

With weary resignation, I turned away from both my parents and walked out of the parlour, setting my face into the stoic mask of the example-giver, calm, patient, forbearing; just like a pious nun. After all, as my father said, I was the first daughter and my sister expected me to set a good example.

Thankfully, my father was wrong.

My sister, Gono, did not expect any such martyr-like example from me. She took one look at my set features and rushed over to me. Her tears re-awakened my own. She clasped my shuddering body in her arms as I poured out my despair to her ears, the only ears that truly heard my pain. My body shuddered with the force of my tears and anger.

'Bastards! Men are all bastards! Useless lumps of pig shit!' Gono raged. 'I wish I were a man. By God, I will reincarnate as a man in my next life and then we'll see who calls the shots. Look at that idiot, Ibe. Already he's a replica of Papa, an *akologholi,* a useless little jerk with no brain cells in his big head. He's not a child anymore, for Christ's sake. He's almost seventeen years now, the same age you were when you married that dwarf. If he were a real man, he would go to Ukari and trash the living daylight out of that short bastard that calls himself your husband. But don't worry sis, don't cry. Everything will be okay soon, you'll see.'

I hugged my little sister tightly, unwilling to separate our bond. I was allowed to spend the night under my father's roof on the proviso that no one found out that I'd done so without my husband's permission and that I left before the crow of the rooster the next day. It was with a weary heart that I dressed up at the crack of dawn and made my feet-dragging way back to my husband's house, the house of my shame and my earthly hell. I did not exchange a word with my father as I left his house for my return journey to Ukari. I managed to smuggle out a few books from my old room - Jane Eyre, David Copperfield and The Water Babies. My books reminded me of what had been and what could have been had Queen Ill-fortune not dealt me such a cruel hand and a bad father. They evoked memories of happier times and to an extent, salvaged my sanity. I felt a strong closeness to Jane Eyre in particular, whose wretchedness and ultimate triumph filled my heart with hope of a better destiny in some distant future.

Just before I got on the Mami-wagon taking me back to Ukari village, Mama ran out and pushed a piece of paper into my hand before rushing back into the house again, ever fearful of incurring my father's wrath for encouraging my perceived rebellion. It was too dark to read the contents of the crumbled piece of paper as the sun was still to chase the moon back to its cold realm. When I finally read the short note, written in the familiar dear hand of my sister, Gono, it was the address of a famed Spiritualist, Pastor Brother Ezekiel of the Cherubim and Seraphim Church of Redemption. My sister's bold calligraphy penned Mama's wishes for me to visit the powerful pastor without delay, as he was the key to my problems. It was an instruction I was happy to obey. I was at the end of my endurance and ready to dine with Lucifer himself if he would free me from my marital yoke.

*****

Pastor Brother Ezekiel proved to be everything I had hoped for and more, far more. He identified and broke all my ancestral curses, binding the demons of infertility with chicken and goat sacrifices, a full body wash in consecrated water, mixed with the blood of my monthly curse and a burnt offering of my shaved pubic hair, the pages of the book of Psalms and a new-born's umbilical cord. I sold my best *Ashoke* ceremonial gown to raise the money to buy the last item from a private midwife and it was worth every last *Naira* note in the end.

Pastor Brother Ezekiel was possessed with the spirit of Arch-angel Michael on the night of my spiritual cleansing. He spoke in tongues, wondrous and mysterious holy words that sent my senses into righteous ecstasy. And when Arch-Angel Michael possessed my trembling body, filling my womb with the holy seeds of fertility, I knew that my sorrows were finally at an end. Queen Ill-fortune had finally met her match in the all-conquering angel of our omnipotent creator, the Arch-Angel Michael himself!

I gave birth to my son exactly nine months to the date of my holy cleansing and my husband aptly named him *Chukwuebuka,* God is great! Every one called him Ebuka, the shortened version of his name. Ebuka's birth healed the pain of my childless marriage, four years of humiliation, abuse and contempt. My sisters-in-law, overnight, metamorphosed from Lucifer to St

Peter, guarding my well-being and that of my son with the same zeal with which St Peter guarded the gates of heaven. Gone were the harsh words, the accusations, the bitter recriminations, the beatings. Even Uzo, the worst of the rotund three, mellowed her hate, bringing me freshly-made *Akamu,* corn pap, for the baby. I knew it was her way of making up for all the gossip she had spread about my *mami-water* mermaid ancestry and accursed infertility. I was ready to accept her peace-offerings. After all, I had been vindicated, made triumphant over Queen Ill-fortune, finally secure in my marital home with a husband who had not lifted a violent hand on my person since the birth of his heir.

Agu threw a lavish party for the baptism of our son. Father O'Keefe officiated the ceremony and consecrated Ebuka with holy water as he read out his two names, Chukwuebuka (which he struggled to pronounce) and Michael, which he proclaimed with loud confidence. I was lavished with new clothes and jewellery for the event and my father's face was full of smiles at the baptism party. I had finally done him proud. Sadly, Pastor Brother Ezekiel was not invited despite being the instrument of my miracle. Father O'Keefe would have frowned at my interaction with that segment of the Christian fraternity. The

Cherubim and Seraphim church was still viewed with suspicion by the Catholic Church due to its practise of mixing Christianity with local traditions. I sent Pastor Brother Ezekiel a handsome gift in an envelope after the ceremony. The guests had been very generous with their donations and money gifts for the new baby.

As the months went by and Ebuka grew stronger, Agu became kinder to me. He began addressing me with the endearment, *Nkem,* my own. My *Adu,* the woven colourful box that held my expensive clothes was filled to capacity. I was treated with respect by the villagers and addressed by the proud title, *Mama Ebuka*. I was now a mother. I had fulfilled my calling as a woman, a daughter and a wife. I had finally earned my place in society and gained acceptance amongst my husband's people.

I soon grew fat on a diet of contentment and pride. As our people say, a beggar who never dreamt of becoming a king will drown himself in ivory amulets from his heels to his chest so that no one will be in doubt of his importance. I was as crass as that stupid beggar, boasting of the beauty, the strength, the cleverness of my son, Ebuka. My eyes were haughty in pride, my voice loud in confidence, my mien, complacent in contentment.

Until the day Queen Ill-fortune paid me an unexpected and devastating visit, wreaking deadly vengeance on me for my contempt of her might. It was only after she left my house that I realised that the moon was a perfect swollen melon. In my pride and folly, I had ceased to keep score, to watch, to follow and dread the changes in the omen-moon.

Until that fatal eve of the New Yam festival, that terrible weltering afternoon when the house-maid brought in the small lifeless body of my son, Ebuka, his features swollen and distorted by the venom of the evil viper, *Echieteka,* tomorrow is too far to live. Queen Ill-fortune had dealt me the most deadly of blows yet and her moon stayed fat in the sky for several nights to mock my sorrow.

The clans-women said that I would not let go of my son's lifeless body; that I clung to him like a bat to its cave, fighting all that tried to prise him from my arms with the strength of ten mad women. They said that even after I had finally been restrained by the men of the clan, my relentless keening had kept the inhabitants of the surrounding compounds awake for several nights. According to them, the mourning food cooked for me by the village women went uneaten and

48

soured in their bowls while my body withered and wasted with the speed of my mind's deterioration.

I remembered none of it. I remembered nothing beyond the cold, cold body of my beautiful son... and the callus laughter of Queen Ill-fortune ringing in my brain, day and night.

The women of the clan beat my housemaid to near-death. Not because of her dereliction of duty resulting in my innocent son picking up the deadly snake with his bare hands while she scampered atop the mango trees in search of the sweet ripe fruits. They beat her instead for breaking the most sacred of taboos - letting my eyes behold the lifeless body of my son. *What self-respecting Igbo person doesn't know that a parent's eyes must never see the corpse of their deceased child?* Such an abomination would bring untold misfortune to the entire clan. Not only had my eyes beheld my dead son, but I had also held his lifeless body in my arms for several hours, ensuring that Queen Ill-fortune's dreaded attention had been caught and drawn to the entire clan! *Ha!* What did I care? As if that terrible deity's attention had ever left my side. Let her visit as much as she likes; go ahead and spread her dark favours on Agu's family and entire clan. Let them know my misery, share my pain and know what it is to play host to that malevolent visitor.

My son was dead. No one would ever again call me "*Mami*" in that sweet baby voice. Arch-Angel Michael had been roundly defeated by Queen Ill-fortune. I was soul-weary, tired of resisting my fate. Whatever evil I had done in my previous existence had to be paid for in full in my present life. I had now paid my dues. Ebuka was gone. I had lost everything. All I wanted was out, freedom to join my son in the dark, cold embrace of death. I knew there would be peace in the sandy warmth of the grave. At least in my next reincarnation, I would finally return with a good *Chi*.

By the time my mind found its way back to the land of the sane, it was too late for me to find my son. Search as I could, ask as I dared, no one would show me where the tiny corpse of my son lay. All I knew was that he was buried in *Ajo-ofia,* the bad bush, a barren and desolate stretch of landscape inhabited by the cursed bodies of the unclean, those who died a cursed death. Their bodies were discarded in the bad bush, un-mourned and forgotten - suicides, murderers, witches and wizards, nightflyers, poisoners, victims of lightning, mothers who died giving birth, children who died before their parents and people who were judged and destroyed by The Tree of Truth.

Nothing grew in *Ajo-ofia* but giant anthills, housing massive termites bloated from gorging on the corpses of the damned. It was no place for my innocent beautiful son, a laughing and happy child once beloved and cherished by all. His little red shoes still lay hidden in my room, buried deep in my *Adu* amongst my expensive wrappers, away from the evil and prying eyes of the clans-women. They would burn those tiny red shoes with the same speed with which they'd burnt all his clothing; wipe out all traces of his existence with the same cold and ruthless efficiency they had cast away his tiny body in *Ajo-ofia,* his grave unmarked by stone or cross, ensuring his name would be forgotten by mankind for all eternity and his spirit would never find its way back to its home to reincarnate amongst its people.

And for what crime? For dying from a poisonous snake bite? For dying too young before his time, before his parents? For allowing his corpse to be seen and held by his grieving mother, thereby bringing the curse of Queen Ill-fortune on the entire clan? What had my innocent baby done to deserve such evil from the entire clan and village?

I wanted to find his grave, to visit that accursed bush where his body lay discarded like bat-eaten mangoes, rancid and worthless. But my cowardly woman's heart feared the vengeful ghosts of the accursed dead that shared the bad bush with my little son. No matter how many Hail Marys I chanted, how many bottles of holy water I drank, how many wooden and metal crucifixes I collected or how many *Jigida* charmed amulets I wore around my waist to ward off evil spirits, my courage refused to reside in my heart and I could never make the long and fearful journey to my child's last resting place and mark his unhallowed grave with a mother's loving touch.

*****

Ukari Forest – 2am

Agu's eyes, closed by death, suddenly snap apart, staring their bloody glare into my eyes, eyes stretched to my ears by heart-thumping terror. My limbs melt, my breathing stops, my heart falls to my stomach as I fight to retain my sanity in the midst of the latest horror that has descended upon me in this forest of the damned. As I struggle to revive my feet, to flee from the zombie ghoul on the raffia mat, his right arm, rotting with peeling flesh, shoots up and grabs my throat, squeezing out my life with a strength and malignancy that is beyond the realms of the living.

I scream - yell - as I struggle to escape from the vengeful decaying demon that had once been my husband. But my voice is silent, my cries, swallowed by my terror. I see the stinking, bloated carcass slowly rise from the forest floor, the raffia mat clinging to its pus-seeping skin. The stench of decay and rank is overpowering, almost stealing the air from my lungs. That bristly and mottled organ is hard against my thighs, rough and painful. IT demands forceful entrance to my secret place, still bruised and hurting from all its previous assaults. The hands on my throat tighten their grip, squeezing, hurting, till I feel the darkness of death pounding in my brain, seeking entry.

Yet, even as death waits impatiently for my soul, even as I feel the deadly pressure on my throat, something in me refuses to give in, to give up without fighting for the one thing that still belongs to me – my life. As pathetic as it is, it's still my own to keep or destroy. I know that if I don't flee, find a way to break through the charmed salt boundary set around me by the witchdoctor, my soul will become entwined with Agu's for all eternity.

For that is the fate of all murderers. Their lives are destined to be taken by their victim's ghosts; to be joined to their victims in death, like joined twins, condemned to an eternity of vengeful justice at the hands of these earth-bound spirits.

Blessed Virgin! I do not want to become a restless dead amongst my other curses and for all eternity, denied the chance of a better reincarnation. I begin to struggle with a desperation born of mind-killing terror, kicking, scratching, screaming, shoving.

My eyes fly awake and I rise to the sound of silence, a graveside stillness that makes me wish for the oblivion of death by its sheer soundless terror. My heart is thudding so loudly I fear I will faint and then truly be damned. With small whimpering cries, I scramble away on bruised knees from Agu's bloated corpse, pulling myself to the very edge of the salt ring that has me chained to The Tree of Truth, shoulders hunched, my armed clasped tightly around my raised knees.

I stare – peer intently into Agu's swollen face, searching, looking for any sign of the terrifying animation I've witnessed in my nightmare. Do his eyes flicker? Do I see his nose twitch? Surely, I hear something that sounds as soft as dandelion pores, a pungent exhalation that blows a sudden chill on my exposed flesh!

I force my eyes to take a brave peep at the jutting monster between his naked thighs, still throbbing in its knobbled evil; the undead tentacle in the lump of fetid rottenness that was my husband. It pulsates with a living strength that defies the rancid body that houses it. Oh Mary Mother of God! Will IT never die? Will IT never wilt? Will IT ever let me go?

Pulling my hair, tangled in filthy clumps on my scalp, I feel like hammering a stone into my skull, to punish my brain for its stupidity. How could I have allowed my guard to slip, to give in to sleep, allowing Agu's vengeful spirit to attempt the possession of my body and chain me to him in eternal servitude? God knows he has enough to be vengeful about. My stupidity and desperation had cost him among other things, his life.

If only I hadn't been so desperate, so frightened. But what mother can hear the pitiful cries of her child and turn a deaf ear? Everything would have been alright if only Ebuka hadn't died, if Enu hadn't come into our family, if I had stayed away from that demon, Ogbunigwe. If only I hadn't been so foolish, so…….

*****

Eight months to the death of my son, Agu took a second wife, Enu. Older than me by several years, she was young enough to provide the male child to replace my late son and ensure the perpetuity of our husband's bloodline. Enu also had the advantage of being a local woman, born in Ukari of Ukari parentage. I was considered a tall woman but Enu towered over me by several fingers. She was a woman of mammoth proportions. Seeing her together with our husband for the first time was a sight I would never forget. Agu could have easily been mistaken for her son but for that strutting walk of his, peculiar to all pocketsize dictators. I would have burst out in a maniac's laughter had my situation not been so dire.

As soon as the wretched woman swaggered her way into our house, Agu threw me out of my room and consigned me to the back quarters of the house, the section reserved for the domestic helps. Enu took over ownership of my room and all the privileges of the main wife, from the domestic helps to the shopping and food management. I couldn't tell which was worse – the scorn of my husband and his sisters or the indifferent pity and contempt of the house-servants, who soon sucked up their way into the new mistress' favour with tales of my anguish. I would see them gathered, sniggering, whispering into their new mistress's ears. My ears would burn as Enu hissed at my back the way one would hiss at a house pest. Yet, I was her senior in rank, the first wife, but our husband had stripped me of my rank and the respect that went with it. At best, I was no higher than the house servants now.

As time went by, I lost all interest in reading, even when the opportunity presented itself. What was the use? Where had all my education landed me? Not as a doctor's or lawyer's wife as Papa had anticipated. I was instead in the back quarters of a man who couldn't string together two words of English if his life depended on it. The sooner I resigned myself to the reality of my life and accepted myself as a village minion, the better I would adapt to my new life.

Less than a year into her marriage, Enu fulfilled expectations with the birth of a son, whose striking resemblance to our husband was confirmed in his name, *Nwanna*, his father's son. On the night of Nwanna's birth, Queen Ill-fortune's gleeful laughter rang so loudly in my head I feared I would lose my sanity. At a point, I cried out in anguish, uncaring what ears might hear my torment - *Please, great deity, leave me alone... forget my existence as the morning skies forget the night stars. Discard me as the tree sheds its dead leaves. Have you not toyed enough with my life so that I am but a wretched husk of humanity, worthless, insignificant, a mere shadow? Why continue noticing this pathetic lump of wretchedness? Why...why?*

My cries went unheard, my pain unseen as I masked my face with celebratory smiles at the wondrous arrival of our husband's heir, Nwanna. I sensed the malice behind the smiles of the clanswomen, heard the velvet spite behind their solicitous enquiries about my well-being – "*Nwunye-anyi,* our wife, did you spend too much time with your kitchen smoke? Look, it has brought charcoal redness to your eyes, you poor woman!"

There was nothing I could do to shield the evidence of my pain, try as I could. My reddened eyes remained puffed with unfinished tears, ready to shed my agony at the slightest excuse. Once, I had known the bliss of holding a child in my arms, suckling his little head on my tender breasts, his skin soft, silky to the touch, his voice beautiful and sweet when he called me *"Mami".* I had nothing now, would never know the glory of motherhood again. The same villagers that had once treated me with respect, now scorned me with indifference. Every honour now went to Enu and her new son. Our husband had ceased to know me as a wife from the day my son died. Now he had another wife and son, I had become an outcast of both man and the gods.

One night, a year to the birth of Nwanna, I awoke to the sound of a child's cries outside my window. It was mournful and muted, yet at the same time, piercing and insistent. I sat up on my bed, its loose springs squeaking out in protest. The cries stopped - just for a few seconds - then resumed with louder intensity. It sounded like a *Bush-Baby,* that nocturnal primate with a child's fingers, which mimics the cries of a new-born baby. It is a cursed creature, sent by enemies to cast evil spells on unsuspecting people. When sent to a woman, it kills all affections the husband has for her, ensuring she'll never become pregnant and have a child. Tricking unwary women with their infant-like cries, these evil creatures assume the form of wicked goblins, raping the women and biting off their toes after the vile act so that people know what had taken place. Consequently, all future children born by the molested women must be killed and buried at the *Ajo-ofia* to ensure the *Bush-Baby* curse is destroyed.

I stumbled through the darkness to my window, to make sure the latch was firmly secured before returning to my bed, my heart thudding in unbridled terror. I *knew* who had sent me the *Bush-Baby – Enu*, my husband's second wife. Not content with taking my husband, my bedroom and my status, she now wished to inflict the vilest of all curses on me by having me molested by the goblin Bush-Baby. *Oh Holy Mary mother of God! Would my travails never end?* I spent the rest of the night in wakeful misery, listening to the incessant cries of that evil abomination till Agu's prize cockerel crowed in the dawn and the unholy cries finally ceased.

For three more nights, the accursed *Bush-Baby* outside my window tormented my sleep. On the fourth night, it entered my room. I awoke to the familiar child-like wails, feeling a terror grip my heart beyond anything I've ever felt since the death of my son. The cries ceased as soon as I opened my eyes. *Something was wrong, very wrong; bad.* The unnatural stillness in my room was heavy with a waiting quality that made the darkness a solid malignant mass.

Covered in cold sweat, I fumbled for the box of matches to light my kerosene lantern. In the thin light of the lamp, I picked out a sudden movement near my *Adu,* the high basket that contained my special clothes, reserved for weddings and Sunday service. Something scuttled to the back of the *Adu,* something the size of a dog, yet faster in motion than any dog I had ever seen.

Then it cried, a sound so piercing and terrible that my heart froze. *Bush-Baby! Oh Holy Maria! Jesus!* What to do? There was no escape through my door as the *Adu* stood behind the wooden door on the inside of my bedroom. My eyes darted wildly around the room, looking for something, anything, to defend myself. The gleaming silver of my crucifix on the small table beckoned like an angel's halo. I reached out my hand to it and felt a sudden chill cover my entire body in goosebumps.

Ebuka, my beautiful, sweet son, stood in front of me; Ebuka, naked as the day he was born, his skin caked in the dirty mud of his unhallowed grave! I wanted to scream…I think I screamed.

I awoke, drenched in cold water, surrounded by Enu, our husband, the fat sisters and the house-servants. Enu held an empty bucket in her hand. I figured she must have doused me in cold water to bring me out of my faint. For a few seconds, my shame dulled my memory, especially when I saw the fury in Agu's eyes. Then recollection returned with terrifying panic.

'Ebbbbbuka!' I stuttered, struggling to speak through the terror that still held my heart in its grip. I cast wild looks around my room as I struggled to my feet, my wet cloths clinging to my skin, bringing shivers to my entire body. 'Ebuka…where's Ebuka? He's here…he's back…'

'Chei! *Tufia!* Heaven forbid evil! The woman is crazy again!' Enu shouted, snapping her fingers to ward off being infected by my lunacy, a cold smirk on her face. '*Onye-ishi,* master, when are you going to get rid of this mad woman, eh? It's not fair that our peace is ruined by her. Your son, Nwanna, needs his sleep, which this crazy woman won't let him have. I think…'

Agu raised his hand, cutting off Enu's tirade with that single gesture. At the same time, he waved away the sisters and the wide-eyed house-helps, his cold eyes fixed on me all the while.

'Return to your room,' he said to Enu without taking his eyes from me. I saw a look of rebellion flash across Enu's eyes as she hesitated. 'Go! Now!' Agu barked. Enu didn't need a second warning. Despite her mammoth size, I've heard her loud yelps on a few occasions, as a result of Agu's fists. Our husband was indiscriminate in his violence, even if I got the lion share.

As the door slammed behind her, Agu approached me, his steps silent, deliberate. I huddled closer to the bed-post, pulling my pillow close, anything to ward off the blows I knew were coming my way.

'So…your son returned to you, did he?' Agu's voice was soft, dangerous. 'You dare mock me with a name that should never be mentioned in my house! You stupid, stupid woman.'

My pillow was useless, as were my cries for mercy. Agu rained his fury on my body, my head, my face, leaving me a bloody, crumbled wreck on the floor when he was done.

The next night, when my son returned to me, I knew better than to scream or faint. I fought my terror and spoke to my son. By the time we were done talking, all my former fears had disappeared. The next night, I had a basin of clean water and new clothes waiting in my room, together with his tiny red shoes I had saved since his death. I washed the grave-mud and death odour off him, oiled his body with palm-kernel oil, combed his thick hair and dressed him up with his new clothes and the red shoes, which still fitted perfectly. Then I carried him in my arms and rocked him till sleep came to me.

When I awoke the next morning, Ebuka was gone and his clothes and little red shoes lay abandoned on my bed. I felt the tears choke my throat at my new loss, a loss now magnified by the brief bliss of motherhood I had experienced in the night. Suddenly, the pain from Agu's brutality on my body returned with throbbing intensity. I had felt nothing since my son returned to me and his disappearance re-awakened all my dormant pains, both mental and physical. For the first time, I contemplated suicide. Surely, death was better than this earthly torment!

The next night when my son came back to me, naked, again caked in filthy mud from his unhallowed grave, with that foul smell of decay still clinging to him despite all my scrubbing and washing, I welcomed him into my arms with indescribable joy. I again carried out the loving chore of cleansing and dressing him, secure in the knowledge that he would be back the following night, till my love held him back for good and he lost the urge to go back to *Ajo-ofia*.

So began my second phase of motherhood. I nursed and loved my dead baby who neither ate nor stayed beyond the light of dawn. No matter what delicacies I offered him, Ebuka would never take a single bite nor drink a sip of water. His eyes remained open through the night and his cold little body would never soak the warmth from my cradling arms. But he was happy to be together with his loving *Mami* again.

And me? My steps grew lighter and my face glowed with ecstasy. I noticed the suspicious looks of the household, the whispers - *'It's the madness…She's too far gone now for help! But Onye-ishi won't do anything about her till she starts running around naked. Just make sure you keep Nwanna away from her. I don't want her tainting my son with her lunacy.'* Enu voiced her thoughts in a voice loud enough for the whole village to hear. *As if I cared for her precious son!* I had my own son with me again and that was enough for me.

It wasn't enough for Ebuka. He started asking me to bring him back for good. He was lonely and sad in *Ajo-ofia,* the bad bush. The cursed soil kept coughing up his corpse, rejecting his body as the humans had rejected it. He was an unclean, a child that had died a cursed death before his parents, doomed to a restless grave in *Ajo-ofia*. It had taken him years to find his way back to our house, a miracle in itself, considering the remoteness of his gravesite. He missed me desperately and wanted to remain with me but he could not return for good till he was reincarnated back to us.

I knew Ebuka's only chance of reincarnation lay with me getting pregnant, enabling him to return through my new birth. But how could I make that happen when our husband no longer touched me as a wife?

The urge to return to Pastor Brother Ezekiel was great. After all, I had him to thank for Ebuka's birth in the first place. But I resisted that temptation with the stubbornness of a Christmas ram being dragged to the butcher's knife. I dared not incur the wrath of Queen Ill-fortune again, who seemed to have forgotten my existence. But our people have a saying – "To fight a demon, you need the devil." Queen Ill-fortune was a demon deity. I would need a demon-savvy witchdoctor to aid my cause and bring back my son to life.

*****

I visited Ogbunigwe's hut at midnight of the next full moon. He would only see supplicants at that specific time. My heart quaked at the sight of the swollen moon, knowing that Queen Ill-fortune was at her most mischievous on such nights. Yet, I had no choice. If I was to have my son back for good, then the only way was to brave the evil deity and seek the famed medicine man, *Ogbunigwe*, he that kills in multitudes.

Ogbunigwe was as fierce-faced as his reputation, tall, marble-featured, coal-skinned and bloody of eyes. His body was knife-carved with intricate designs too mysterious for me to decipher. His voice when he spoke to me, was deep, yet raspy, full of authority and ancient knowledge. The aura of menace about him terrified me even more than the macabre place he lived, set deep in the forest and littered with numerous human skulls and dead animal carcasses. The metallic smell of blood was strong, overpowering, coupled with another strange odour I could not fathom. The great medicine man was dressed in nothing but a loin-cloth and multiple amulets and charms.

As I stepped through the low door of his hut, I noticed that the cement flooring of the room was polished with blood. Briefly, the thought flickered in my mind, *'What will Father O'Keefe think of me if he knew where I was?'* I couldn't believe that I, Desdemona, once an aspiring teacher and a devout Catholic, had now descended to this level of fetishness. I waved the thought away. *We are all what our* Chi *decides for us. Who can say what is right and what is wrong?*

After all, didn't King Saul himself visit the Witch of Endor in the Bible and spoke to God's prophet, Samuel?

As I looked around Ogbunigwe's hut, I recalled my first and last visit to another of his kind. Next to Ogbunigwe, the decrepit charlatan my sister-in-law had taken me to visit all those many years gone, seemed like an ignorant apprentice, a total novice in the art of wizardry. I bowed my head and fell to my knees before the great Juju-man.

'Great One, please, hear the pleas of your handmaiden.' I could neither control the tremor in my voice nor the quake in my body. Even in the midnight chill, my body was coated with sweat. 'My husband no longer touches me as a wife and I am a woman without a child. My childbearing years are shortening and my departed son is now a restless dead. He cannot reincarnate back to his clan without a pregnancy in my belly. Help me, great and wise One. Give me the pregnancy I seek. Give me back my son. Chain my husband to my side, so that my belly may once more swell with the seeds of a child and the bloodline is preserved,' my tears flowed unchecked as I beat my chest repeatedly with my fists.

Ogbunigwe was silent for several minutes, staring down at me from his great height, his face inscrutable, like the jagged rocks surrounding his abode.

'Are you prepared to pay the price?' His voice was low, deep, terrible.

'I have saved enough money,' I said, reaching to the lumpy knot at the edge of my wrapper, where my folded Naira notes were hidden.

'Foolish woman! Keep your money,' his hand waved away my offering. 'Listen with your ears and pay heed to my words. I repeat, are you prepared to pay the price?'

Then I knew. And yet I did not know. I suddenly recalled another saying of my people – *never dine with the devil without a very long spoon, in case you need to make a speedy escape.* A favour from the devil always came with a price in blood. *But whose blood? Whose death?* I could already sense the presence of Queen Ill-fortune at my side, mocking me, laughing at my dilemma. Her glee decided me. I was done with being the play-thing of the queen of misery.

'I am ready, Great One,' my voice was resolute, with no signs of its earlier tremor. 'I am ready to pay the price.'

'On your head be it. Before the gods, I wash my hands of any guilt and blame. I am but a messenger of the gods. Your contract is with them, not me. You have entered this agreement of your own free will and so shall it be. There is no turning back now. Give me your hand.' With a swift flicker, Ogbunigwe pierced the skin of my thumb with a blade, drawing the blood in a thick spurt. I saw the red drops hit the floor of his shrine, merging into the blood-polish with a hiss that had me almost bolting from the room. From nowhere, smoke suddenly filled the room, as if a thick fog had descended from the skies. The smell of blood was now truly overpowering. My head was swimming, my eyes watering. My breath come out in short gasps. I saw movements in the fog, quick darting motions by figures I could not decipher. They seemed human, pale and ghastly, yet, too insubstantial to the sight. And surely, no human could move with such speed, even faster than hurricane. *What on Amadioha's earth were they?*

Ogbunigwe gave me a list of items I needed to bring to him for the preparation of the charms. When I heard the list, my blood almost froze in my veins. They included the hair from my dead child's skull, our husband's under-garment, a vial of my menstrual blood, the blood from a week-old baby boy and several other animal and human parts and herbs too numerous to recount. He also wanted hair from Nwanna's head,

70

Nwanna, our husband's new son. I felt my resolve falter at that last item. Why Nwanna's hair? Why not hair from any other child? I voiced my thoughts but the great medicine-man hushed my words with a glare that put the terror in my heart. I wanted to flee from the skull-littered shrine, to hide away from the terrible visage of the witchdoctor. But I recalled his words, *"There is no turning back now."* I also remembered the melancholy face of my son, Ebuka and the arrogant swagger of Enu. I knew then what I had to do.

'It shall be done, Great One,' I bowed my head again, stooping low to kiss the ringed toes of Ogbunigwe's bare feet. 'It shall be done.'

*****

Ogbunigwe's list was truly daunting, almost impossible to secure. But as our people say, *there is nothing the eyes will see that will cause them to shed blood-tears*. A desperate need will always find a miracle. My will to bring back my son was as strong as an elephant's charge. I found my miracle in my wonderful sister, Gono, who had gone ahead to become a successful head-teacher at a top secondary school, one of the handful of female head-teachers from our country, rubbing shoulders with the white Irish nuns who ran our education institutions.

As my father had long dreaded, Gono had indeed refused to give him a befitting son-in-law and dowry, preferring to earn and keep her own money instead. She had become a very wealthy and respected woman who some people predicted would have a successful political career in the new political parties that had won us our independence from the Queen of England. Men were now seeing the hidden beauty in my sister which our father had failed to recognise on account of her dark skin hue. But Gono had my wretched marriage as a constant reminder of what that vile institution harboured for women. She vowed never to relinquish her freedom and wealth to any man.

Gono gave me the exorbitant sum I requested for the purchase of most of the items demanded by the medicine man, Ogbunigwe. She neither asked, nor did I volunteer the reason for my need. As always, she was happy in my happiness and I again thanked Our Virgin Mary for blessing me with such a loving sister, whose kindness I did not deserve.

Afterwards, for several days and nights, I agonised over the terrifying trip I had to make to *Ajo-ofia* to obtain a palmful of my dead child's hair. It was a trip which I had always lacked the courage to attempt, a journey I could not avoid, a visit that had been waiting to be made since the day they dumped my son's little body in the unhallowed grounds of *Ajo-ofia.* It was a trip now inevitable in order to bring my son back to life.

For three nights in a row, I attempted to cut the hair off Ebuka's head when he visited me. I washed him as was my habit, washing off the brown mud of his unhallowed grave and cleaning the corpse odour that continued to cling to his little body. I used a small scissors to cut off a generous amount of his hair, which remained thick and lush despite the ravages of the grave. Yet, every morning when I awoke, the hair, just like my son, would be gone, leaving me with nothing but the little red shoes and tiny clothes that remained as new as the day I bought them.

My son told me that I must go to *Ajo-ofia* to get his hair. He said he would lead me to his grave. He told me that his grave was a shallow grave, barely an arm-length in depth, as was the way with all unhallowed graves. Accursed corpses require no respect or protocol. I could easily dig open his grave with nothing more than my farming hoe. He said it was a job I could complete in the course of a single night.

Ebuka knew why I needed his hair and the knowledge made him happier than I'd ever seen since he returned to me. It was strange, the contradiction in his age and demeanour. In size, he had not aged a day beyond the three years he was when he died. Yet, his speech and reasoning were that of an *Ozo*, a wise and titled old peer of the clan. He calmly informed me that he would not come back to me until the day I became filled with the seeds of his reincarnation.

'But my son, how will you know when I get pregnant if you don't visit your poor *Mami*?' I asked, my eyes pleading, my voice cajoling.

'I will know, *Mami*,' was all he said. 'I will know.'

And so it was, that on a moonlit night of still air and sleepless insects, I made my stealthy journey to *Ajo-ofia*, accompanied only by my son and my farming hoe. I had agonised over embarking on that trip on a night when the moon hung round and low in the skies, knowing that Queen Ill-fortune was most alert on such a night. Yet, it would take an infusion of the hearts of a thousand warriors to get me to attempt that terrible journey under a black sky. I steeled myself to brave the mischief of that demon deity of bad-luck.

I started off just after midnight. I soon developed the vision of the night bat and the agility of the forest monkey as the journey progressed. I engaged in lively conversation with my son to rein in my terror. Ebuka was as sure-footed as the bush antelope as he navigated through wild vines and erosion gullies, leading me further away from Ukari village and deeper into the forest. The night seems to go on forever till suddenly, I found myself in a desert-like landscape populated with nothing but giant anthills and uncountable mounds that housed the corpses of the damned. Like a macabre farm, the mounds grew ghastly white masks, each, fortified with charms and potions to chain in the evil dead within the confines of the bad bush. A foul smell pervaded the corpse-farm, an odour of badness and decay; a vile smell that I'd tried in vain to wash off from my son's body.

My heart froze. My speech ceased. My head began to swell and expand and my breathing hung. All sounds stopped, vanished, as if cocked inside a sound-proof bottle. The noisy insects that had accompanied us through the night, the barking dogs, the hooting owls, all ceased their clamour. Even the very air seemed to succumb to the stillness of the desolate and chilling landscape. In the unnatural silence, I heard the thudding of my heart as if the drums of the masquerade dancers beat. I heard the harshness of my breathing and the roaring in my ears.

Then I saw them…*oh Jesus, Mary Mother of God*…I saw them all, the soulless inhabitants of the accursed land, *Ajo-ofia,* the doomed outcasts of the gods and men, the unclean! Gathered in a silent, waiting crowd, hollowed eyes dripping blood as black as tar, each posed in the manner of their demise, they impaled me to the ground by their appalling visage. A young mother with a rotten foetus dangling between her wide thighs; a large man with a rope tight against his impossibly-angled neck; an albino that glowed inhumanly white beneath the brightness of the moon, his body bloated and battered from the beating that caused his demise; a tiny baby wailing and writhing on the ground, his wide mouth exposing a full set of upper teeth. They were the abominations of nature and the rejects of men.

Amongst them was my son, my beautiful, sweet Ebuka, standing silently in the midst of the other small spectres, each doomed for dying before their parents or being born with abominations; a set of teeth, an extra finger, a single testicle. One second, Ebuka was by my side, his tiny hand gripped firmly in my right hand. Then in a blink, he was gone, gone without a sound, without me seeing his departure, only to appear amongst the ghoulish gathering of the damned, the cursed inhabitants of the unhallowed grounds of *Ajo-ofia*.

The sound of my hoe hitting the ground resonated like a thousand footsteps in the awful silence of the burial ground. It also released the voices of the apparitions, who started to howl in an unearthly cacophony that chilled the marrow in my bones. My voice joined their discordance, terror and panic cloaking my screams. Prayers spilled from my lips, babbles, the distinct sounds of supreme lunacy. Inside my head, Queen Ill-fortune shrieked in glee, her cackle as manic as my screams. Above us, the moon grew fatter and brighter, revealing the ghoulish figures in all their undead horror.

I tried to run, turned to flee, feeling the hot water of terror flood my thighs. I stumbled against a mask…*no*…the mask rose against my feet as if flung by an invisible hand. Then all the other white masks joined the attack like a sea of skulls, hurling themselves against my face, battering my body and my head till I fell onto a soft grave, feeling the mud cover my face, fill my screaming mouth. It was the same mud that clung to my son, the vile grave-mud of the unhallowed ground I'd tried in vain to wash off my son.

My fall stilled the masks. They fell to the ground with muffled thumps. From the corner of my eyes, I saw them scuttle away, like the crabs on the beach of River Niger, each returning to the grave-mound they guarded, their hollowed eyes watchful, dark and terrifying. In the sudden stillness, I heard another sound, a noise like the roar of the winds. And suddenly, they were everywhere, the ghosts of the damned, in front of me, behind me, at my right side and left side. And when the light of the moon dimmed above us, I glanced up to see the flying ones, the witches and *Amosu,* night-flyers, who had carried on their nefarious art even to the grave.

I felt their hands on me; cold hands, clammy hands, pus-wet hands, peeling hands, skeletal hands. Reeking bodies swamped me, seeking the warmth of my blood, the light of my humanity, my very soul. I tried to push, to crawl to safety on hands and knees, to be free of the repulsive touch of the foul undead. But I was but a woman, a weak and foolish human who should have known better than to challenge the might of the queen of malignancy on her most potent night.

But desperation was never a person of caution or reason. Desperation would dare the gates of hell and the wrath of Queen Ill-fortune to fulfil its goals. Desperation gave me the voice to scream out my son's name, to call for his aid and his intercession. Desperation fuelled my garbled explanations, my pleas for their forgiveness, my supplications for their help in finding my son's grave amongst the hundreds of unmarked mounds that grew in that accursed farm of corpses.

Suddenly, I was free - free of hands, of bodies, of voices, of the pulsating hate that had engulfed me and left me cowering on the cold hard soil of *Ajo-ofia.* Once again, my son was by my side, his little hands filled with an impossible strength, raising me to my feet, his face sad, *oh Jesu,* so very sad. I wanted to die and lie with him in that bad bush for eternity. *How can any mother bear to see her child abandoned in such a desolate and terrible place? How could I ever sleep in the warmth of my room when my only child wandered in the dark wilderness of these cursed grounds? How could I walk amongst the living when I knew that my son walked amongst the damned, the restless and angry souls of the accursed?*

As if he read my thoughts, Ebuka pointed to a small grave barely the size of a yam-tuber mound in a flourishing farm. It was guarded by a repulsive white mask that resembled a leering goblin. I shuddered as my eyes encountered that accursed object, reluctant to bring my person within its malignant reach. My heart still quaked with the recent memory of the white masks' vicious attack on me.

My son motioned me to dig, his small hands holding up my discarded hoe. Once again, my resolve was re-ignited as I stumbled my way to the small mound and started to dig. Through that moonlit night, I dug till the sweat lay on my body like a bucketful of water; till my palms went raw and bloody; till my joints ached as one crushed by a palm-tree; till my eyes ceased to see anything but brown hard soil; till my breath rushed in staggered gasps through open mouth and nostrils clogged by dirt;

Till…. till I finally struck the brittle bones of my poor, poor son, dumped in that terrible grave without the dignity of a coffin.

I began to howl. I slumped on the dirt floor of the grave and wailed - keened - mourning my dead son all over again as if he had died anew. The pain was as raw as the day the evil viper, *Echieteka,* stole him from me. My heart burnt with anger and pain, fury at the callous way they had discarded my son's body and a hurting pain that threatened to steal what was left of my sanity. I felt the presence of the ghosts, felt their compassion surround me as I tore the hair from my scalp, knocked my forehead on my hunched knees, beat the ground with clenched fists and bawled my pain into the cold dark grave of my son. I felt his little hands on my face, stroking my wet cheeks, his small cold body nestling against me, his thin arms around my neck. I held him close, so tight, I would have squeezed the life force from his body if there was any left to destroy.

'I'm so sorry, my son,' I choked between sobs. 'I'm so sorry. Forgive your poor *Mami* for not protecting you, for letting them do this to you.'

'Don't cry, *Mami*,' his voice was muffle against my chest. 'Don't cry, please *Mami*. Look, my hair is still here, see?' Ebuka pointed to his tiny skeleton which indeed still harboured a long bush of hair. That was the day I realised that hair was immortal. And it finally made sense why Ogbunigwe had demanded that particular item. Only immortality could confer life. My son's immortal hair would reincarnate him back to life. Nwanna's living hair would link the bloodline, ensuring a successful reincarnation.

I did not need a pair of scissors. The hair left my son's skull in an easy clump, filling my hand with its kinky soft texture.

'You have to go now, *Mami,* before the sun rises or there will be no one to show you the way back to Ukari. We have to sleep when the morning dawns. Come, let me take you back now.'

I allowed my son to lead me out of that terrible place, my eyes filled with tears, my heart breaking with sorrow at the tragic plight of those pathetic souls that haunted the grounds of *Ajo-ofia.* I knew some of them were guilty of the crimes that had consigned them to the bad-bush. But most of them were innocent, like my son, like those poor teethed babies. Yet, all of them were equally damned for eternity. *But not my son, not my sweet innocent baby. By* Amadioha *and all the gods, I'll free him from that terrible curse and return him to the loving fold of his family.* I now had the final and most precious item demanded by Ogbunigwe, the great witchdoctor. Ebuka's hair would be the final piece in the charms that would secure the affections of our husband once again and germinate my womb with my son's reincarnated foetus.

*****

When the door of my bedroom swung open a couple of weeks later and Agu stepped into my room, I knew that Ogbunigwe had lived up to his reputation. Even before he began stripping off his clothes, I knew from Agu's face that he had not come to inflict violence on my body. From the minute I covered my face with the foul-smelling oil given me by Ogbunigwe, I noticed a growing look of desire on Agu's face. And when he unexpectedly called me by the long-forgotten endearment, *"Nkem"*, my own, I knew that he finally belonged to me, at least in body, if not soul. Already, a cup of palm-wine laced with the cloudy liquid the medicine man had given me to feed our husband stood by my bedside, a drink which also had to be spiked with the residue of his semen before he drank it.

Afterwards, when Agu had drank the charmed wine and once again mounted me, I noticed a difference in his *Amu*. It looked and felt double its original size and remained solidly erect even after his release. I saw the look of baffled pleasure on Agu's face as he observed his enlarged and turgid organ. It was the look of a young boy discovering his first tuft of manly beard.

Over the following weeks, Agu continued to visit my room every night. His desire was insatiable and my body soon grew weary of the incessant demands made on it, coupled with the fact that his visits were affecting my son's. Ebuka had not paid me a single visit from that terrible night he led me to his grave to collect his hair from the skeletal husk that lay beneath the shallow grave at *Ajo-Ofia. Holy Mary! Jesus our Saviour!* I still shudder, still wake up in sweats, still glance behind me in unspeakable terror at the memory of that dreadful night.

As the weeks turned into months, Agu's nightly visits gradually increased to afternoon and evening visits. The intimate name, *Nkem,* never left his lips when he addressed me, even in front of strangers. Soon, malicious tongues began to wag, fuelled by Enu's spite. The words "Witch" and "Mami-water" cropped up once again in reference to me. They were tags I hadn't heard since my son's death gave birth to new names, "*Akula",* mad woman.

But this time, their insults left me cold. Despite the element of truth in their accusations, I felt none of the guilt and shame I'd felt in the days I was falsely accused. What did I care about their feelings as long as I brought back my son to life? The Holy Virgin knew I was paying my own heavy price, enduring the rough and incessant attentions of our husband to achieve my goal. My secret place was raw from the persistent demands made on it by our husband.

And yet, despite the passing months and the increased frequency of Agu's carnal visits, my belly refused to germinate with the seeds of fertility. Nothing grew inside my soured womb. But something began to grow on our husband.

*****

The first mole appeared on Agu's *Amu* on a Sunday afternoon. I know the precise time and date because I remember being dragged into my room as soon as I returned from Sunday Mass and mounted before I could even undo my *Enigogoro* head-scarf. I also remember feeling soiled and defiled by the act, considering I had just been sanctified by the Holy Communion taken from Father O'Keefe's white hands.

After the act was over, I noticed Agu starring at his *Amu,* which as always, jutted up towards the low ceiling of my room, bloated with useless seeds that could not fertilize my womb. I instantly noticed the spot on his organ, a spot more like a giant mole than anything else I could imagine. It formed a solid round mass at the tip of his *Amu,* its reddish hue contrasting starkly with the blackness of that organ. *Chickenpox!* That was my first thought; *Agu has chickenpox!* Trust the wretched man to do everything differently. Other people got the pox on their faces but not Agu. Oh no! He had to go get it on his blighted *Amu*.

By the next day, four more moles appeared and within a week, the entire length of his *Amu* was covered with the unsightly red moles. It was about this time that I noticed a difference in his possession of me. It felt as if he performed the act for a reason other than desire, as if something else was driving his frenzied thrusts, an itch perhaps, an uncontrollable urge to scratch, relieve the irritation in his skin. But why use me? Why wouldn't he keep away from me till his pox or whatever it was ailing his organ was cured?

Because of Ogbunigwe's charms, you fool! The mocking voice in my head was as nasty as Queen Ill-fortune's laughter. I'd asked for our husband to be enslaved by desire and I had my wish. Something else told me those wretched charmed drinks I had fed him over the course of several weeks were equally responsible for the disgusting moles that were fast turning his *Amu* into a twisted grotesque appendage.

Conjugal exercises had never been pleasant with our husband, even at the best of times. Now, they were just awful, terrible acts of torture that tore up the tender skin of my circumcised womanhood and left me dreading the simple act of weeing or washing. My days were now lived in terror of those hurried footsteps headed to my room, knowing that my objections would be quashed by violent hands and thrusting hips. I was raw and bleeding both inside and out but our husband was oblivious to my pain. All he knew was the driving desire that kept him chained to my bedside. He would not discuss the state of his *Amu* with me. In fact, he seemed determined to ignore the ghastly thing, despite the fact that other alien bits had joined the moles, long spiky hairs and worm-like welts.

I tried not to look at that monstrosity. Jesus knows just how much I tried to keep my eyes away from it. But the eye is the master of curiosity. It will look where it should not and seek where it is forbidden. So, my eyes followed the gradual distortion of that organ, observing the festering malignancy of that benighted appendage as crusted pus was replaced by fresh eruptions and I wished....*dear Lord*...how I wished I could sever that evil with a sharp knife and free us both from our nightmare.

We were now the talk of the whole village. Agu no longer stepped out of the house, seeing as he could not wear anything save the loose wrapper he kept secured around his waist. His visit to his *Dibia* had not cured his ailment, neither had all the ointments and antibiotics prescribed by the doctors at Park Lane Hospital. Ogbunigwe was more powerful than Agu's witchdoctor and nothing could ease our nightmare. I had tried to get an antidote from Ogbunigwe, something to cure our husband's organ and free me from the pain inflicted by that weapon. But the powerful medicine man had been like a stranger to me, aloof, cold. He reminded me that I'd made the choice of my own free will. The consequences were therefore mine to bear. He could not help me.

I remained a prisoner in my room, unable to walk without bowed thighs, writhing in agony from the lacerations inflicted by that punishing weapon. Enu and the three fat sisters shouted to all who would listen that I had chained our husband with witchcraft, that he had lost his mind as I had lost mine. His business was failing and his workers were running lawless. Enu was pregnant with yet another child and our husband ignored that fact and provided little for her comfort. The news of Enu's pregnancy almost drove me wild with jealousy. Why should she have all the luck, a living son and another easy pregnancy, when I had been going through months of torture to achieve the same fate without success? Clearly, the blasted woman was born under a very good *Chi* despite her meanness.

Except she wasn't after all.

On a dark rainy night, Nwanna got the runs. All night, I heard the sound of the housemaids rushing up and down the stairs as they emptied the child's potty. My room was still at the servants' quarters so I could keep tabs on their comings and goings. Our husband had wanted to return me to my old room which Enu occupied but I didn't want to leave the room that was my only link to my son. Ebuka must never come and not find me in my little room at the end of the servants' corridor.

Enu burst into my room a couple of hours later, rousing our husband from his deep sleep in my bed.

'Your son is dying and you lie here like an idiot,' she shouted at Agu. Her eyes were red and puffy, her hair dishevelled.

'What's wrong with Nwanna? Can I help?' I asked. I felt a sudden pity for the woman. Despite everything, she was still a mother, experiencing a mother's hurt at her child's suffering.

'Keep away from my child, you witch,' Enu glared at me, dousing my goodwill with her spite. I shrugged and turned away, feigning disinterest. Agu dragged himself up from my bed, waving Enu away.

'I'll be with you soon,' he said. 'Send for the driver to take him to Park Lane hospital.'

Enu stalked out of my room, slamming the door behind her.

'Nkem, I'll be back soon, ok?' Agu said, looking apologetic and guilty at the same time, as if he were committing a crime by attending to his sick son instead of spending time with me. Ogbunigwe's charms had really done the works on him, I thought with regret as I watched him hobble out of my room. I had not spiked his drinks in months yet his *Amu* refused to heal and his slavish devotion to me refused to wan. If only I could convert that *attachment to a pregnancy.*

Nwanna died that same night. Even the white doctors at Park Lane hospital could not perform their usual miracles. They said it was cholera, the deadly sickness of the intestines. Enu said it was witchcraft. I had finally killed her son with evil juju, as I had long intended since his birth.

The accusation chilled my bones, filling my heart with terror. *Oh Holy Mary! Don't let Nwanna's death have anything to do with my visit to Ogbunigwe and that tiny quantity of hair I'd taken from Nwanna's comb!* For several days following Nwanna's death I paced around my room, enduring sleepless night after sleepless night. *How could I live with myself if I had a hand in that innocent child's death? How could I possibly forgive myself if I had been instrumental in sending that poor child to join my son at Ajo-ofia, the dreadful corpse-farm of the doomed?*

I derived no pleasure at the thought that Enu's child now shared the same fate as my son, having died of a deadly disease before its parents. What mother would wish the same torture on a fellow mother? Who could bear the thought of another innocent child confined to that tragic, desolate, unhallowed ground?

Enu's incessant wails and howls gave me no peace, just as my troubled thoughts gave me no sleep. Nwanna's hair I'd stolen was only supposed to re-ignite my son's hair, give it the living spark it needed to bring Ebuka back and link him to his father's bloodline, enabling his speedy reincarnation. The charm was not supposed to harm the child in any way. The harm had already been done to our husband; that guilt I freely acknowledged to myself. I could live with the damage done to our husband as I was sharing the effects of it. Agu was no innocent or saint and

I still remembered the horrors he'd put me through before Ogbunigwe's charms mellowed him. Nwanna was a different story. Nwanna was an innocent child.

I found my way to Ogbunigwe's hut for the fourth and final time. From the resigned look in his eyes when he saw me, I knew he had been expecting me.

'Nothing was supposed to happen to the child,' I screamed at him, tears pouring down my cheeks. 'You told me his hair was only needed to link my son's return to his bloodline.'

'Foolish woman!' His voice was scornful, albeit I detected a hint of compassion in his bloodshot eyes. 'I did warn you, didn't I? I am only a mouthpiece to the oracle and the gods never lie, not in my lifetime, nor in the lifetimes of my grandfather and great grandfather. I come from a long line of shrine-keepers and our juju have never failed.'

'Then why am I not pregnant? Why has my son not returned to me yet?' My voice was shrill in the dead silence of the night.

'A life for a life, a son for a son. Fear not, the bloodline is not broken. The oracle never lies. Return to your home, woman, and disturb me no more. My patience with you now wears thin.'

The witchdoctor waved me away with a casual flick of his hand, as if I was no more than a troublesome gnat, as if he hadn't just destroyed my life with his words, as if the death of an innocent child by his actions was no more than a splash of water on a Sunday gown.

I stumbled out of his hut and into the warm blackness of the night. My body was shivering uncontrollably. My heart was pounding painfully and a loud voice kept screaming, *no! no! no!* inside my head. *What have I done? Oh dear Jesus, what have I done?*

*****

Following Nwanna's death, Enu and the three fat sisters called several meetings of the clan to air their suspicions and vent their rage. The clansmen consulted several witchdoctors, who all pointed their fingers at me. They said that the curse of Queen Ill-fortune had been brought upon the family by my actions when my son died. They claimed that I had an unholy union with some powerful deities which defied their own powers. The house of Agu, son of Onori, was a doomed one. The only way to break the curse was to sever my link to the family.

The elders reached a decision that I was to be sent back to my father's house without delay. I read the fear and repulsion in their averted eyes as they told me my fate. The only eyes that held no fear was Enu's. If hatred alone could kill, I would have been struck dead in seconds. Her eyes were the only gaze I could not hold in that large gathering of clansmen and women.

Our husband vetoed their ruling, telling them in no uncertain terms that I was his wife of no regrets, as he put it. He said that if anyone was to leave his house, it was Enu, not I. I heard Enu's sudden gasp, echoed by the rest of the family at Agu's words. His unusual stance confirmed all their suspicions but there was little they could do but wait, scheme, bide their time.

Until the day Agu finally succumbed to the infection that had journeyed from his deformed *Amu* to his veins, poisoning his blood and stealing his breath. He died in my bedroom, right on my bed, still trying to mount me even as death pulled him to its black door. The last words I heard from his lips were *"Nkem"*, my own, repeated over and over till his speech was silenced by eternity.

And I suddenly found myself at the mercy of all the enemies I had made in that accursed village, Ukari, helpless, childless and with no-one to protect me from their collective hate. I had no one to speak for me, plead my cause and spare me from the nightmare of my ordeal in the accursed forest of Ukari and the terrifying judgement of *The Tree of Truth.*

*****

Ukari Forest – 5:15am

Above me, heaven suddenly opens its mouth and spews down a thunderstorm on mankind. God's eyes flash His wrath across the skies and His anger roars over the world. In seconds, I am drenched, the rain washing the matted filth and blood from my body.

I raise my face to the skies. My mouth is open as I drink in God's holy water of my salvation; real water at last, not the corpse water I've endured for days. The water rejuvenates me. It also rejuvenates the world of the living - and of the dead.

I see them. Suddenly, I see them in the deep gloom of the forest. They are everywhere; soulless spectres, the restless spirits of all the victims of The Tree of Truth. They crowd around the tree, howling, pleading their case, begging forgiveness for past crimes, cursing, laughing; the pitiful laughter of the insane. They fly against the tree, through the tree, around the tree. They're drawn to the tree like moth to flame, powerless to leave the scene of their demise or the towering judge that sentenced them to sleepless eternity.

I recognise some of their faces; Ugomma the witch, Adaku the husband poisoner, one-eyed Chiadi, the child-napper and Ijeoma the night-flyer. The great tree had judged them all guilty, just as it might yet find me guilty. It seems to have a peculiar penchant for the evil souls of women. I do not want to be judged by The Tree of Truth. I fear I may not survive its wrath. I pray I do not become an unclean. Ajo-ofia is no place for eternal rest.

I see my son, Ebuka, hovering beyond the ring of salt. He is murky, coated in dirt and a strange darkness that renders him almost indistinct. My heart swells with delight then shrivels with terror at the look in his eyes. They blaze with hate, with rejection. He points at me, an accusing finger and I hear his voice, louder than the thunder that had heralded the storm.

'You lied to me,' he screams. 'You lied! You cannot bring me back because I don't belong to Agu's Obi, his ancestral compound. His blood does not flow in my veins so I can never be reborn

to his bloodline. I can never return anywhere. Only Nwanna can go back. His bloodline is intact. His mother is pregnant. You have doomed me to Ajo-ofia for eternity. I hate you, Mami, I hate you.'

I am wailing as I see my son fade into the night, the night that has suddenly turned as bright as day, lit up by the engorged moon.

Then, I see Nwanna. He flies like all the other spectres, hovering in the clearing, laughing, his voice tingling like little bells, his child's eyes happy, innocent. They bear me no malice, no hatred for my deeds. He glows with a dazzling brightness that is almost blinding in its intensity. Then he winks out, just like a star. And I am all alone with my guilt and my shame. The rain pounds down on me, relentless, merciless.

It has all been for nothing...nothing. After everything, all my suffering, all my hopes, my plans, everything. In the end, it has all been for nothing. If only I had gone back to Pastor Brother Ezekiel rather than that accursed witchdoctor, Ogbunigwe. If only I'd been born under a brighter Chi.

I hear a rustle. My head swivels. I see the waifs melt into The Tree of Truth, disappear into the massive trunk. The bark turns a sickly grey colour and the roots begin to heave. Oh Holy

Mary! The Tree is alive! It moves! My husband's corpse stirs, sluggishly, blindly, its arms lifting, slowly. A bloated hand gropes its way to its Amu. It clasps the erect vileness and starts to yank in a grotesque act of masturbation. I gag, my stomach heaving, my muscles contracting, aching, hurting.

The head turns, silently, heavily, towards me, where I cower at the edge of the salt ring. I begin to shudder. My entire body is one continuous rattle, my teeth, my bones. Oh Holy Mary, sweet mother of God, don't let him open his eyes, please... keep his eyes shut...

The lids lift and I see those eyes - bloody, black. They stare at me, fix me with their dead glare. I shut my lids and cover my head with my arms. The heavens continue to pour and I hear my moans, whimpers that sound like Agu's dog when it is whipped for misbehaving. I hear another sound, a croak, like a strangled man's dying grunt. Then I hear the words, repeated over and over and over and over...

'Nkem...Nkem...Nkem...'

I jump to my feet and scream. I remember too late the salt ring, the charmed circle made by the powerful witchdoctors to keep me trapped under The Tree of Truth. I hit an invisible wall. Bright lights explode inside my head as I stumble back, falling, falling, right atop the rotten carcass of my randy husband. I feel arms encircle me, strong arms, skin slimy against mine, sleeked by decay and death. The stench is overpowering and I am suddenly re-living my dreams, my night-terrors only a few hours past.

Just as in my nightmare, I feel the hard thrust of that rotting, jutting deformity against my thighs, feel the touch of those putrid hands pushing, prising my thighs apart with a strength not of the living. The pain is excruciating, unbearable. I hear that awful gurgling sound repeat the accursed name, "Nkem" into my ears. My soul is pulled, dragged from my being by a malignant force beyond the realm of the living.

And I am screaming, shrieking. Queen Ill-fortune is cackling, crowing with unholy glee. The fat moon smiles down benignly at my unholy ravishment and impending death. God is thundering, roaring, helpless as He's always been in the face of mankind's tragedy. Our husband is grunting, panting. The spectres gather closer, their ashen faces greedy for my dying soul, eager to welcome me into their foul and restless fold.

From a distance, I hear the sound of the approaching villagers, murder in their voices. A small smile twists my bruised lips. They will be too late. I can already sense my soul fleeing, fighting for release from my dying body. I am happy to give it its freedom. I am ready to be judged, to end this accursed cycle and heaven willing, begin a better one. If nothing else, I shall share the same unhallowed grounds with my son and be with him for as long as the gods wish. It is a better fate than one of eternal sexual servitude to our husband, who is still panting his pleasure on my immobile, dying body. I feel nothing now, not the rain, not the pain, not even the fear.

I cast my dimming eyes at The Tree of Truth, awaiting its final judgement. But The Tree of Truth... The Tree of Truth is silent.

*****

Night Market (Oja-ale)

"You pay for what you get, you own what you pay for…and sooner or later, whatever you own comes back home to you."
Stephen King – "IT"

The girl came out of nowhere. Hunched on the back seat of his white Land Rover Discovery, Alan Pearson saw her through the rainy blackness of the narrow road. The headlamps picked out the drenched figure by the grassy verge. Her clothes clung wetly to her body, defining the contours in a way that left no doubt of her sex and youth. That was why he ordered his driver to pull over; that and the fact that it was late, almost midnight on the car's digital clock. The stormy night magnified the wild isolation of the terrain. It was no place for a young girl to be by herself, especially in a country like the one he lived in.

Everyone knew the dangers of Nigerian roads, day or night. Armed robbers, kidnappers and terrorists competed with corrupt policemen and out-of-control soldiers at various ad-hoc checkpoints, wreaking terror on unwary travellers. Alan needed little reminder that he was an easy crime target, diplomat or not. He was a white man, perceived as a bearer of dollars and pounds, not to mention a potential ransom hostage for the various criminal factions operating in the country. It was Embassy policy not to offer bribes at these checkpoints. But Alan had learnt that it made life easier to just hand over a wad of *Naira* notes to the checkpoint tyrants and get waved through with wide smiles and loud cheers

Olu, his driver was reluctant to stop, driving on for several seconds after Alan had instructed him to pull over. He reminded Alan that the girl could be a member of an armed robbery gang, a decoy sent to lure gullible fools into their trap. Alan silently acknowledged the truth in Olu's words. But a stronger truth ruled his heart. *What self-respecting Englishman would abandon a woman in distress?* The girl was clearly in dire straits. He saw the fear in the frantic wave of her hands as Olu reversed their four-wheel to her. He wound down the window, his hands ineffectual in shielding his face from the rain that blew into the car.

'Would you like a lift?' he shouted, his words almost drowned by the sudden clasp of thunder that rumbled the earth. The girl nodded, twisting her shawl tightly around her face. *Fat lot of good that would do to keep the rain off her head,* Alan thought, watching the water trail down her flowered cotton kaftan, melting the cloth into her body. He pushed open the door, inviting the girl into the car. He heard the deep sigh of disgust coming from the driver's seat. Olu wasn't impressed by his chivalry. Not that Alan blamed the man. After all, Olu would have to clean up the mud and dry out the car.

'*Oshe,* sir,' the girl's voice was soft, almost a whisper.

'You're welcome,' Alan said, proud of his limited grasp of the Yoruba language. 'Olu, ask her where she's going and if it's on our way, drop her off or at the safest location you can find.'

Olu muttered a low oath in Yoruba and turned to face their passenger. 'Where you dey go?' Olu barked the question, his face as fierce as his voice. The girl's response was in the same soft husk. Alan listened as his driver and the girl talked, their exchange too fast for him to understand.

But he couldn't miss the condescension in Olu's tone and the submissive fear in the girl's whispered response. Alan shook his head with a weary sigh, stifling his exasperation. He'd long ceased to be irritated by Olu's high-handed manner with anyone who wasn't white, rich or in military uniform. The man's arrogance put the most pompous English butler to shame.

His loyalty and honesty however, were unquestionable. In a country rife with corruption and exploitation, where everyone, including the beggars, were out to rip off everyone else, Olu was a rarity, a godsend he was fortunate to have as his official driver. Olu treated Alan as his personal property, convinced every woman wanted a piece of Alan's body and everyone else wanted to exploit his position at the High Commission for a British Visa.

As the commercial attaché, Alan had spent the last three days at a trade fair in Benin City, negotiating lucrative deals for British companies seeking expansion into Africa's largest economy. They had left Benin just after midday and would have been back at his house in Lagos in hours but for an unplanned detour. A ghastly accident along the express road had caused a pile-up and queues so long, they'd decided to seek a different route back to Lagos.

Except that a host of misfortunes had landed them in their present dismal predicament. They were hopelessly lost in the middle of a violent thunderstorm, driving through a desolate stretch of road somewhere close to midnight. Were he of a superstitious disposition, Alan would've been convinced that an invisible, malevolent hand was against them. He left all that however, to his driver, Olu, who was convinced supernatural forces were at work in the most mundane of circumstances.

The detour they'd taken had turned out a dead end, thanks to the ravages of erosion, which had eaten deep into the road, splitting it into two un-joinable paths. There were no warning signs to motorists of the danger ahead and it was a testament to Olu's driving expertise that they hadn't plunged into that terrible abyss at the speed they'd been going.

The experience had shaken them enough to dim their senses and intelligence. Otherwise, how else could one explain their foolhardy actions in asking for directions and accepting the instructions of the next decrepit-looking villager they'd met? Alan had long discovered that one thing Nigerians shared in common with the Englishman is a reluctance to admit they didn't have the answer to every problem. 'No problem,' was the national response to every request, no matter how impossible. Ask a Nigerian man if he could turn day into night and without batting an eyelid, he would reply 'No problem', with that ever-ready affable smile.

Two hours after following the villager's directions, they had enough problems to last them a lifetime. They were still driving round like headless chickens, seeking that magical expanse of asphalt that would signal a motorway, civilization of some sort, a road to somewhere, possibly, Lagos, their final destination.

The sudden braking of the car flung Alan forward, almost dashing his head against the front seat, but for the firm hold of his seat belt. Olu pulled the jeep to a halt in the middle of the road and killed the engine. He jumped out of the car, leaving his door wide open, automatically lighting up the car with the electronic lighting system. Wet, muggy air flooded the car, diluting the chill of the air-conditioning. The back door pulled open and Olu lunged forward like a man possessed. He started pulling the girl by her arm, intent on dragging her from the vehicle. He screamed at her in Yoruba. Alan didn't need a translator to tell him Olu was cursing the girl in the vilest manner possible.

'Olu! What the hell! Are you crazy or what? What's got into you?' The girl's loud cries drowned out Alan's voice. She grasped his arm with surprisingly strong hands for one so small, her fingers like pincers, digging into his flesh.

'*E gbami o!* Help me, sir! *E joo*, please!' Her voice was shrill, desperate.

'Olu, let her go at once…do you hear me? At once, I said.' Alan's voice was harsh. 'Hell! What's the matter with you, my man? Get back into the car at once…at once.'

Olu slammed the door with such force the entire car rattled. He jumped back into his seat, wiping the rain from his face. He shut the driver's door and once more, the car was plunged in the familiar darkness, punctured only by the regular flashes of lightning. They had not met any other car in over an hour.

'Mister Alan, the girl is bad. She is a very bad girl, sir. She must leave this car or she will bring us bad luck,' Olu turned round to face him, before glaring at the girl. Alan saw something in his black pupils, the look of an arachnophobe that sees a bloated tarantula crawling up his bed – revulsion and terror. He curbed his instinctive impulse to laugh out at Olu's hysteria. Experience had taught him that these people took their superstitions seriously. It would never do to mock them.

'Olu, as a Christian, I'm sure you're aware that Jesus fraternised with prostitutes and lepers and we both know he didn't die from AIDS or Ebola,' Alan' voice was gentle, like a mother soothing a bruised child in a playground accident. 'So what if the poor girl is a prostitute? I'm sure neither of us will be jumping into bed with her and the last time I checked, AIDS still isn't airborne. So, why don't we find our way out of this infernal place and get ourselves back to Lagos as quickly as we can, eh?' A thought occurred to Alan. 'In fact, why don't you ask the girl for directions? She's clearly local to these parts and just might be our salvation tonight. You never know. One good turn deserving another and all, eh?'

Alan glanced at the girl, who was huddled at the far end of the seat, her shoulder pressed tight against the door. She still held her wet shawl tightly to her face, blocking her features. He saw the shuddering motion of her shoulders and realised she was crying. *Poor thing!* Who knew what horrors had dragged her into the murky world of the thriving flesh market. It infuriated Alan to witness the glaring inequalities amongst the Nigerian population, the corrupt enrichment of the privileged few against the enslavement of the rest of the citizens. The poor girl huddled in his car could well be a genius for all he knew but poverty had consigned her to prostitution and abuse. The least he could do for her was to give her a lift to safety and perhaps three thousand *Naira* to tide her through the week. In England, £10 was barely enough to feed a dog for a week. But thankfully, its local equivalent would be sufficient to meet the girl's needs for a couple of days. He would have liked to give more but was low on local currency. He doubted if Olu would offer any assistance, not with the look on his face. He'd seen raging bulls look meeker than Olu presently did.

'Mister Alan, the girl is not a prostitute, sir,' Olu's voice was pitched as one addressing an imbecile, each word punctuated, every letter stressed. 'She is a Quarter-to-Dead, sir.'

This time, Alan abandoned all decorum and burst into loud laughter. 'A Quarter-to-Dead! That's a new one,' he chuckled, shaking his head in amazement. Just when he thought he'd heard all the outlandish expressions in the English dictionary that only Nigerians could come up with, Olu sprang yet another massacre of Her Majesty's English on him.

'Pray, let me into the secret,' Alan said, ignoring Olu's frown of displeasure at his merriment. If the fool insisted on his superstitious drivel, then he deserved everything he got. Alan was suddenly in need of light entertainment at Olu's expense. 'So, what exactly is a Quarter-to-Dead then? Wait…don't tell me. Let me guess,' Alan turned to face the girl, a grave look on his face, struggling to reign in his mirth at Olu's frustrated hiss. The girl remained mute, her face hidden behind her shawl, looking into the night as if they did not exist in her lonely world. 'I see what you mean. I see the clock of doom hanging over her head.' Suddenly, he'd had enough of the farce. 'Olu, just drive, ok? The girl is not dying and even if she's told you she is, is that any reason to abandon her to her fate on this dangerous road?'

A sudden flash of lightning and clasp of thunder reminded him of their plight. 'Olu, make you start the engine now, my man,' Alan instinctively reverted back to the local lingo, a form of Pigeon English he found both amusing and fascinating. There was a music to it that was irresistible to him. He'd had to catch himself on several occasions from using it in his normal daily interactions with fellow diplomats.

'Mister Alan, I beg you, let me remove this woman from the car now,' Olu's voice held an urgent ring, almost desperate. Before Alan could respond, the car was flooded again in near-blinding brightness as Olu switched on the interior lights. Alan blinked, blinded by the light. 'Mister Alan, ask the woman to remove her scarf from her face, I beg you. Just use your hand remove her scarf and you go see the thing that she is.'

The fear was back in Olu's voice. He unconsciously reverted to the Pigeon English he scorned to use in the presence of his white employers. Alan turned to the girl without a second's thought. Good English manners demanded better of him but he couldn't have stopped himself from looking in her direction if a

112

knife was held to his throat. It had to do with the fear in Olu's voice, his unusual choice of words. *When did it become normal to describe a girl as a thing?*

The girl pressed herself harder against the door, pulling further away from Alan. He saw the glistening blackness of her pupils through the narrow slit of her shawl. They were wide in fear. He'd seen the same helpless terror in the eyes of trapped foxes during the few hunts he'd attended in the past with his parents, before the cruelty of the sport put him off it for good. Her fear tugged something in his heart. He felt a sudden fury at Olu, an anger that was as much directed at himself for being a party to the poor girl's shabby treatment.

'I've heard enough of your gibberish for the night,' Alan's voice was harsh, icy. 'Not another word out of you or you can start looking for a new job tomorrow. Now start the car and get going. And switch off the blasted light while you're at it.'

For a few seconds, it seemed as if Olu would defy his orders. His black pupils flashed, his gaze alternating rapidly between Alan and the girl before finally turning away from them. He switched off the light with a loud hiss and turned on the engine. Soon, they were on their way again, fighting the rain, the potholes and the dense darkness of the alien territory. Occasionally, Alan saw a brightly lit mansion amidst several lamp-lit mud huts, their loud generators breaking the otherwise grave silence of the road. *Quintessential Nigeria,* he thought. *The obscenely rich flagrantly flaunting their corruptly-acquired wealth to the pathetically destitute and finding nothing morally reprehensible in their egotistical, vulgar displays.*

The girl crouched quietly in her huddled corner, like a lost mouse in a cat-guarded kitchen. Alan let her be, pretending intense interest in his mobile phone, which as expected, had no signal. Thank heavens he'd been able to get a call through to Laura when they'd taken their first wrong turn of the long night. Otherwise by now, she would be going silently crazy with worry. Even so, he knew his wife would be worried out of her wits. They'd been lost for much longer than he'd anticipated. He didn't want to imagine the number of cups of Earl Grey tea Laura must have consumed in the course of the night.

He caught a slight movement from the girl from the corner of his eyes. She quickly turned away when he sent a reassuring smile her way. He wondered if he was being prudent in using his diplomatic mobile phone with its coded contact numbers in the presence of the girl. Its loss or theft would be a serious disciplinary incidence. But he doubted if the young girl in the car had any interest in anything other than getting to wherever she was headed to at such an unholy hour and horrific weather. Thankfully, the rain appeared to be easing and the roads widening, as more electric-lit houses cropped up, pushing the trees further back from the roads.

Soon, the roads became busier with cars, dilapidated *Molue* buses and *Keke-Marwa* tricycle taxis, all fighting for road dominance, horns blaring with manic persistence and deafening pitch. Pedestrians and wayside hawkers jostled for ground space while the flashing bulbs of police cars strove to out-shine the flickering street lights and rapidly changing traffic lights. Long queues of cars formed on multi-laned roads, as self-deputised traffic wardens in police uniforms tried to assist the traffic lights with the usual disastrous consequences. They happily waved traffic on when the lights were on red, forgetting to stop vehicles who were obeying the green lights from the opposite direction. Angry horns and screamed curses ensued, with a few free-for-all fist-fights, all calmly observed by the incompetent policemen masquerading as traffic wardens. In no time, arrests were made, with the police demanding on-the-spot bribes to let the hapless motorists free.

The general air of chaos and mania brought a broad smile to Alan's face. *Lagos! Good old fucking Lagos!* Against all odds, they had found their way back to the sleepless city of endless day. The girl had brought them good luck after all; just as he'd said to Olu, one good turn deserving another. He was home and he didn't use the word lightly. Lagos was his home in every sense. The Island city, with its collection of crazy people from all corners of the world, its congested roads, its wild night-life and organised chaos, had insidiously woven its way into Alan's bloodstream. As if to truly welcome him into its whore arms, Lagos had sent its lagoon-bred mosquitoes to make a mockery of the anti-malaria medication he'd taken in England before his journey to Nigeria. He was struck down with the deadly disease within weeks of his arrival to Lagos and for a while, it had been a case of touch and go as the British High Commission considered flying him straight back to England.

But as suddenly as it had struck, the illness vanished without any after-effects. One day he was lying on his sweat-drenched sheets, shivering uncontrollably with the chills, the aches, the hallucinations and pains that accompanied the

116

disease. The next day, he was fever-free, alert and pain-free, with a raging appetite that demanded instant satisfaction. He had received his baptism into the City of Lagos fraternity. He was a bona-fide *Lagosian.*

The doctors said it was a near-miracle, that he had the constitution of an ox. Alan put it down to his fitness and the loving care of his wife, Laura. Years of jogging, horse-riding and cycling had firmed his body to athletic perfection. People assumed he was several years younger than his thirty-seven years. With his grey-green eyes and sun-bleached wavy hair, he knew with a certain degree of vanity that the excessive attention he got from the local female population had more to do with his looks than his job at the High Commission.

Alan had been warned - just as other diplomats on rookie posts in Nigeria - about the temptations posed by the dangerously attractive Nigerian women, especially to foreign diplomats, whom they viewed as their easy tickets to visas and foreign citizenship. American and British diplomats were the most sought after by these ruthless sirens. In fact, there was a voluminous book of indiscretions at the High Commission, where all staff had to record every single intimate encounter they had with the locals. The chap who manned the book was a good friend of Alan's and had once given him a peep at its salacious contents. His mind had boggled at some of the recorded encounters he'd read, the gullibility and stupidity of supposedly intelligent British men and the manipulative ingenuity of the Nigerian women.

Alan guessed he should be grateful for Laura's presence in Lagos, which kept him out of the reach of the white female expatriates, who were as desperate as their local sisters for erotic liaisons with eligible men. Unlike the Lagos ladies, Alan found that the British females in general, accepted the boundaries set by his married status, albeit with reluctance. He still got the occasional flirtatious invitations from some faded blonde desperadoes. It was a different ball-game with the Lagos women, especially the socialites. Poor Laura was no match to those seductive, over-confident barracudas, with their sophisticated and ruthless allure. *Bisi!* Alan's face relaxed in a small smile at the thought of his glamorous secretary.

Save for Olu's zealous sentinel, Alan knew without a hint of self-deceit, that his amorous report would have long peppered the pages of that notorious red book of indiscretions at the High Commission. It would take a man with blood of ice to resist the dangerous charms of Lagos socialites. There was an edginess to them that Alan had never encountered in any of his previous relationships; something in the way they looked at a man, as if he were a delicious bowl of ice-cream offered to a weary traveller in a hot, barren desert. They walked - sashayed - as if they owned the world, modern day Cleopatras to all men named Anthony or otherwise. He was as terrified as he was mesmerised by their dark allure, somewhat like Adam must have felt the first time God delivered Eve into his safe, garden paradise.

But he was a married man, perhaps not happily noosed but nonetheless bound in Church of England wedlock to the most loving and solicitous wife any man could wish for. *Laura.* Petite, blonde Laura with the coldest hands and warmest heart in the universe, the only white person that wore cardigans in Africa and drank endless cups of Earl Grey tea under the sweltering Nigerian sun.

In their nine years of marriage, Laura had accompanied him to every single posting without complaint, leaving friends and family as each new posting arose. Spain and China had been enjoyable interludes for Laura, with her incessant need for warmth. But so far, Nigeria hadn't been

119

the great hit he had hoped for. Laura hadn't taken to Lagos as he had.

A loud blast, followed by an equally loud curse from Olu, interrupted Alan's musings. There was a peculiar motion to the car that was unmistakeable, like a woman trying to walk on one broken heel.

'Flat tyre, sir,' Olu's comment was unnecessary. Alan knew a flat when he felt it. 'See the bad luck this devil witch come give us now.' Olu's hiss was loud and long as he drove for several more minutes in search of a safe place to stop in the busy road. Alan knew better than to respond to Olu's comments. The fool was still seething over their passenger's presence in their car. Anyone stupid enough to blame a flat tyre on a hapless young girl minding her own business hiding underneath her soggy shawl, deserved to be ignored.

Olu manoeuvred the car to a space that wasn't quite a kerb but wide enough to keep them from the dangers of the congested road. Alan looked at the girl, sitting quietly in her corner of the car. He was suddenly overcome with a strong desire to see her face, perhaps, read her tragic story on her features – *the life and times of a young Nigerian street-walker. Poor thing.* Olu jumped out of the car, slamming the door behind him and murmuring querulously under his breath as he made his way to the rear of the Discovery, where the spare tyre adorned the boot like a black rosette.

Olu's exit acted like a shot of adrenaline to the girl. She sat up from her huddled position, wrapping her shawl even tighter over her face. The movement released a strange odour that was both sour and pungent at the same time, like a mixture of rotting fruits and rotten fish. As the smell hit his nostrils, Alan realised that he wasn't experiencing it for the first time. The smell had been present in the car for quite a while, from the time the girl joined him in the back seat of the Discovery. The ruckus with Olu, coupled with the storm and their dire straits had clouded his senses. The odour had taken back seat in his sensory perceptions, somewhat like the dull headaches of a chronic migraine sufferer. You knew it was there but as long as it stayed muted, you were happy to live with its inconvenience, ignore its existence the best you could.

Until the big one struck again, the mother and father of all headaches, the blinding throb of pure, undiluted agony. That was what Alan now experienced as the girl turned to face him. He gagged, struggling to breathe in the rank, cloying enclosure of the car. His finger instinctively pressed the electronic window buttons, pushing down again and again in frenzied desperation. It took him a few terrible seconds to realise that the engine was switched off, killing the electronic function of the car. The window stayed wound up.

He felt the girl's hand on his arm. It had the same unexpected strength he recalled from her last contact with him, only stronger, much more powerful, like a metal clamp on soft flesh. Another sensation, unpleasant, repulsive, crawled across his skin. His mind travelled the speed of light to an earlier time, a warm summer day in his parents' vast mansion in rural Shropshire; freshly mowed lawns under a lazy summer sun. He was seven or eight years and Keith Bowman-Myers was visiting with his parents. They'd weaved through thick, mature foliage, playing tag and other silly games little boys got up to, even though Keith was now a new teenager, thirteen years at his last birthday not too long ago. But Keith was cool. He didn't act all big or know-it-all like Alan's big sister, Sarah, who thought she was as grown up as mommy, just because she got the yucky blood thing that girls get. He was glad he wasn't a girl.

Suddenly, Keith turned to Alan and asked if he wanted to see something special.

'Yes, oh yes please,' Alan was all eager and excited.

'Ok, shut your eyes and promise not to open them till I say so,' Keith instructed. Alan obeyed. He heard a rustling sound, loud uneven breathing, sounds of excitement similar to his own. Keith's hand reached for his own. It felt clammy and hot. Alan didn't like its sweaty warmth on his own.

'Remember, keep your eyes shut,' Keith's voice was hoarse, as if he had a cold. Alan nodded, feeling his own excitement build, drowning out the unpleasant sensation of Keith's moist hand.

Suddenly, he felt something slide into his hand, something warm, silky, hard, something vaguely familiar, yet oddly strange, not nice...*uh-uh*. His lids snapped apart. He looked down and saw Keith's penis snuggled in his hand. Keith clasped his wrist, urging him closer, drawing him nearer to his naked thighs.

Alan's stomach churned, a sickening sensation layering his skin in goosebumps. Shock, disgust and fear warred within him and the piercing scream he gave was a culmination of all three. Keith let go of his wrist, surprise and terror replacing the hazy glaze in his pupils. Alan heard his mother's voice calling out to him, her feet rushing towards them even as Keith pulled up his trousers, his movements hurried and furtive, his face as red as the plum in cook's basket.

He'd rushed past his mother, desperate to hide, hide the truth from her, hide the shame from himself. He washed his hands till his palms hurt. With the exception of his wife, he never told anyone what had happened in the garden that idyllic summer's day. Keith never visited again. For Alan, that day marked the end of his childhood, the death of innocence. He would never again trust any older boy or forget the unwholesome and unclean sensation he'd experienced that day when his hand made contact with Keith's aroused penis; a sensation he now felt all over again at the girl's touch on his arm.

Alan tried to pull away, break contact with her. But she held fast, as if she'd read his thoughts, his aversion to her touch and wanted to punish him for them.

'*Oyinbo*, white man, give me something,' her voice was strong, even commanding. Gone was the husky wail of the drenched waif he had rescued from the storm. 'I say give me something now or you be deaf?'

As she spoke, a foul rankness oozed from her mouth, like a mushroom cloud of decay. Alan felt his head swim. For a second, he was convinced he would faint from the suffocating reek. Her hand tightened its clasp on his arm and again, the unpleasant sensation churned his stomach. He wanted to remove her hand but he was suddenly afraid to touch her skin. He looked into her eyes and recoiled, repulsed by the leer he saw in the black pupils. *Dear Lord! Did the woman actually believe he was interested in anything she had to offer?* Even if he were that way inclined (which he wasn't and would never be) he would seek out a higher class of prostitute than the stinking whore in his car.

He reached for his wallet, his movements frantic, hurried. Better give her the money and send her on her way. He pulled out a wad of *Naira* notes and gave them to her. He had planned to give her the money anyway, with or without her demanding for it. He wished she hadn't asked in such a repulsive manner, that she'd let him be her kind benefactor without ruining his goodwill with her vile greed.

'Keep your money,' her voice was dismissive, even contemptuous. Her eyes darted round the car in a shifty and rapid scan. They settled on Laura's cardigan, the lilac M&S cardigan with the mother-of-pearl buttons. Laura kept it as a spare for when the car's air-conditioning system got too chilly for her. The girl grabbed the cardigan before Alan realised her intent. She pushed it under her armpits and made for the door. Instinctively, he stretched out his arm to stop her. Not because he gave a hoot about the cardigan or its value. Laura had loads of cardigans floating around the house. No; his action was purely an act of principle and outrage. He'd be damned if he let anyone rob him in such a blatant fashion, especially when he'd gone out of his way to be kind. He grabbed hold of her shawl in restraint. His action caught her unawares and before her raised hand could hold up the shawl, it fell from her head to the carpeted floor of the car.

Their screams were simultaneous; hers, a shriek of panic, Alan's, a shout of horror. What he saw before him, what he glimpsed before Olu yanked his door wide open, was the mummified skull of an ancient corpse, ghastly and hideous; a foul and unholy thing that could only have been spawned in absolute evil. The paper-thin skin clung to her face like a withered scalp. Where the nose should have been was a yawning black hole. Her lips were drawn back, revealing hideously blackened teeth. The wisps of hair still clinging to her scalp was as silvery as a winter moon and her eyes sunk so deep into her skull that she appeared almost skeletal. The smell of rotting fruits and rotten fish was all pervasive, even with the car door now open.

In a twinkling, the girl…*the thing*…leapt out of the car, running in a clumsy manner, her gait similar to a that of an old drunk after a night of vodka bingeing.

'Mister Alan! What happen? Wetin the devil woman do to you?' Olu's eyes followed the fleeing figure of the girl as she disappeared into one of the filthy alleyways that carved across Lagos Island like a maniac's maze. His voice dragged Alan back from his terror. He shook his head, trying to bring back sanity, normalcy, to the bizarre situation. He felt the rapid thudding of his heart beneath his pale blue cotton shirt and his breath came out in short, hard gasps. A drop of sweat trickled down the side of his face. He raised his hand to wipe it. They were trembling like storm-tossed leaves. *Hell! What on earth just happened? That girl… that loathsome thing… did he really see the nightmare his mind was forcing him to confront?*

Again, Alan saw the gruesome image in his mind's eye, the near-bald head with its withered face that was more a death-mask than a human head. Not even an AIDS victim at death's door could look that shrivelled. What he'd seen was something foul, rotten, reeking of corruption and the grave.

'I told you she is Quarter-to-Dead but you refuse to listen. I smell *Oja-ale*, the Night Market, on the girl immediately she enter our motor. It is the smell of the dead. Anyone who enter that market must sell their life to the ghosts that trade there. Once they sell their life till they pass half-past-life and reach quarter-to-dead, then they get the smell of *Oja-ale*. Soon that girl will reach dead-o'clock and her life go finish. Mister Alan, we don see evil with our two eyes today! *Chei!*'

Olu's steady monotone had a calming effect on Alan till his loud exclamation dragged back Alan's racing thoughts. He looked around him, his eyes wide with shock. He noticed the wet shawl on the floor of the car amidst the scattered *Naira* notes. The crawling sensation returned to his skin.

'Take that filthy thing out of the car at once,' he ordered, pointing a shaky finger at the shawl. Olu rushed round the other side of the car to obey, although he refused to touch the cloth, using the cross wrench of the car jack instead to toss out the offending shawl. Alan again saw the fear in Olu's face as he discarded the shawl with the cross wrench. He didn't have to guess the train of Olu's thoughts...*superstitious fool had talked himself into terror with all that drivel about quarter-to-deads and half-past-lifes.*

Then he realised that Laura's cardigan was gone. The foul thing had escaped with it after all. An uneasy feeling settled in his stomach. Something didn't feel right. Why would the girl...the thing, (he must stop ascribing any human qualities to that evil abomination) refuse the money and take the cardigan instead? Admittedly, she was drenched to the skin and no doubt needed the warmth of the cardigan. Still, why would someone like her turn down the money? The thought of Laura's cardigan on that creature made him sick to the gut. Suddenly, all he wanted to do was to get home to Laura, to her clean, pure love and be cleansed of the foul evil he'd just encountered. His head felt clogged by the putrid smell the thing had emitted. He feared the smell would never leave his nostrils again.

'I told you that girl is bad luck. She is the one that make our tyre go flat so she can do evil juju on us. Only by the blood of Jesus that we are alive now, I swear,' Olu's voice was starting to grate on Alan's nerves.

'Just get into the car and get going,' Alan snapped. 'We've wasted enough time as it is. And not another word about the girl. Make sure you don't mention any of this nonsense to Madam either.'

'Yes sir,' Olu's voice was sullen. Alan felt a twinge of regret for his abruptness. Olu was only trying to help in his usual over-zealous manner. But Alan was tired and still shaken by the weird incident, despite his attempt to shield his emotions from Olu. He just wanted to get home without further delay and unnecessary chatter. All Olu needed was a small opening to talk him to insanity. The man could talk for the whole of England and Ireland put together.

*****

Laura was waiting up for him as he'd known she would, the ubiquitous cup of Earl Grey tea cradled in her hands. Moses, their houseboy, let him in through the front door before rushing out to collect Alan's travelling luggage from the Discovery, together with some fresh fruits he'd picked up from a mini road-side market in Benin City.

'Darling, you look absolutely ghastly, you poor thing,' Laura kissed his left cheek gently, her tea-warmed hand tender on his brows, massaging away his tension. Alan saw the startled look on her face as he pulled her tightly into his arms, covering her lips with his in a deep kiss, merging their bodies closer, harder. He felt some of the badness leaving his body, the unholy taint of the creature's touch fading away in the warmth of his wife's arms. *Why had it taken his sudden brush with evil to make him see the goodness in his wife, her uncomplicated essence?*

'Alan…darling, are you alright?' Laura's face was clouded, uncertainty tingeing her pale blue pupils. He knew his uncharacteristic display of passion had taken her by surprise. A tacit understanding in their relationship meant Laura made the advances when her myriad of imagined and real illnesses permitted. He blamed his frequent absences from home for her anxiety, amongst other things.

'I'm fine… just fine,' Alan forced a laugh, embarrassed by his temporary loss of control. 'God! It feels great to be home again. Dreadful journey, absolutely ghastly. You don't know the half of it.'

'I made some Shepherd's Pie and rhubarb crumble for you. They'll only take a few minutes to warm up in the microwave. Why don't you go upstairs for a quick shower? I'll send Moses up with a drink for you while I get your supper ready, ok?' Laura reached up and kissed him, this time on the lips, stroking his brows in the familiar gesture that brought a lump to his throat. *What the hell was the matter with him, getting all emotional like a sissy?* Laura wouldn't thank him for going all mushy of a sudden, not after nine years of marriage. Alan ruffled her hair with an air of casual affection before heading up the spiral staircase for a much-craved shower. Forget the shower – it would take a thorough dowsing in a great pool of Olu's holy water arsenal to cleanse the foulness in his memory. Even in the sterile elegance of his home, the odour of decayed fruits and rotten fish still clung to his nostrils.

Alan wasn't a superstitious man but he wasn't a blind fool either. There was evil in the world, just as there was good. Take Ted Bundy, Harold Shipman or Fred West for instance. Yes, there was evil in the world, alright. One prayed never to come into contact with it, went about one's daily existence with an unconscious awareness of evil, never expecting to be tainted by it. Evil was something that happened to other people, never oneself.

Except that evil is omnipresent and can turn up when and where it wills. Tonight, evil had chosen to claw its terrible path into his life. Olu had called it Quarter-to-Dead (in hindsight, a truly apt name) but Alan had his own name for the foul thing he'd seen in his car. Pure evil, absolute corruption. *What lunacy had possessed him in the first place to stop for a total stranger in the middle of the night?* Even Olu had had better sense than he did. So much for the superiority of the master and the inferiority of the servant. Teach him next time he felt the urge to flaunt the superiority of English values to the natives in his ego-driven bid for self-aggrandisement. *Damn!* He would have to think up a plausible reason for the loss of Laura's M&S lilac cardigan.

Over the next few weeks, Alan went about his life with almost the same normalcy as prior to his brush with evil. Without his knowing, his life had suddenly divided into two distinct parts – before the evil thing and after the evil thing. It was as if nothing else had ever existed or mattered prior to that singular encounter; not his marriage, his first posting abroad, not even the previous monumental divide of "before and after the Keith thing". Happy Hour at the High Commission village club became "Happy Hour *before* the evil thing or Happy Hour *after* the evil thing". Dinner at the American Ambassador's house became Dinner *before or after* the evil thing and so on. Even his relationship with his wife had now broken into the two distinct *before* and *after* in his subconscious.

One good thing that came out of it all was the new feelings it awakened in him for his wife, a new tenderness and gratitude for Laura's love. The Laura of *before,* had been to Alan at most, a convenient appendage, frankly irritating with her endless cups of Earl Grey tea, M&S cardigans and numerous mysterious illnesses, all of which led to a singular diagnoses from uncountable doctors – anxiety. He wished he could place his finger on what it was that Laura was anxious about and sort it out for her. But it was like searching for a pin in the proverbial haystack. All he could come up with was boredom and narrow-mindedness.

Laura's preference for the company of fellow Europeans, her desperate determination to cling to anything British in their latest posting, aroused a feeling of mild contempt and irritation in Alan. If only she made an effort to get to know the Nigerians, learnt something about their culture, saw the poverty and suffering around her, then perhaps she would have less time to wallow in self-pity and be anxious about God knew what. Alan's determination to immerse himself in the local culture had been a kind of domestic rebellion, an attempt to rile Laura out of her superior complacency. His demands for *Amala* and *Ewedu,* the typical Yoruba dishes which he didn't really enjoy and his wearing of the

occasional colourful native garb were all attempts
to shock Laura's English sensibilities. Even his
proficiency in Pigeon English had been yet
another form of rebellion.

Except it had attracted the attention of his
ambassador, who saw in Alan a potential asset to
the empire's ulterior goals in its former colony.
Soon, more and more duties were delegated to
Alan, duties that involved a great deal of domestic
travelling and close interaction with all strata of
the society. On a daily basis, Alan met up with
politicians, military chieftains, business moguls,
union leaders, bankers, traders, manufacturers,
importers, local chieftain and even dubious
pastors from popular Pentecostal churches. His
proficiency in Pigeon English and his affability
opened doors for him, albeit, his secretary, Bisi,
claimed it was all down to his good looks and
easy charm.

Bisi was his number one fan, his ego-
booster, what the *Igbo* tribes called *"Oti-mkpu"*.
Alan couldn't pronounce the word but he knew its
exact meaning. It had no equivalent in the English
dictionary or way of life. The closest meaning he
came up with was a Press agent to a celebrity,
whose duty was to sell all the positives of the
celebrity to the general public via well-crafted
press releases and interviews. Perhaps, those Press

agents flattered the celebrities in private. Alan couldn't tell.

What he knew however, what he'd witnessed, was the *Oti-mkpu* in impressive jaw-dropping action at a wedding ceremony in Enugu, the main city of the *Igbo* tribe of Nigeria. The *Oti-mkpu* shouted the praises of his master to all and sundry, piling accolades and fantastical names on him, literally hopping from one foot to the other in a frenzy of flattery. Alan was informed that every rich man worth his mettle in *Igbo* culture had his own *Oti-mkpu* or praise-singer. Most times, these men and women weren't even in the paid employment of their particular champion and merely derived joy in letting the world see their hero's virtues by volunteering their voices in lavish public praise.

Bisi didn't go quite that far in public, what with being his personal secretary and all. But in the privacy of his office, she made zero effort to hide her admiration. It shamed him to admit that he was flattered by her open adoration of him. What man of flesh and blood could resist the unabashed adulation of a beautiful woman? And Bisi was beautiful – stunning. She was also a mega-carat Lagos socialite or *Sisi-Eko* as they were popularly called, beautiful, social butterflies with endless connections and access to the hottest parties and exclusive clubs. Tall, slender, full-busted and articulate, Bisi was a British graduate from Keele University, Alan's alumni. That was part of the reason why he'd chosen her in preference to the other interviewees; that, and the instant physical attraction he'd felt for her.

As a secretary, Bisi was an absolute disaster and several times, Alan had toyed with the idea of relieving her of her post after yet another costly error on her part. But one look into those sultry heavily-kohled eyes and a flirtatious stroke from her exquisitely manicured hands and he once again turned putty. Bisi was the true queen of glam, with her short tight skirts, six-inch Louboutin shoes and mind-spinning Yves Saint Laurent perfumes. Alan had spent countless hours covertly studying her voluptuous curves, fighting a losing battle against her blatant seduction.

Prior to the evil thing, he had flirted with the idea of starting something with Bisi, taking their steamy relationship to its final erotic conclusion. He wouldn't be the only one breaking his marital vows with local women. If one went by the contents of that voluminous book of indiscretion "upstairs", several of his colleagues, past and present, had already sampled the exotic pleasures of Nigerian women. In fact, a few had even gone the whole hog and married their girlfriends, remaining in the country after their posting and acquiring full Nigerian citizenship in the process.

Bisi was more than ready for a liaison with him, illicit or otherwise. She'd never hidden her amorous intentions despite the brittle humour of her flirtatious advances. Maybe if Laura was more forthcoming in the bedroom he wouldn't entertain such dangerous fancies. But he mustn't put the blame solely on Laura. At the end of the day, he knew it all boiled down to his own weakness and infatuation with Bisi.

The encounter with the evil thing cured Alan of his amorous insanity where his secretary was concerned. It turned him into a new husband, a different man in the deepest part of his heart. He didn't display the changes for the world to see but he knew they were there, that his soul had metamorphosed like a caterpillar into a butterfly. These days, he kissed his wife more, exercised more patience and understanding with her anxiety bouts and generally tried to spend as much of his free time with her as was possible. Laura smiled more often and drank less tea. And in the bedroom, she was more adventurous than before, almost the same girl he had courted and married nine years ago. It was like a new honeymoon in his marriage.

Bisi noticed the change in Alan. He no longer laughed or joked with her as much as before, no longer bent quite as low or close to her abundant hair extensions when he delivered a file for corrections. He was creating a deliberate and calculated distance between them, in the hope that she would quit the job in a huff and spare him the torture of dismissing her.

Bisi had a temper. Her voluble outbursts were notorious across the High Commission departments. How many times had Alan listened to her rant in Yoruba at some offending expatriate who couldn't understand a word of her screams? At those crazy times, her expensively-acquired, impeccable British accent was thrown to the winds in her fit of fury while she swore blue murder in an impressive mixture of Yoruba and Pigeon English.

Bisi's response to Alan's new personae had gone from amusement to bafflement in the weeks following his fateful encounter with the evil thing. She was now in the sullen stage, fixing him with cold stares and loud hisses each time they met, which was several times in the course of the day. Alan knew the explosion would occur any time soon. Bisi was like a volcano piped for eruption. When that happened, he would have no choice but to relieve her of her post. But Bisi would probably resign before he could give her the sack. Her pride would never permit a dismissal.

Alan knew he would miss her when she left – dreadfully. Even with the way things were now with Laura, the strong attraction to Bisi remained. But it would be foolhardy to retain the old status quo. Why put temptation in the way of his reformation? With Bisi safely out of his life, he could finally give his full attention to his marriage and hopefully, regain his mental fidelity.

*****

Exactly four weeks to his fateful encounter with the evil thing, Laura had her first nightmare. Nothing prepared Alan for the horror that came into his life that night. They had made love, shared a glass of Sauvignon Blanc before settling in for the night. Sleep had been almost instantaneous, the gentle hum of their air-conditioning unit lulling them into contented slumber.

The scream dragged him out of his sleep; the scream and the painful punches pummelling his naked body. His groggy mind tried to make sense of the random attack as the punches continued to rain on his body. *Armed robbers*!

140

That was his first thought. Bleeding armed robbers; the bane of everyone's life in Nigeria, rich and poor, black and white. You weren't a bona-fide citizen of the Lagos metropolis until you'd earned your war-badge by surviving an armed robbery attack.

Alan had been expecting them ever since he first arrived in Lagos. He had a security man, Femi, (or gate-man, as they were commonly called). But Femi was really there to keep out unwanted visitors rather than deter an armed robbery attack. When the ruthless gang of thieves visited, all the gatemen in the world couldn't keep them away from your bedroom. The first time Alan arrived in Nigeria, he'd noticed that all the doors and windows in the houses were fortified with heavy-duty metal bars or burglar-proofs as they were called. Even his own house in the posh Ikoyi area of Lagos, sported reinforced metal bars in every window and door. But they might as well be feather bars for all the good they did. When those Kalashnikov-bearing thugs came calling, they arrived as visitors with a mafia-like offer you couldn't refuse – "let us in without fuss or we let ourselves in with maximum fuss". Only a fool or a lunatic would opt to risk his life by refusing to unbolt his door with minimum delay.

In most cases, a looting and a beating with some rapes were the worst a robbed household would endure. They might also be forced to rustle up a meal and drinks to refresh the robbers for their next victim. Death only occurred when there was resistance or when the robbers were so high on drugs they became trigger happy. Or it could be a contract killing masked as a robbery but that was a different story. Calling the police was a waste of mobile phone credit. They loved their lives much more than yours and would not engage in unequal gunfire with Kamikaze opponents armed with superior weapons. A victim could expect to see the police a couple of hours after the attack at best. The usual excuses of lack of patrol cars, petrol or armed officers would be given, with demands for bribery cash from the robbery victims.

All these thoughts flashed through Alan's mind in the few seconds it took him to realise that his assailant was none other than his wife. By then, he'd managed to restrain Laura's flaying arms, holding her tightly in his arms while she whimpered against his chest, her body drenched in cold sweat. He turned on the bedside lamp, feeling Laura's hot breath on his skin, fast and hard. Her body shuddered in silent sobs, her tears dampening the hair on his chest.

'Earlie…what's the matter?' Alan automatically reverted to his pet-name for her on account of her addiction to Earl Grey tea. 'My dear, what happened?' he lifted her face, wiping her tears with an unsteady hand. He was still shaken by her midnight attack. The colour had drained from Laura's face and she looked almost the colour of their white bathroom tiles. 'Earlie, look at me…come on, talk to me. Did you have a nightmare? Is it the migraine again? What's wrong?'

'It was horrible…horrible,' Laura spoke in-between hiccups, her voice low, whispery. 'All these people in a market, Africans…a kind of Night Market with different stalls and tables and kiosks. Except they're selling nothing…nothing; no clothes, no foodstuff, no furniture… nothing. And the smell…' Alan felt Laura shudder in his arms as she pressed her face into his chest again. He felt a sudden chill in his heart though he couldn't figure out where his fear was coming from. 'Everything was silent in that market, eerie, scary. Even though there were lots of people there, I didn't hear a sound. Just this awful, cloying smell and a terrifying silent darkness. And their faces…' Laura shuddered again. 'Alan, I couldn't see their faces no matter how much I looked,' Laura's voice shook with such terror

Alan feared she would break out in another hysterical scream. 'It was creepy, like something you see in a demonic ritual in a Hammer House Horror film. They were all covered with this horrible dark cowl as if they were monks in an ancient abbey. Then suddenly, this girl comes out of a stall. She's young but there's also something old about her…I can't explain it. She's covered in that black hood like the rest of the people in that weird Night Market. She walks towards me…a sort of limping gait… and something about her frightens me even more than the others. I can't see her face but I know I don't want to see it. As she draws nearer, I notice something strangely familiar about her. And then I see what she's wearing….'

Again Laura paused, her voice trailing into the cold air of their air-conditioned room. Alan didn't need her to finish the story, didn't want to hear the rest of her nightmare. The chill in his heart was spreading to every part of his body. It was all he could do not to bolt from the bed, shut his ears to the horror he knew was coming.

'Alan, she was wearing my cardigan. I know it sounds crazy and I'm wondering if I really saw what I saw in my dream. But I'll almost wager an arm that that girl was wearing my M&S lilac cardigan, the one I keep in the car as a spare.'

Before Alan could speak, Laura jumped out of the bed like one injected with adrenalin. 'I need to find that cardigan. I'll ring Moses and ask him to get it from the car immediately. I need to see it, to be sure it was just a stupid nightmare…but it felt so real…so real.' Laura pulled on her night gown, her arms stick-thin like the rest of her body. Fleetingly, Alan wished again she would add some curves, get a body more like Bisi's. He quickly pushed away the traitorous thought, bolting from the bed like one stung by a wasp.

'Dearest, why don't you leave things till morning?' he took her by the arm, guiding her back towards the bed. 'It's not fair to disturb Moses' sleep. Poor lad works hard enough as it is, what with taking on both outdoors and indoor chores since the gardener left. I'm sure your cardigan is in the Discovery. It's just a silly nightmare; can happen to any one of us. Come on now, let's catch some sleep, otherwise I'll be late to work come morning and Bisi will start calling like the world's coming to an end.'

Alan knew he was being devious by bringing Bisi's name into the conversation but it was the only thing he could think of at the spur of the moment to distract his wife and keep her away from the car till he came up with a plausible story in the morning. He needed to speak first with Olu, warn him to keep his big mouth shut about the girl they'd given a lift, even though Olu knew nothing about the stolen cardigan. All Laura needed to know was that a strange girl had been in their car and her imagination would run riot, triggering another attack of anxiety.

Alan knew his wife could not stand his secretary, a kind of female intuition thing, jealousy perhaps. Most women would be envious of Bisi's striking beauty and arrogant confidence. Laura had asked him to get Bisi dismissed or transferred to a different department at the very least. Surely, with Bisi being an LE staff, locally engaged High Commission staff, it would be easy to get rid of her. He'd explained that things didn't work that way as Laura of all people ought to know but that he would look into it. He had meant to sack Bisi or at least get her to resign in the immediate aftermath of the evil thing. Heaven knew that was his honest intention.

But so far, Bisi had held her temper and surprisingly, become more efficient at her job. It was as if her anger towards Alan spurred her to excel in her job, as if she needed to show him she could do the work and do it brilliantly too. She also seemed to have taken his cue and no longer flirted with him, treating him with cold indifference and what he could only term as professional disdain. It was as if she'd never told him his posh English accent brought the wetness to her knickers; as if she'd never ran her ring-decked fingers over his trouser-encased manhood, stroking it to turgid discomfort, promising him paradise and beyond, if only he would lose his stupid, out-dated scruples and follow her home.

Alan missed their old relationship, mourned what could have been. Seeing Bisi still distracted his thoughts, stirred unwanted feelings in him. But a deal was a deal and he had no business thinking about Bisi, especially at this critical moment when his life was unravelling before his eyes; when his wife was recounting creepy dreams of events she knew nothing about; when he desperately needed to get Laura back into bed while he worked things through in his mind and tried to make some sense out of a senseless situation.

Thankfully, Bisi's name worked the old magic. Laura didn't want to get calls from Bisi or listen to him speaking to his gorgeous secretary. After several minutes of silent thoughts, Laura returned to their bed, her movements slow, hesitant, as if she were frightened of their cotton-sheeted king-size bed. It was a long time before either of them went back to sleep.

The next morning, he was dressed and out of the house before Laura woke up. The nightmare of the previous night had worn her out. Alan was equally tired but a more pressing problem drove him out of the house and straight to his office. He would be gone before Laura awoke to search the car for her blasted cardigan. He planned to miss her calls to his mobile till he got home. Time enough to answer questions about the whereabouts of the cardigan then. He was more troubled by her nightmare. *How on earth had she dreamt of the evil thing he'd picked up from the road? How could she dream about the Night Market Olu had talked about?* He knew Olu hadn't mentioned anything to Laura. He valued his job too much to blab. *And the cardigan; how did Laura know…dream about the true fate of her cardigan?* The questions ran through Alan's mind through that day and for several more days, as he tried to make sense out of the impossible.

He succeeded in convincing Laura that her cardigan had either been displaced or stolen during his last journey to the Benin Trade Fair. He wasn't sure if she bought his story or not but at least, she stopped asking and searching for it. And after a few days, the haunted look in her face

148

disappeared and bedtime became once again a place for loving and sleeping.

Until the evil returned, turning their lives into a pantomime of horror. Exactly a week to her first dream, Laura awoke in tears and terror. Just like the first time, Laura went back to the Night Market again. Everything was just as before – the stalls without wares, the silent traders in their dark cowls, the awful smell of decay, the eerie silence of the market place and the strange girl wearing her M&S lilac cardigan. Except this time, Laura finally saw their faces. Alan knew what she'd seen in her nightmare even before she told him in a terrified stammer. He too had seen the unspeakable horror, shared a car with the loathsome evil underneath the shawl. *How could he ever forget that ancient, withered, mummified skull atop the perfectly formed body of a healthy young woman?*

What Laura had seen in her second nightmare was a Night Market heaving with tens, even hundreds, of those spooky mummified creatures. Alan couldn't imagine Laura's terror, didn't even try. He was experiencing his own nightmare, albeit, a different type of terror. He knew what Laura didn't know, a truth his wife didn't share. Discovering what he knew would drive Laura to insanity. He wasn't even sure if he

149

too still had control of his own reason. *Was it possible that witches existed, the kind of witches one read about in stories and saw in films, casting evil spells, assuming other terrifying forms and possessing souls?* He was struggling to give a name to what Laura was experiencing, find a rational explanation for the fact that a foul girl-creature he'd given a lift in his car had somehow found her way into his wife's dreams. But why Laura, who had never met her…it? Why not himself or even Olu?

The following morning after Laura's second nightmare, Alan decided to fish for information from Olu. Not that he believed any of his driver's superstitious drivel and all that nonsense about Quarter-to-Deads and Half-past-Lifes. But research is everything as he'd learnt during his undergraduate years as a law student at Keele University. Research gave you vital knowledge and prepared you for whatever you had to face in life. Research came in every form and his talk with Olu would be nothing more than another form of research.

As he expected, Olu couldn't wait to fill him in with information about *Oja-ale,* the so-called Night Market of the dead.

'Mister Alan, everyone know about that evil market,' Olu said, his voice the voice of doom and wisdom. 'It opens only on Sundays, which is why every Pastor prays for protection against the dead traders at *Oja-ale* at Sunday devotions. In that market, you can buy anything at all you want….anything. If you want money or fame, you can buy them at *Oja-ale*. If it is an eye or leg you want, you can buy it there. Anything at all you want, those dead traders will sell it to you. But they don't trade in money. They trade with your life. A person can only shop in that market four times and once you enter, you cannot leave without buying something. That is their rule. Each time they sell you something, you must pay them with a quarter of your life. Those dead traders know how long everybody has to live, so they never buy from anybody who is old because old people don't have enough life to trade. That's why they only like young, healthy people. Each time they buy your life, they store up their life-tank and when they have bought enough years to return them to the age they were when they died, then they will return to life again. We call them *"Come-backs"*. Everybody knows what a *Come-back* looks like. They get albino eyes and always wear sunglasses, even at night. That's why whenever you see any of these beautiful Lagos girls wearing their sunglasses, always try and see their eyes to make sure they're not a *Come-back*.

151

Many people have seen their dead relatives in different towns, living life just like a normal person.'

Olu paused in his narrative, manoeuvring a tricky spot in the Kingsway Road. 'The people who go to *Oja-ale* to sell their lives must go back to that market when they reach Dead o'clock and die. That market is their own heaven and hell. They cannot enter Christian heaven because they're not given Christian funeral but buried in cursed unholy grounds. The first time they visit and sell one quarter of their life, you will not see anything different in them. When they go back for a second time and reach Half-past-Life, their hair will just go pure white like a very old person and start falling out. Just like that.' Olu snapped his fingers before returning his hand to the wheel.

Alan listened with fascination, unable to believe the incredible fable being recounted to him as gospel truth. No wonder the continent was so backward. With this kind of superstitious mumbo-jumbo driving the lives of the people, even the most educated amongst them, how on earth could they be expected to fully embrace the advances of the new millennium?

'By the time they reach Quarter-to-Dead, their skin will just become like a very old person's skin and they will start smelling very strongly of death. Everybody starts running away from them because they know that they're now the walking dead and they can steal your life too if you're not careful.'

'Why would someone want to keep going back to this Night Market to keep selling their lives over and over again after the first time?' Alan asked, interested despite himself. 'I mean, why not just stop after you've got whatever it is that sent you shopping from the dead in the first place?'

'Aahh! Mister Alan, you don't know these dead people,' Olu laughed, a harsh sound. 'They're greedy like those *Igbo* traders at Ladipo Market. Once they get you, they will not let you go till they have sold everything they have. Even if you refuse to buy after the first time, they have their ways of tempting you back into the market. Sometimes, they even offer you two deals on the same day so they can get half of your life in one sale, instead of just one quarter. I heard of a woman who sold her whole life in just one day of trading at *Oja-ale*. One Sunday, she left her house in the village to find a doctor for her only son, who had sickle cell and was dying. When she left the village that afternoon, she was a young woman, not even thirty years, strong and healthy. She didn't return till midnight. In fact, her people were beginning to worry that she might have met some misfortune on the way. Then she came home and went straight to her son where the priest was giving the child the last sacrament. She was walking like a very old woman, her back stooped, her steps very slow. People did not even recognise her till she spoke. But the smell on her chased everyone away, just like that smell on the girl we picked up. That's when they knew she had gone to *Oja-ale* to buy health for her dying son. As soon as the woman touched the boy and said the secret word the dead traders gave her, that child rose from his bed as if he was never sick. His fever and pains disappeared and he never suffered from sickle cell again in his life. His mother died that same night and was buried in the cursed forest because as I said, you can't give decent Christian funeral to people who die *Oja-ale* death. It is an evil death.'

Olu paused to give his pass to the security men at the High Commission gate before driving into the large compound. Alan had just one final question to complete his research.

'How interesting. Tell me, can these dead traders at the Night Market get into people's dreams or can they make people, absolute strangers, even white people, visit their market by force? Incidentally, where is this notorious Night

Market? Is it in Lagos?' Olu jumped out of the car to retrieve Alan's briefcase and his files.

'Mister Alan, I don't know where that market is and I don't want to know. God forbid! What is my business with the dead? All I know is that they have powers, very strong juju. They can enter people's dreams if they want. They can do anything. But I hear that they normally need something that belongs to you, a personal thing like cloth, trinket, hair or even your urine to gain power over your mind. That's why that day I kept watching the girl in the rear mirror because I don't want her to cut my hair and possess my mind. You are very lucky all she stole from you was money.'

Alan felt his heart lurch, felt that terrible chill crawl up his spine. *Laura's M &S cardigan.* The evil thing had spurned his money for the cardigan. Was it coincidence or was there some truth in Olu's story after all? Surely not. Science and logic were against it all, people returning to life in solid form when their corpses had rotted in their graves; a Night Market ran by the dead who traded with human lives. Absolute rubbish. Ask them to take you to that market and hey ho, what d'you know? Suddenly, no one knows the location of the market. Exactly as he suspected, all hogwash. Laura must be feeding off his own

155

fears. He'd read an article about women who shared the same house and all got their monthlies the same day. People had been known to experience similar dreams just from living in close proximity to each other and how much closer could two people be than Laura and himself had become?

For the rest of that day, Alan found himself wondering each time he saw a woman in sunglasses, resisting the strong urge to remove the dark glasses and see the eyes behind. *Albino eyes indeed.* What did that prove apart from the fact that he was fast turning into an ignorant fool like his driver?

*****

The following Sunday, Alan found himself as taut as a wire, his nerves glass-fragile as he waited for the night and what he prayed would never occur. The rest of the week had passed without incident. Laura had experienced no more nightmares and even though she went to sleep in a heightened state of anxiety, nothing disturbed her slumber and she enjoyed restful nights. Alan knew he was being silly, almost as ignorant as the superstitious locals he scorned, by giving any credence to Olu's prattling about dead traders and

Quarter-to-deads. He was giving more sinister importance to the creature's theft of Laura's cardigan than was the real case. Still, try as he could, the dread image refused to dislodge from his thoughts and by bedtime on Sunday night, he was unable to make love to Laura, just kissing her goodnight and turning over, feigning sleep.

At some point, his sleep pretence must have turned to reality because the next time he woke up, Laura was screaming as if she had been stung by a thousand scorpions. Alan had almost grown accustomed to her nightmare screams but this time it was different. Her shrieks were sustained, relentless, terrifying. His blood turned cold, a heavy feeling in his heart. *It was true after all…Olu's story had all been fact. Somehow, the evil thing he picked up on the wayside had gained control over his wife's mind through the theft of Laura's cardigan.*

Alan held his wife in his arms, tightly, seized by a desperate desire to protect her, shield her from the horror he had invited into their lives by his folly. A sudden shiver ran through his body. Laura's skin was as cold as refrigerated mutton. She shuddered, shaking all over, her teeth rattling uncontrollably. Alan held her close, trying to infuse his own warmth into her body. He never knew the human body could be that cold. What if

Laura were coming down with malaria on top of everything else? Laura wouldn't survive a malaria attack. He'd been through it and knew why it used to be called "the white man's death".

Alan ran his hand over Laura's forehead and underneath her neck. No temperature. Of course there was no fever, idiot that he was, not with the sub-zero temperature of her body. He checked her pulse, pressing his fingers against her neck and her wrists. They raced faster than a Formula One car. Something was definitely wrong with Laura beyond the nightmare but he couldn't put his finger on it. Laura wasn't talking either. In fact, she now seemed to be going into a zombiefied state, numb, senseless, her gaze fixed somewhere towards their bedroom door.

Alan followed her gaze and froze. Suddenly, his heart started thudding as hard as Laura's own against his chest. The panelled oak door was slightly ajar. He would have sworn he'd shut it and locked it as he always did every night. Either they had an intruder in the house…in their bedroom…or Laura had opened the door and forgot to shut it. It seemed the most logical explanation, otherwise, he would have heard someone break in. That door was as strong as they came, with the strongest lock the High Commission could purchase.

He laid Laura back against the bed and tucked the thin duvet tightly around her. He stooped to pull on his pyjama bottoms before picking up his mobile phone by the bedside. He looked around for something to use as a weapon but all he found were a pair of Laura's knitting needles with something already knitted halfway. They would have to do and Laura would have to start her knitting all over again. He pulled a long grey needle from the wool and made his way towards the open door, his bare feet silent on the cool, tiled flooring of their bedroom. He felt the heavy thudding of his heart, the dryness of his mouth and the rapid burst of his breathing as he drew closer to the open door. *What if someone was waiting just outside, pressed against the wall, out of sight yet within reach, armed with a knife or his golf stick which were usually in the downstairs gym?*

Alan stepped out of the bedroom, his arm raised in attack. At the same time, he switched on the light, flooding the wide landing in welcome brightness. He was panting as if he'd ran a marathon and the sweat hung in beads on his forehead. His eyes scanned his surroundings. The *Fulani* girl in the large painting on the wall smiled down at him, her beads as rainbow crystals under the bright illumination of the overhead chandelier.

The shiny marbled flooring reflected the shadows of the various potted cacti lining the long corridor while the imposing Benin bronze mask watched sentinel over the hall. The wide spiral staircase with its gilded railings was clear of intruders.

Alan cocked his ears, listening out for any alien sounds as he made his silent way down the stairs. All he heard were the familiar noises of the house, the tick-tock of the great Grandfather clock his father had given him on his wedding day, a family heirloom which he took with him to all his postings like a wooden mascot. His ears picked out the gentle humming of the various air-conditioning units around the house, the swishy watery sounds coming from the giant fish tank in the downstairs living room as well as the louder hums of the fridges and freezers in the kitchen and dining room. He also picked out the muted noise of the generator outside the house. NEPA, the Nigerian Electric Power Authority, must have cut off their supply while they slept, triggering the automated electric generator. *What else was new?*

His scouting convinced him that there was no one in the house with them. He checked that all the doors and windows were firmly secured. Finally, he inspected the anti-burglar metal bars on the doors to ensure they hadn't been tampered with, before returning upstairs to their bedroom.

Laura lay as he'd left her, a frozen look on her face, her eyes still glued to the doorway. Alan shut the door behind him, locking and rechecking it was firmly locked before returning to their bed once more. He pulled Laura into his arms, again surprised by the coldness of her skin.

'Dearest, I've just done a thorough check and there's nothing to worry about,' he stroked her hair, sweat-dampened and limp, planting a gentle kiss on the top of her head. They smelled of summer fruits and clean freshness. He inhaled deeply, pulling the duvet over himself. Then he paused, his arm suspended, a frown on his face. He sniffed, inhaled again, like a dog searching for its bone where it should've been but wasn't. *A smell...out of place in his bedroom, in his house...yet, something familiar about it, a familiarity that wasn't pleasant, one that invoked sudden panic in his heart.* Alan sniffed again, getting out of the bed for the second time that night.

He started walking round the room, opening wardrobe doors, drawers, en-suit bathroom door, searching, sniffing, trying to recollect...*afraid to remember*. He wandered back into the bedroom from the bathroom. The smell was stronger in the bedroom, though still faint. The unpleasant sensation remained with him as he

161

returned to their bed. Laura turned to him, her eyes clear with awareness, a terrible awareness. Alan had never seen such terror in anyone's eyes in his life. She looked like someone that had just seen their own corpse.

'The girl was here,' Laura said, her voice almost a whisper. Alan had to stoop low to hear her.

'What girl? There's no one here, Earlie. Believe me, I checked every room in the house. The doors and windows are all shut. We are alone in the house. You just had another nightmare that's all.' He wondered if Laura's anxiety bouts had taken a new turn and evolved into sleepwalking. That would explain the open door of their bedroom. *Dear God.* That was all they needed, on top of her night-terrors.

'The girl was here,' Laura repeated as if she didn't hear a word he said. Her voice was louder, hysterical. 'She said I could have my cardigan back if I wanted but that I must pay her for it. But I don't want it anymore…not now…she was wearing it. I told her she could keep it but she wouldn't listen. She kept telling me to come to the market and buy it back…' Laura's voice suddenly trailed off as her eyes wandered away to the distant place Alan could not see, a place that drained the blood from her face and started the shivers in her body again.

Alan's heart froze. The crawling feeling crept up his spine like the feathery touch of a graveside spectre. *The smell…the girl…the evil thing.* That was what he smelled in their bedroom. It was back in his life. Evil had found its way into his home, crawled out of Laura's dreams into their bedroom. There was no other explanation for Laura's words. He couldn't put it down to the nightmares anymore, not now that he recognised that smell in their bedroom, the foul odour of rotting fruits and rotten fish.

'She touched me…she touched…oh my God! Alan, it touched me, the thing touched me… touched me… cold hands… smell…horrible… oh dear God, what is it? Who is she? What does she want from me?' Laura was screaming, her voice hysterical, her hands gripping his arms, tight, manic. 'I know the market… I've seen it… in the dreams… I've been there. It's horrible, terrifying. I don't want to go there but I'm afraid she won't leave me alone till I go there. Help me, Alan… please help me.'

Alan felt his throat constrict at the pleading tone in Laura's voice, her implicit trust in his ability to make everything okay. How could he tell her that he was responsible for her torments, that he brought that evil into her life by his own folly? He had to put an end to it somehow. He had to get back that M&S cardigan from the foul thing. Olu would have to find the way to the blasted market since he seemed to know so much about it already. Alan would have to cloak the order as professional necessity, a need to discover new markets for British businesses. Wouldn't do to let the chap think he'd bought into his ignorant drivel regardless of the terrible truth he now accepted. But he must put an end to all this horror before next Sunday. He doubted if Laura could survive another experience such as tonight's.

Several hours and a couple of sleeping pills later, Laura finally slept and Alan lay on his side, eyes free of sleep, wondering where it would all lead, when and how it would all end.

*****

Olu was adamant that he would not find or visit the Night Market of the dead. He was almost on his knees in his desperation to convince Alan to abandon his foolhardy decision to visit the market. Alan debated whether to disclose Laura's Sunday night-terrors and the theft of her cardigan by the evil thing. That would convince Olu and definitely change his attitude. But then, it would come at a very high cost to Alan. He would become no better than the natives and would lose his credibility and the respect of his driver. Worse, what if the truth ever came out and his colleagues heard about it? He would never hold up his head again in civilized society. No, he couldn't take the risk of confiding in his driver. Olu would have to find someone else to take him to the market.

In the end, that was the deal he reached with his driver - find me someone who will take me to the Night Market and I'll pay both of you handsomely. Olu turned down any rewards for himself but agreed to make enquiries and find a scout. Three days later, on a Wednesday, Olu brought an old man to his house after work. The old man knew the way and would take Alan there on Saturday, show him the location of the market and collect his reward. Alan would have to find his way back to the market on the Sunday when the dead traded. Alan paid the deposit for the hiring of a vehicle to take them there. He couldn't take his official car without his official driver, Olu, and his official driver was being a real wimp. The old man took the money and agreed to turn up on Saturday morning. The deal was done.

They set off early, before the normal traffic congestion hit the roads. Alan kissed Laura goodbye, telling her to expect him back late. He didn't want her to see the disreputable company he was keeping, a decrepit-looking old man and the young, scruffy driver with his rakish hat and faded Malcolm X T-shirt.

The hired car, an old jalopy, had no air-conditioning and in minutes, Alan felt the sweat staining his navy polo shirt and tan chinos. The driver talked incessantly in between singing along to some loud *Fela* afro-beat music. Alan didn't mind the music as much as he minded the lad's raucous and tuneless singing. Alan was partial to the late Fela Ransome Kuti, a true visionary in his opinion. The guy fought Nigerian corruption the only way he knew how – with his music. Fela's untimely death was both a loss to the music industry as well as to the average impoverished Nigerian, for whom he's been a mouthpiece.

They had turned a blind corner when Alan saw the large trailer hurtling towards them at a speed it had no business doing in the narrow road. It took him a second to realise that his driver was bent low, changing the Fela cassette in the deck, unaware of the danger coming their way. His shout coincided with that of the old man. The driver made a last minute ditch to avoid collision,

Nuzo Onoh

swerving sharply to the left. Alan heard the loud report of a burst tyre and screaming wheels. It sent the car in a lethal spin. The driver fought the wheels but it was a lost battle. The last thing Alan recalled was the trailer looming close, deadly close, together with the shrieks of terror in their car. He thought his screams were one of them. He wasn't sure. By then it didn't matter any way.

*****

He awoke to a world without light, a world of blank pages, where all that was real was his pain, a mind-numbing pain that was beyond endurance. His body was a mass of throbs and hurt. The pain was concentrated in his head and his abdomen. Beyond his stomach, he felt nothing, just a blessed numbness, as if in compensation for the torture that ravaged his upper torso. *What was wrong with him? Where was he? Why wasn't someone doing something about his pain? Why was the room in pitch darkness?*

Alan forced his eyes open, felt his lids come apart as he opened them to sight. All he saw was the infernal blackness, a darkness so dense it felt like an impenetrable solid mass. He raised his hand to his face to feel his eyes. Yes, they were

167

indeed open but for some reason, powerless against the unyielding blackness.

He called out, hearing the raspy croak of his voice with a sense of puzzlement. Why did he get the feeling that his voice sounded different from the hoarse sounds he made? He cleared his throat, prepared to pitch his voice louder. A hand settled on his brows, stilling his voice. It was a soft hand, gentle, tender, yet cold. A faint memory stirred in the fogginess of his mind, a memory of hot drinks…. *think…think. Earl Grey tea! That was it…Earl Grey tea! But what did it mean? What did Earl Grey tea have to do with the gentle, cold hand that was massaging his brows in rhythmic soothing strokes?*

Again, a memory resurfaced in his subconscious. Cardigan! Lots of cardigans….a woman…no, two women, maybe three. He pushed away the thoughts. They hurt his head too much.

'It's okay, darling. I'm here. Everything's just fine. Just relax, ok? You're in the best hospital in the country and in the best hands. Your doctor is French. Isn't that lovely? So you see, you have nothing to worry about. Your Earlie will take care of you. Sleep now…sleep.'

The voice was as gentle as the hand on his brows, soft and feminine, kind. Alan felt himself relaxing, his muscles un-tensing, allowing the voice to sooth away his pain. He felt the drowsiness pull down his lids, drawing him into a deeper darkness than the one in the strange room. Just before he succumbed to the call of sleep, a final question floated through his fuzzled mind, light and whispery like a butterfly's perch on a flower bud – *who on earth was he? What was his name?*

He found out his name the next time he awoke. The voice that identified itself as his doctor called him by the name, Alan. *Alan who?* He was too weak to ask the question or any other question. But the doctor filled him in with the information anyway. He had been in a ghastly car accident. He was lucky to be alive, the sole survivor of the crash. He had sustained extensive head injuries, which accounted for his loss of sight. It was too soon to determine the extent of his loss till the tests came back. Alan wished they hadn't given him that piece of news, that they had just left things the way they were so he could go on blaming NEPA…*who on earth was NEPA and why should he blame this NEPA guy or woman for his loss of sight?*

The doctor, who should have been the twin brother of his compatriot, the Marquis de

Sade, continued with his sadistic news. Apparently, his injuries were not restricted to his eyes alone. He was also paralysed from his waist down. Again, tests were being done to determine the extent of the damage. In the meantime, rest was all he needed. He was lucky to have such a devoted wife by his side. She had not left his bedside since the night he was brought into the hospital over three days ago.

His wife? He was married to the woman with the kind voice and gentle, cold hands, the one that called herself Early? Strange name, Early. Pity she wasn't early enough to prevent the accident that had ruined his life. No way would he live as a blind cripple, completely dependent on people for his needs, even this wife he knew nothing about. He'd rather put a gun to his head, which was already fucking messed up anyway. He couldn't even remember his own name.

Alan eventually managed to ask the doctor some questions, several questions. His questions gave rise to more questions, this time targeted at him. Did he not remember anything? Nothing at all about the accident? What about his name? His wife? His job? Where he lived? Nothing? Absolutely nothing?

Of course he remembered something. He hadn't gone completely bonkers. *Not yet.* He remembered his sister, Sarah. He also remembered that he worked for the British High Commission... incidentally, had they been notified about his accident? Yes? Good to hear the guys from Consulate had been visiting daily and were arranging to fly him back to England... *just a minute... fly him back to England? Why on earth would they want to do such a silly thing when they had good doctors in Spain?*

By the time it dawned on Alan that he was at the International SOS Clinic in Lagos, Nigeria, and not in Spain as he'd thought, he realised that his problems were far worse than he'd thought.

*****

One night, exactly a week following his accident, Alan woke up with his mind as clear as the brook that meandered across his parents' vast grounds in Shropshire. He had gone to sleep still grappling with the fact that he was a man of thirty-seven years and not in his late twenties as he's thought; trying to cope with the knowledge that several years of his life was lost to him for good. No matter how positive Dr Fournier sounded about his prospects, Alan wasn't deceived. The amnesia was there to stay, just like his blindness and paralysis.

Except that the good doctor had been right all along. Alan awoke sometime past midnight with his memory returned in its brilliant, wonderful entirety. *Laura!* Of course, his wife was Laura and not *Early* as he'd stupidly thought. He'd given her the name after all… *Earlie,* after Earl Grey Tea, her addiction. These days she drank even more of the bloody stuff since the evil thing entered their lives. *The evil thing!*

Alan's heart began pounding, racing so fast he thought he would faint. It all came back in a flood of terrible recall. The loathsome creature he'd given a lift, the Night Market of the dead, Laura's night terrors, his trip to the market. Except he never made it there. *Had they somehow stopped him from making that trip?* He shook his head violently. He mustn't start thinking like Olu, his driver, who had been visiting him every day in hospital and whom he hadn't remembered till now. Alan felt a pang as he recalled the happy face of the young driver with his Malcolm X t-shirt and Fela music. He had died together with the old man in the accident. And all his fault. They would've never made that trip but for the lure of his bribe. *Blood money.* He must get Olu to take something to their families, his personal compensation for his role in their demise.

Alan remembered something else. The doctor said he was being flown back to England in a couple of days as he was now strong enough to cope with the flight. He had to stop them. No way was he flying to England when Laura's life, their lives, depended on his remaining in Nigeria and recovering that cardigan from the evil thing. But how? The task had become even more monumental with his paralysis and blindness. Suddenly, he wished he hadn't remembered, that his mind had remained in its clouded paradise. Worst of all, he would now have to complete an official report on why he was in that un-approved vehicle at an unknown location at the time of his accident. He didn't have the foggiest idea of the story to give the High Commission.

Everyone was ecstatic at the return of his memory. The medical staff cheered and his driver Olu pumped his hands several times in joy. And Bisi... darling, beautiful, magnificent Bisi, his secretary, who had spent almost as much time as Laura at his bedside despite the fact that he couldn't recall her name or her face, couldn't recall just how much she affected his body, seemed to had forgotten their spat. She couldn't hold back her sobs as he said her name with recognition. He felt the warmth of her tears on his cheeks when she bent to kiss him on the lips, the

173

first time ever that she'd done that. He felt his heart lurch at the contact of their lips, felt the pain of regret constrict his throat. Even if there had ever been any chance of anything happening between them, it was now truly over. What woman would want a blind man in a wheelchair?

The only person that wasn't as ecstatic about his recovery was his wife, the last person he'd have expected to give him the lukewarm reception he received. Laura tried to act enthusiastic and pleased for him. But he knew her moods, the different nuances of her voice. That was one of the advantages to recovering his memory – remembering the idiosyncrasies of the people he knew and therefore knowing when they lied. He wished he could see Laura's face, read her eyes and find out why she wasn't too pleased with the return of his memory.

Doctor Fournier commented on Laura's looks the next time he did his rounds, saying she needed to rest as she wasn't looking too well herself. Her husband was out of death's doors and could afford to do without her presence by his bedside for a day or two. Alan felt guilty for his thoughts. He was a selfish bugger. Here he was more concerned about how people reacted to his blasted memory when poor Laura had been run ragged caring for him. Little wonder the poor dear sounded tired. Again, Alan felt the anger and frustration rage in his heart. He had to make a full recovery and face the fact that his marriage was over. No way would he consign Laura to a life of drudgery caring for his worthless carcass.

After his memory returned, Alan's recovery accelerated, as if injected with a super booster from planet Krypton. Exactly a week following the return of his memory, he regained the full use of his legs. Doctor Fournier and his team were gobsmacked to say the least. Their tests had indicated his incapacity was a permanent one or as near permanent as could be expected from limbs crushed by a thousand-ton weight. Just like when he'd beat the malaria attack, they called it a miracle. Yet again, Alan put it down to Laura's single-minded devotion, her selfless attention to his every need, sacrificing her time and her energy tending to him. That and of course the expert care of his team of expatriate doctors at the International SOS Clinic.

Alan tried to ask Laura about the dreams a few times after regaining his memory. But she brushed away his concern, telling him everything was alright, just fine. She was free of the nightmares. Alan wanted to believe her, wanted to accept that the evil that had terrorised their lives was finally gone for good. Perhaps, the ghoulish traders at the Night Market had been behind his accident after all. Now that they had exacted their revenge or whatever it was they had against him and his wife, they had decided to leave them alone. *So why did he continue to feel a sense of disquiet? Why did he sense that all was not as Laura made it out to be? Was she trying to be brave for his sake, spare him the worry and shield him from the truth? Why did doctor Fournier keep harping on Laura's health, constantly urging her to rest? What exactly was going on? There was something about the French accent that he didn't trust.*

In the end, Alan could only come up with one conclusion. The evil thing was till haunting his wife and she was keeping the truth from him. Laura was too besotted with him to play false with any other man, even if he was now just a blind man. So it had to be the evil he had unwittingly invite into their lives. The haunting was clearly taking its toll on Laura and therefore, he still had to make that visit to the dreaded Night Market, somehow. Thankfully, he had the use of his legs again and who knows? His sight might just come back some day, hopefully soon. In the meantime, all he could do was to be there for Laura, share the night terrors and protect her as best he could in their home. He would start by demanding his discharge from the hospital. As wonderful as the staff were, as lovely as his private room was, he just wanted to go back to his own home and convalescence. Somehow, he knew he would find it easier to navigate his way around his house than was the case in the hospital.

A few days after returning to his Ikoyi home, Laura made a strange request. She asked him to invite Bisi to their home. Laura said she wanted to thank Bisi for the care she'd shown while Alan was hospitalised. She felt ashamed for her former hostility towards Bisi and just wanted to make up for it by having her over for dinner. Alan was stunned yet thrilled by the change in Laura. He was also humbled by her dignity. It took a big heart to admit one was wrong and make amends. He was also ashamed of his past with Bisi, the feelings she still elicited in his heart despite everything. The memory of the brief kiss they'd shared in his hospital room resurrected all the old desires. *God! How he wished he had his sight again.* Seeing the blonde, fragile beauty of his wife might cure him of his infatuation with his glamorous secretary.

Dinner with Bisi was a huge success. Laura went out of her way to be the most gracious hostess he could wish for. The conversation flowed as freely as the drinks and soon, both women were giggling like old friends, exchanging information about shops and fashion. Laura expressed her admiration for one of Bisi's numerous gold rings. Bisi in her usual lavish magnanimity, offered Laura the ring. Laura resisted, though not wholeheartedly. It was a beautiful ring and way too expensive to give away. Bisi waved away Laura's protests and pulled off the ring. They fitted Laura's middle finger perfectly. The two women cooed over it, wishing Alan could see just how lovely the ring was on Laura's finger. Alan couldn't see it but knew it was just as pretty as the new best friends said it was. He smiled, feeling a sense of contentment and peace for the first time since his accident. Laura sounded really happy, in fact, happier than he'd heard her sound in a long time. Maybe she was telling the truth when she said the haunting was over; maybe there was hope for them to live a normal life once again, despite his blindness.

The High Commission hadn't made any permanent arrangements regarding his future. He was still on sick leave with full pay. It might be best to retire on a full pension and take Laura back to England. Poor thing had never settled well in Nigeria and would welcome the chance to return to England with its damp, grey weather and uniform brick houses. He would hate to leave Lagos and everything he loved in the city. But for Laura, he would make that sacrifice. She had made so many sacrifices for him that moving back to the UK was the least he could do for her.

*****

Two weeks later, Alan took Laura back to England. He accompanied her corpse in the Virgin Atlantic flight from Lagos to Heathrow airport, where he was met by Laura's brother, his parents and numerous friends and colleagues from the Foreign & Commonwealth Office. The coffin was transferred into the hearse, en-route Shropshire, in a cavalcade of black limousines. An onlooker would have sworn a celebrity was being buried, such was the number of mourners that turned up to support Alan. Friends and business contacts flew in from Nigeria. They included some Ministers, state governors and business moguls. Alan never realised the high regard in which he was held in his adopted country till Laura's death. The lump hardened in his throat yet again, a tumour that had lodged with unmovable tenacity since the fateful night his world ended.

Laura was cremated the following day, a day that was as damp and dreary as the moods of the guests. Her ashes were kept in the ornamental urn that his sister, Sarah, had bought especially for Alan. It had the name, Earlie, inscribed on it and Alan encased several bags of Laura's favourite beverage in the urn with her ashes. It felt the right thing to do.

As Alan shook hands with the funeral guests and accepted their condolences, he grappled with the silent horror that still gripped his heart. He felt a dizzy weirdness. Everything felt surreal, like an alien in a strange place. He was overwhelmed by the sea of predominantly black-clad mourners he saw. How different from Lagos with its vibrant colours; Lagos, that whore city that had taken the young, sweet life of his wife in the cruellest way.

Why? Why did she do it? Why didn't she talk to him first? Why didn't he suspect what was going on till it was too late? The same questions that had tormented him since the day he discovered the truth about his wife and lost her forever, surfaced again in Alan's tormented mind.

The official story was that Laura had caught a deadly tropical disease, somewhat like

Ebola, though the autopsy was inconclusive. Its progress had been rapid and aggressive, ravaging her organs within days of her getting infected. The few people that saw her corpse agreed that they had never seen anything quite like it. How could anyone literally turn into a shrivelled mummy in a matter of days? The Deputy High Commissioner still struggled to look Alan in the eyes. They shared a secret too gruesome, too intimate, to allow the previous ease of their relationship. Like everyone else, the Deputy High Commissioner wondered what would have reduced a young and healthy woman to the terrible death mask they had seen in Alan's bedroom.

Alan knew what. He discovered the truth the very day he got back his sight. But by then it was too late. The terrifying smell of rotting fruit and rotten fish had taken possession of his house and Laura reeked of the dead stench of the Night Market. She'd locked herself inside their bedroom and wouldn't let him in. But she spoke to him and he made himself listen despite the choking stench of the foul smell that wafted out of their bedroom.

She had done it all for him. The evil thing wearing her cardigan had promised her that she could buy back Alan's memory, his sight and his legs at the Night Market. It would show her how

181

to get to the evil market place. How could she resist? It was killing her to see him lying in that infernal hospital bed like rotten vegetable, all broken up, a shadow of the husband she loved and worshipped. She wanted her husband back and would do anything to get him back to the way he was before. And the evil thing had promised not to haunt her dreams or her home anymore if Laura made that one purchase.

Except that the ghoul had not kept its promise. It demanded a quarter of Laura's life for each transaction or all her life in a single trade-off. Laura had accepted the first deal and battered away a quarter of her life for Alan's memory. She had felt no different after that initial transaction, apart from a draining tiredness. Seeing Alan's recovery of his memory had proven the efficacy of the Night Market's weird remedy. She hadn't planned to return to that terrible market of the dead. But the evil thing started haunting the house on a daily basis. Laura had opened the doorway to its possession by her unholy transaction and it could enter their bedroom at will, day or night. In the end, Laura had done what she had to do to end the haunting.

It had been easy to make the second trade; again, a quarter of her life in exchange for his legs. That was when she started seeing the changes, especially in her hair. By the time Alan left the hospital, Laura was already hooked on L'Oréal hair dyes to hide the sudden premature greying of her hair. She was starting to age. People were commenting about her looks, kindly putting it down to the stress of Alan's tragedies. There was only so far she could hide the terrible physical changes occurring in her body. She hated what she had become and could not go on living with the torture of the incessant hauntings.

The other ghouls from the Night Market had joined forces with the evil thing to persecute Laura, hounding her by day and by night, urging her to complete the transaction she had started. They hit her and pulled her hair, bit her and spat on her. It was an unremitting hounding that proved too much for her to cope with. How could she tell Alan what was going on? How could she convince him that she wasn't crazy when she knew just how scornful he was of the natives and their superstitious mumbo jumbo? He probably didn't believe a word of what she'd just confessed but it didn't matter anymore.

She had made the final visit to the Night Market and traded away the other half of her life in one deadly transaction, buying back his eyesight, the most prized of all his lost senses. She had concluded the transaction that very night.

183

Alan would get back his sight before the crack of dawn. Maybe then he would believe her. She didn't want him to see her as she now was. It would kill her for him to see the ghoulish nightmare she had become.

He tried to tell her that he believe her, that he could see, that nothing mattered to him except her, that he loved her beyond words could express, that he was sorry… so, so sorry for what he had done. But Laura was deaf to his pleas. Her final request was to be cremated, burnt to cinders so that no one would see the abomination she had become.

By the time Alan called the Deputy High Commissioner and they broke down his bedroom door, Laura had downed two bottles of sleeping pills with half a bottle of whiskey. She hid away the empty bottles so that no one would know what she had done and resuscitate her. She had also left a suicide letter by her bedside. Alan had not read the letter. There was no truth in it beyond the horror he already knew. He left it to the Deputy High Commissioner to read and keep and decipher. He knew a diplomatic scandal would be averted at all costs.

He didn't want the ambulance team to save Laura after seeing the horror that had once been his wife. For the first time, Alan wished he had remained blind, had never gained back his sight to see the gruesome and fearful sight that would remain with him to his dying day.

His howls had been sustained, hard and choking, spurred by guilt and shame.

*****

Laura's death plunged him into a state of apathy. For days after her cremation, he wandered aimlessly around the vast grounds of his parents' estate in the countryside. The fresh spring air, fragranced by the flourishing plant life, failed to lift his dark mood. A listless air hung over him, a gloom that neither the slavish devotion of the family's Jack Russell nor the incessant pestering of his twin nephews could lift. His medical leave had been converted to compassionate leave. There was nothing physically wrong with him anymore. In fact, his incredible recovery was still a source of amazement to the hospital personnel and the entire High Commission staff, who had all witnessed the extent of his injuries and had doubted his survival.

Fool that he was. That should have been his first sign that something was terribly wrong. No man makes such an instantaneous recovery from the kind of damage his body had sustained without raising suspicious brows. He should have confided in Laura, made her see that he believed her and didn't think she was as ignorant as the superstitious locals. His arrogance and pride had driven her away. He had killed her as surely as if he'd forced the damned pills down her throat with his bare hands.

Alan pushed away the morbid thoughts - for the umpteenth time. It was better to think of nothing, leave his mind as blank as a white board, feel the blood flow through his veins, pumping his heart, sustaining his worthless life. He didn't plan to return to Nigeria after his compassionate leave. There was nothing there for him anymore. Everyone he loved was in England, his parents, his sister, his nephews and Laura... Laura's ashes that stayed by his bedside day and night, listening to his choked confessions and teary apologies. He liked to believe that she heard him, that she had forgiven him. It was because of her that he considered ending his diplomatic career. She'd never liked Nigeria, as if she had a premonition of what the country held for her. It seemed only right that he now stayed behind in her beloved England with her. He would return to Nigeria for the final time in a couple of weeks to pack up their belongings and say his goodbyes to their staff.

The decision lifted a weight off Alan's shoulders, a weight he hadn't realised he'd been labouring under since Laura died. His mother was glad about his news. She wanted him close to home, safe in England. His father was reserved about it, telling him not to rush into a decision while he still mourned his wife. He had built up an enviable career in the diplomatic service which he shouldn't throw away so impulsively. His sister, Sarah, shared their father's sentiments although she asked him to request a cross-posting to England or somewhere safe in the Eurozone. Alan agreed to consider all their suggestions, albeit his mind was already made up about relocating back to England.

The following night, he got a call from Bisi, a call that would plunge him right back to the horror he'd thought he had escaped for good. Alan hadn't been answering his mobile in recent days, weary of the constant calls by well-wishers determined to remind him of his loss. But Bisi was different. He'd almost forgotten all about her and felt a slight pang of guilt when he saw her name light up his mobile's caller-id. It was a two-fold guilt – guilt for the speed with which he had forgotten Bisi and guilt for speaking with her next to Laura's ashes. It felt like infidelity to him, disrespect for Laura's remains. Quickly, he walked out of his old bedroom in his parents' house and answered the call in his mother's flower-filled Morning Room.

'You bastard! You and your fucking wife!' Bisi's voice was shrill – livid - worse than he'd ever heard her sound, even at the peak of her notorious rages at the High Commission. 'If you think you and that bag of bones you married will use me for your evil juju, then I've got news for you. You won't succeed, d'you hear me, you asshole. You won't succeed.' Bisi was now crying, her screams coming in choked husks.

'Bisi, for Christ's sake, calm down woman.' Alan struggled to control his anger. *How dare the bitch call Laura a bag of bones?* 'I don't know what's got into you but whatever it is, I'd appreciate it if you refrain from calling my wife names, when she can no longer defend herself. I expected better of you.' Alan's voice was cold. *How could he have thought for one second that Bisi had class and finesse?*

'Fuck you and your bloody expectations, Mr high and mighty fucking Pearson,' Bisi screamed again, almost killing his eardrums. 'I thought we were friends, even more than friends. Instead, you go and stab me in the back. I should have suspected something fishy when you invited me to dinner in your house after your nasty behaviour to me before your accident. And the way that witch, Laura, fussed over my ring. I should have known it was all false. I hate you, Alan Pearson. You're not a man at all, just a fake. But I'll show you that no one messes with me. My father is the Oba of Lagos' chief *Babalawo* in case you don't know, the top witchdoctor in Lagos. His medicine is more powerful than you and your wife's and all her demon friends in that wretched Night Market. Just wait and see.'

Bisi hung up on him and Alan slumped on the nearest seat, breathing hard. He felt the horror crawling up his spine with icy fingers. His heart was racing so fast he feared a stroke. *Night Market.* The words reverberated in his head. Bisi had definitely said those two awful words. *Night Market.* He hadn't imagined it. He wanted to call her back, get her to repeat her words. Perhaps he misheard her, allowed his imagination to make up phrases that were never uttered. But his mouth was so dry he doubted his voice would come out of its dry well.

He stood up and began to pace the room, his bare feet soundless on the Ottoman rug in his mother's exquisitely-furnished Morning Room, set in the east wing of the mansion. In the morning, the sun would burst through the high windows, lighting up the room in a dazzling brilliance of colours. But for the moment, the chandeliers did an equally effective job for the night. He needed light and brightness as one needed oxygen. He couldn't face a second of darkness. *Night Market*. Bisi had definitely said those words. He had to know for sure.

Alan speed-dialled Bisi. She answered at the sixth ring, as if she was debating whether or not to speak with him.

'Bisi, I can see you're pretty upset about something,' he tried to keep his voice civil. 'That much I gathered from your call. However, you leave me in the dark as to the nature of my offence. You seem to believe that Laura and I are somehow responsible for some harm against you and I confess total ignorance. What's happened and what's all this crazy talk about Juju and Night…stuff?' Alan couldn't get himself to speak out the dreadful words.

'Are you telling me that you don't know anything about the Night Market?' Bisi's voice was dowsed in icy scepticism. 'You want me to believe that you and your wife didn't set me up so she could get my ring?'

Alan tried to still the heavy pounding in his heart. He wanted to speak, deny Bisi's accusations. But his words were trapped behind

190

the terror that gripped his heart in an icy block. *He couldn't possibly be hearing what Bisi was saying... just his mind sending horrible words to his ears.*

'Hello... Alan, are you still there?' Bisi's voice exploded in his head like a shotgun. 'I knew it. I knew you were lying, you sod. You knew all about the Night Market, didn't you? Listen to me, you bugger. If you know what's good for you, you'd better come back here at once and sort this out. You people will not use my life to bring back your wife. As far as I'm concerned, she can rot in that market for eternity. I warned her last night not to bother me again because I am not afraid of any *Oyinbo* white woman's ghost, especially not her skinny arse. Call me when you return.'

For the second time that strange night, Bisi hung up on him. This time, Alan didn't try to call her back. He didn't want to hear anything more Bisi had to say. His limbs felt as if they were made of yoghurt rather than bones. His thoughts raced wildly in his mind, struggling to cope with the horror Bisi had dropped into his life with such casual brutality. *Laura was alive!* Somewhere in the murky depths of Lagos, his wife lingered in a dark silent world of the living dead, waiting for her release from her earthly hell. All those wasted nights crying and talking to an urn-full of ashes

191

when he could have been in Nigeria fixing the mess he'd made. *What was it Olu had said?* Something about the Night Market being the final resting place of those who sold off their lives; their unhallowed grave till they could repurchase their lives again to return as albino-eyed *Comebacks*.

Alan dragged himself from the chair and poured himself a stiff glass of Scotch whiskey. He downed it in a single gulp, feeling the fiery liquid burn his throat. He poured another shot, then a third. Soon, he felt a mellow cheer replace the terror in his heart. *One for the road.* He filled the glass for the final time and stumbled his way up the wide staircase to the bedroom he shared with Laura's ashes. He started packing his suitcase, his actions frenzied, clumsy. *To think he'd once laughed off the lore of the Night Market and treated the narrator with derision and contempt. Poor Olu!*

Alan felt oddly unworried about his metamorphosis, the fact that things like dead traders and purchased lives were now as normal to him as if he'd grown up in the ghettos of Ajegunle. *Hadn't he always known that Lagos had stamped its DNA in his blood with that virulent Malaria attack? No one amongst his family or colleagues would believe how native his mind had gone. What did they know? Stuck in the false security of their artificial world in the West, they knew nothing about the ancient truths, the existential world, the secrets behind the beginning of mankind? Africa! The cradle of life! The guardians of the ancient mysteries of life and death! Yes, he would return to Africa and set poor Laura free, even if it meant selling his own life in exchange for hers.*

*****

The flights were cancelled – a summer strike by immigration officers at Heathrow and Gatwick. Then Alan's father suffered a coronary attack. A chain of events converged to ensure his trip back to Lagos was delayed for another week. By the time he finally boarded the Virgin Atlantic flight back to Lagos, he had ceased to bother about the myriad of misfortunes that had dogged his every step since his decision to return to Nigeria.

He'd run over Bertie, the family Jack Russell, as he backed out of their garage. Then his mobile was stolen at the hospital canteen while he awaited news of his father's condition. He'd almost gone berserk with the loss of all his contacts. *Beware what you ask for, you just might get it.* The old phrase ran over and over in his mind in the days following the theft of his Samsung. He'd wanted peace, craved to be left alone by well-wishers. Now he was left alone by the entire world. No one could get through to him neither could he get through to them. The pre-Nokia days of knowing phone numbers by heart were long gone.

It was therefore of little surprise to him when he boarded the plane and realised that he'd forgotten to charge his new mobile in his rush to catch the flight out of London. *They knew he was coming and they were doing everything in their power to keep him away.* A cold smile twisted his lips. He ordered a glass of Bloody Mary and several screw-top bottles of Sauvignon Blanc from the glamorous red-clad hostess, the black hostess with the dangerous arse that reminded him of Bisi.

Bisi. She was like a fever in his blood, a virus he couldn't rid himself of no matter how hard he tried. There was unfinished business between them but it could wait. Other urgent matters required his undivided attention. *Twit.* What made him think Bisi was still interested in him after the way he'd treated her, not to mention her torment by Laura's ghost?

Alan didn't need to be told what Bisi was going through at the stroke of midnight on Sunday nights. He'd witnessed it first-hand after the evil thing stole Laura's M&S lilac cardigan. Laura had taken Bisi's ring to gain possession of her soul. She must have known she was doomed by the time she made the second visit to the Night Market. What better revenge on the woman she'd perceived as "the other woman", than to buy back her life with Bisi's own? He recalled Olu saying that the Night Market traders required a personal belonging to aid their possession. Olu had said lots of other things too. Alan wished he had paid better attention.

He slept through the six-hour flight, oblivious to the annoying cries of the babies, the spicy smell of rice and stew and the occasional minor turbulence when the plane went through the clouds. The flight landed at *Murtala Muhammed International Airport* just after 05:00hrs. Alan could barely make it out of the plane. He was experiencing the father of all hangovers. His eyes felt gritty, his mouth dry, while the throbbing in his temple threatened to destroy what was left of his sight.

He fought his way through the airport touts that harassed him for foreign currency in exchange for the *Naira* and bagged himself a taxi.

The High Commission would have had a vehicle waiting for him had they known he was travelling back into Nigeria. They would have also made arrangements with the immigration guys to ensure he experienced minimum delay on arrival. Alan was breaking every code in the DSP, (the red-bound volumes of the Diplomatic Service Procedures, which ruled on everything) by entering the country incognito without clearance from the highest quarters. But, as Rhett Butler would have said, he frankly didn't give a damn. He was leaving the diplomatic service anyway. When Laura returned as a *Come-back*, he doubted if anyone at the High Commission would swallow his story that he'd married her twin. If everything Olu had said was true, (and he had no reason to doubt Olu anymore, not after what he'd already witnessed) then Laura would be coming back to him as soon as she found the perfect buyer at that macabre market of the dead. But he'd make damned sure Bisi wasn't her doomed victim. No way would he allow any harm to come to Bisi.

Soon, the taxi passed the Eko Bridge, exited Awolowo Road and in just under an hour, Alan found himself back at his official residence in the exclusive Ikoyi area of Lagos State. The taxi driver hit his horn, loudly and persistently. Alan's gateman sauntered out, his face set in an irritated frown at the sight of the taxi. When he saw the passenger, he let out a shout that was both joyous and alarmed and ran to open the high, metal, electric gates. His shouts roused the other members of the compound, who resided in the Boys' Quarters, reserved for the domestic staff. Moses ran out to collect his luggage while the new gardener rushed out with his long duster to clean the spider webs he'd allowed to gather during Alan's long absence. Alan didn't mind. He was used to the eye-service culture of his local workers. That was Nigerians for you – *last minute dot com,* the only country that succeeded to grow trees overnight on the occasion of Bill Clinton's famous visit to Abuja. One morning the road leading to the international airport was no more than a barren stretch of dusty asphalt. By the next morning when Bill Clinton's convoy cruised along the road into the Capital territory, tall, lush, mature trees had lined the road, sprung overnight by the miracles of *Julius Berger* German engineering.

   He let himself into the house. An intense feeling of loss overwhelmed him afresh. He could almost smell Laura's Estee lauder perfume in the hall. He never realised how much he'd dreaded returning to their house till he smelt a different scent from the rotting fruits and rotten fish he'd expected.

Alan sank into the deep leather sofa in their main reception room, feeling his head pound anew. Everywhere he looked had some bits of Laura stamped on them; the floral table lamps, the bookshelf stacked with her favourite Catherine Cookson novels, a pale blue M&S cardigan hugging the high-backed chair, a spare pair of her reading glasses. It was as if she had just stepped out of the room. He reached into his hand-luggage and brought out the urn with her ashes. He placed it on her mahogany writing bureau, next to her *Laura Ashley* curved mantle clock. The name his sister had engraved on the urn brought a lump to his throat.

Suddenly, he felt like making himself a cup of Earl Grey tea, craved the feel of one of Laura's China teacups in his hand. He never knew he could miss Laura so much. He had taken her love for granted, just as a fool takes the devotion of a loyal dog as norm. Returning to the last house they had shared brought home his loss in a manner he never anticipated. He was wracked with guilt and pain, craving her arms around him, the gentle husk of her voice, her fragility and undemanding love. Laura had made the ultimate sacrifice for him, just as she had done throughout their nine years of marriage. He had done the taking, always expecting and receiving her giving as his due. Little wonder he had worn her out with his needs, reduced her to an anxious wreck with his criticisms and impatience. Why had he married her in the first place if all he wanted was to mould her into his clone? He should have married a woman like Bisi if that was what he wanted all along, someone that was selfish, driven, strong and ruthless.

Moses walked in with a cold bottle of beer, despite the early hour. He asked if he should prepare some breakfast, perhaps a fruit cocktail for Master. Alan shook his head. He wasn't hungry, hadn't felt the need for food in a very long time. His trousers hung on him and his belts were pulled several notches tighter around his waist. The last time he'd looked in the mirror in the plane's toilet, his feature had taunted him with their gauntness. These days, his eyes looked greyer than green due to the bleary coating of his sustained alcohol binges. Again, he didn't give a damn. It wasn't as if he were out in the dating world or had a wife or lover to impress. If he could live with himself, then others had better damn well live with his looks or stick it in their fucking pipes and smoke it. And by others, he specifically referred to the stuffy staff of the British High Commission.

He downed the chilled beer straight from the bottle and plugged in his mobile on recharge. As if on cue, the message alerts began coming in manic succession, as if they'd been frantically queuing up for his attention for months. Alan opened the first message. It was from the Deputy High Commissioner. Could he get back to them as soon as he got the text? Very urgent. Three more messages from the Deputy High Commissioner in the same vein. Another one from His Excellency, The High Commissioner himself, asking Alan to get in touch as soon as he could.

Alan deleted the messages. They were tying themselves up in knots because they'd found out he'd travelled back into the country without clearance. *Fuck them all.* He had better things to do with his life than to listen to them wittering on about protocols and the lot. He started making his way up to his bedroom.

The bell rang. He halted midway up the stairs. Moses ran out of the kitchen and rushed to answer the bell. He opened the door and screamed, a piercing scream that had Alan stumbling down the stairs in panic. Moses rushed past him, exiting the house through one of the back doors, still screaming. Alan followed Moses' fleeing form in bafflement. *What on earth had gotten into the lad? One could swear that he had seen a ghost... a ghost! Laura!*

Alan's heart began thudding. He felt the sudden trembling of his body. He looked around desperately, wanting to flee, just like Moses. His feet remained frozen on the spot just below the stairs. The front door swung wide open and Bisi walked in.

'Bisi!' her name burst from his lips as relief surged through his body. For one terrible second there, he'd thought that Laura had returned, that Moses had seen the ghost of his late wife at their doorstep. 'Bisi! God, am I glad to see you. Incidentally, you look absolutely gorgeous, as usual,' he leaned forward to hug her. 'How are you? How did you know I was back?'

He led Bisi into the reception room he'd just vacated and offered her a drink. She headed straight to the sofa and sunk into it with a deep sigh. Alan noticed that she looked exhausted, as if she'd just complete a gruelling Sahara marathon minus the sweat. As always, Bisi was impeccably made up, her full lips luscious and red, her hair extensions, wavy and long. Her black skirt was as short and tight as ever and a thin, gold anklet gleamed wickedly above her Louboutine-encased feet as she elegantly crossed her long legs. He felt himself trapped by the familiar lust as his eyes caught her exposed thighs.

Then he caught her glancing at the urn of Laura's ashes before turning away quickly, her lips twisted as if she'd seen something unpleasant. Her actions killed his desire. He felt a sudden irritation at her arrogance. Bisi had no right to disrespect his wife in Laura's own house.

'I've only just come back this morning as you can see,' he said, pointing to his hand luggage still on the leather sofa where he'd left it. 'I wish you'd let me know you were coming so I could freshen up. As it is, I'm rather bushed and desperately need a shower. So, if you don't mind waiting, I'll just sort myself out and be back with you in a few minutes,' he waved an expansive arm. 'Feel free to get yourself anything from the kitchen, though I can't guarantee you'll find much in there, seeing as we've...I've been away,' he turned away from Bisi before the tight lump in his throat dislodged in a shameful flood of tears. *When would he get used to using the singular "I" rather than the "We" that had encompassed his marriage to Laura?*

Bisi nodded, her head still resting on the back of the sofa. He couldn't see her eyes behind the dark Gucci glasses she wore, for which he was thankful. He wasn't ready to face the accusations and hostility he knew were lurking beneath them. He escaped to his bedroom, pausing briefly outside the door to still the pounding in his chest. The memory of the last time he'd been in that room still haunted him; Laura, withered and dead, her mummified skin almost as black as an African's. And the smell, the foul stench of the Night Market, the reek of death.

Alan pushed the door open and entered the bedroom. He looked around him, forcing himself to take in Laura's things in the room without breaking down. He wandered over to their dressing room through the connecting door and opened one of the wall-lined wardrobes. It was jam-packed with Laura's clothes. He pulled out a floral nightgown from one of the shelves and pressed it to his face. It smelled of fresh laundry. Like a man possessed he ransacked all her drawers, pressing clothes against his nose, seeking the distinct smell of his wife, that subtle blend of clean skin, baby powder and Estee Lauder. But it was as if Laura's scent had died with her. There was nothing of her left in the house but the external soulless possessions.

Alan felt his eyes pool as his body shuddered with uncontrollable grief. He allowed the tears to flow, gave reign to the ever-present guilt even as he staggered to the bathroom. He turned on the shower and stepped in, allowing the tepid water to rinse away his tears together with the soapsuds. Gradually, he felt a calm settle over him. A release of tension like a physical burden lifted from his shoulders. He dried himself with a towel and walked back into the bedroom.

He stopped. Bisi was in the bedroom, sitting at the edge of the bed. In her hand, she cradled a cup of steaming liquid. Alan picked out the familiar smell of Earl Grey tea. *What the heck?*

'Bisi, I don't know what game you're playing but this isn't the time or the place for it,' his voice was icy as he quickly wrapped the towel around his nakedness. 'Now, if you'll excuse me, I need to get dressed. I'll meet you downstairs in a few minutes,' he turned away, waiting for her to leave the room. He heard the soft sighing of the mattress as she stood up, the click of her high Louboutine heels against the tiled floor of the room.

Suddenly, her arms were around him, gentle, tender, as she pressed herself against his naked back. Her hands were on his nipples, cold hands, rubbing, squeezing, exquisitely. He shivered, feeling himself harden as her tongue licked his skin, warm and moist, planting little kisses across his shoulders, his neck. Her hands continued their torture of his body, reaching down underneath his towel to cup his engorged penis. He let out a small gasp as she stroked him, massaged him, rubbed him, squeezed him, slowly, rhythmically… *oh dear lord… he didn't want to come… had to hold it… had to stop her… not right… no… no… yes… oh yes…* He pumped himself into her hand, fast, hard, his bucking hips taut. His eyes glazed over as he felt his seed spill into her hand, sleeking it into hot molasses. His knees buckled and he collapsed to the floor. His breath came fast and hard and the ever ready tears merged with his sweat.

He had betrayed Laura, yet again, right in their bedroom, with her ashes downstairs in the living room while her spirit languished away at the accursed Night Market. He couldn't blame Bisi or the alcohol for it. It was what he had always wanted, fantasied about. He couldn't even do the Bill Clinton on her and dismiss it because there had been no actual penetration. Infidelity was infidelity by any other name.

He felt Bisi lie down beside him, felt her hand on his brows, massaging, gently, tenderly. He jerked away from her, feeling his heart race.

'What's the matter darling? Didn't you like it?' Bisi's voice was soft, whispery, her accent unmistakeably English. *Laura's voice.*

Alan scrambled away, his eyes widened by horror. He saw Bisi rise from the floor, coming towards him, her steps slow, seductive.

'I thought this was what you wanted,' she said, still in Laura's soft husk. 'I thought you would be happier if you had me in *her* body. Do you think I didn't know how you felt about her, how you looked at the African girls?' she paused, just a few steps from him. Her face took on a faraway expression. He wished she'd remove the blasted sunglasses. 'They didn't want me in the Night Market, you know,' she continued, a bitter smile twisting her lips. 'I was as dead as them but I was the only white trader amongst them. Just shows racism never ends, even amongst the dead.' Bisi shrugged her shoulders. It was so reminiscent of Laura he almost gasped. 'I did everything to leave that nasty market. Yet, even though I had Bisi's ring, I couldn't make her visit the market no matter how much I haunted her. Her father was some big-shot witchdoctor and had given her some protective charms. Bet you didn't know she came from such a fetish background with all her hoity-toity ways,' there was a malicious spite in Laura's voice... *no*...Bisi's voice, which was starting to freak him out. If he shut his eyes, he could swear it was his wife speaking. But he daren't let down his guard, not for one second.

Alan wished he hadn't drank all that alcohol; that his mind was sharp enough to deal with the creepy situation he was faced with.

'The other traders wanted me out so bad they would do anything to get rid of me. So they joined forces with me and Bisi couldn't fight all of us. I bought her life in a single transaction, her body in exchange for mine. She's always wanted to be white, the tart. So now she can be me when she buys enough lives. At least that's what she thinks. She'll have to find my body first, won't she? But I think that was it in that dreadful urn downstairs. You must get rid of it, darling. Anyway, the last time I saw Bisi, which was yesterday, she was in my old stall in the Night Market, cursing me in every vile Yoruba word under the earth. I'm rather surprised the High Commission hasn't contacted you to let you know she's dead. Took a nasty stumble on the stairs. Mind you, I've always thought those ridiculous high Louboutine shoes were rather dangerous. Now we know, don't we?' she gave a little giggle.

Alan felt the icy chill layer his skin in goosebumps, felt the painful throbbing of his temples. His mind tried to grapple with what Bisi was saying but his heart wouldn't accept it. It was all a trick, nothing more than a sick trick by Bisi to get into his pants and stop him from rescuing

Laura from the Night Market. So what if she sounded uncannily like his late wife? She'd had an English education after all and had known Laura well enough. It wouldn't take much for her to mimic Laura's voice, even thought it was the best mimicry he'd ever heard.

'Get away from me,' he shouted, rushing to the door and holding it open. 'Get out of my house right now and stay the hell away from me from now on. And incidentally, you're fired.' *There! He'd done it, what he should have done all along, fired the conniving bitch. God! What a fucking psycho!*

Bisi stood where she was, looking at him through her dark sunglasses, a mocking, yet sad smile on her face. Then she did something strange. She drew all the curtains till the room was flooded in dazzling sunlight. She turned on all the lights in the bedroom, her movements as sure as a dragon returning to its lair.

'I could tell you that on the day we met at Adrian Parkes' summer barbeque, I was wearing a flowered, sleeveless dress while you wore a pair of black jeans and a pale blue polo shirt. I could also tell you that we had our first kiss less than five hours later when you drove me home because I don't drive as you know, having failed my driving test five times. I could go further to tell you that the last time we talked about starting a family when we were in Spain, we had agreed that my thirtieth birthday would be the date. Isn't it ironical that I died just a few months to that date?' She started walking towards Alan. 'But you and I know all about that filthy, little pervert, Keith Bowman-Myers and what he tried to get little Alan to do with his naughty, horrid thingy, don't we?' her laugh was shrill, evil.

By now, a voice was screaming silently in his head... *oh God! It's true... it's Laura... Laura... oh dear God, no... no...* 'I guess you will only believe what you see. You've always been a cynical bugger. Why don't you look down; go on, look on the floor, look to the walls and see if you can find my shadow.'

He looked. *Dear Jesus, he looked.* He couldn't help it. His eyes scanned the room, seeking her shadow, that dark twin to all humanity. He saw his own shadow, defined, strong, against the brilliant light. But he could find no shadow for her. She laughed, mocked him, flaying her arms, kicking her legs, twirling round, all the while asking, taunting, 'Can you find my shadow? Can you find my shadow?' There was malice and glee in her voice that chilled him to the bones.

By the time she reached him where he stood frozen by the open doorway, Alan had stopped searching. He knew he could never find her shadow. He finally accepted the truth, the terrifying truth that he was stuck with a wife that loathed him as much as she'd once loved him, a warped spirit in the body of the woman he'd lusted after. The Night Market had left its mark on Laura. Olu hadn't told him the whole truth; that they come back but they come back spoiled, tainted, like the rotten stench of that evil market of the dead.

Alan shut his eyes, just like a child shutting out the wardrobe monster. The sweat poured down his body in rivulets. He could feel his limbs getting weaker, his breath coming faster, wheezy, like an asthmatic. He didn't need her to remove her glasses anymore. He didn't want her to pull off those dark designer shades as she was now doing with slow deliberate hands. He didn't want to look into her eyes, didn't want to see the final proof of Bisi's demise. A painful lump lodged in his throat. *Bisi. Sassy, beautiful, sexy Bisi; gone forever, trapped in the unhallowed grounds of that infernal market of the dead.*

He felt her hand on his face, on his brows, cold hands, stroking, massaging, gently, tenderly.

Alan forced his eyes open and gazed into the pale, mocking, dancing eyes of an albino.

*****

Our Bones Shall Rise Again

"The Flight of the Eagle is a source of great envy to the Kite" – Igbo proverb

(Part One)

He awoke to the sounds of drums, a frenzied beating of ancient hands on weathered leather which was the signature rhythm of the mysterious Izaga masquerade fraternity. Oba sat up on his elevated mud-bed, the thin raffia of the mat sheet rustling in the deep silence of the night. His heart was thudding rapidly in his ribs, his eyes wide, suddenly bereft of sleep. *Who on Amadioha's earth was beating the Izaga drums at that unholy hour? Who dared beat the Izaga without his say so?*

In the near solid blackness of his stuffy hut, his eyes picked out the small figures of his two sons, Obinna and Uchenna, stretched out on their raffia mats adjacent to his bed. Like him, the boys were in semi-nude states and likely covered in sweat due to the airless humidity of the hut.

Staring at them, Oba shook his head, a weary expression on his face. Even in their sleep, the two boys displayed their individual spirits. Lying on his side, his first son, *Uchenna* (his father's mind), had both hands tucked in safely between plump thighs – the typical position of a weakling, a coward that would never show his hands to an enemy in an open and fair fight. At almost ten years, Uchenna had already shown himself to be a habitual liar, a greedy and indolent boy who took more pride in his food and his status as the first-born son of the great witchdoctor, Oba, rather than soiling his hands in a day's hard work at the farm. Oba's heart despaired at the prospect of moulding the boy into a worthy first son, capable of leading the family and the village whenever he was eventually called to join the ancestors.

His eyes settled on his second son, Obinna, lying in reckless abandon next to his big brother, arms and legs flung wide apart. The frown in his brows disappeared as his fierce features softened in an unusual tender smile. *Obinna, his father's heart.* Never was a son's name more apt. If only mankind held the keys to creation, he would alter the sequence of birth and confer the first-born title on Obinna….*and give him the gift of speech as well. Or perhaps not.* Perhaps, his tongue was the price demanded by the Great Spirits for the uncanny gift they had given the child, an awesome power that might be lost should the boy regain his tongue. But what a leader he would make should he master the art of speech!

Already, the boy commanded the respect of both his peers and the older boys in the masquerade age-grade, not to mention the elders of the clans. The respect wasn't just as a result of his incredible psychic powers. It lay in the clearness of his gaze, a transparency that revealed the strength and purity of the heart beneath. Oba could not count the number of times Obinna had returned home with bruises, occasioned from a fight in defence of another, usually his cowardly good-for-nothing older brother, Uchenna. Only the Great Spirits knew that if Uchenna had been someone else's child, Oba wouldn't even let him play with his own kids or hang around his *Obi,* his ancestral compound.

Unfortunately, one can never choose the spirits that will reincarnate in one's children. Oba already knew that Uchenna was none other than Isichie, his late uncle-in-law, a useless wretch, notorious in the ten villages for his cowardice, sliminess and drunkenness. Isichie's death from poisoning had been a cause for celebration rather than mourning. Oba hadn't even bothered to use his powers to seek the truth from the oracle and bring the poisoner to justice. His wife, Ugodiya, had pestered him for weeks to find her uncle's killer and wreck terrible vengeance on him. But she might as well ask him to reincarnate as a woman in his next life. Whoever the sly assassin was, had done the family a favour in getting rid of the useless drunk.

Except the blasted man had had the last laugh in the end, returning back to the family that'd despised him in the guise of Oba's first son, Uchenna. Even the way the boy walked reflected the indolent strut of Isichie, not to mention his light skin tone and incorrigible proclivity to gluttony and sloth, just like Oba's late uncle-in-law. It was a struggle to love the boy or the wife that brought him into the clan. But what could he do? For better or worse, Uchenna was his *Okpala*, his first son, who would one day inherit his *Obi* and his trade should the gods so will. He had no choice but to raise and love him the best he could.

The violent sound of crashing drums broke through his ruminations, speeding his legs to the doorway of his hut. With an impatient hand, Oba pushed aside the raffia mat that hung over the exit, the only door in the large rounded hut. Outside, the full moon lit up the *Obi*, turning the night into a silent dusk, somewhere between day and night, not too bright, yet not too dark. The sandy soil of the *Obi* was like gold dust under the full moon and the shadow cast by The Great Shrine Tree in the centre of the *Obi,* stretched across the entire hamlet like a giant black claw.

Across the compound, by the goat pen, the brown mongrel lifted its head and gave a half-hearted bark before settling back to its sleep on

218

recognising the master of the *Obi*. The dog was oblivious to the unholy din of the *Izaga* drums, which continued to invade the peace of sleep till the entire hamlet was filled with people, wide-eyed and frightened village men, desperately seeking answers to the unearthly drumming from their great witchdoctor. As if guided by an invisible hand, they all gathered under The Great Shrine Tree, huddled in terror.

'Who is it, great Oba? For whom does the drums beat? Tell us which family will be losing a son, please?'

The questions came from numerous voices, voices which under normal circumstances would instil fear and respect in their women-folk and children, but which now rang with the sound of weakness and terror. Before Oba could respond, a sudden hush fell on the crowd as all eyes turned to the direction of a tall woman striding towards them, her bearing erect, her right eye, fierce. She favoured one leg as she walked and a milky haze clouded the sight in her left eye. As she drew closer, one could make out the missing right ear beneath thick grey hair, matted in clumps. She was the only female in the assemblage of men.

The men bowed deeply to her, murmuring greetings in hushed voices.

'Great Mother, we greet you! May these eyes that behold you never go blind.'

She acknowledged their respect with a curt nod as she walked directly towards Oba, who was already rushing to meet her.

'Mama, Great Mother, I greet you. May these eyes that behold you never go blind,' Oba's bow was deep and low as he took hold of his mother's hand. The village men observed mother and son in awed silence, one broad of shoulders, the other, broad of hips, both tall and fierce-looking, both missing identical right ears. The woman was of an indeterminate age, which lay somewhere between middle and old life-lines. She was tall, over six feet in height and towered over most of the men in the *Obi*. In the bright light of the full moon, her chest shimmered with the thick curly hair that matted her exposed cleavage and jawline. She was nude to the waist, her body covered in dark artworks carved into her skin with a blade. The drawings were like skulls, symbolising the number of times she had encountered the terrifying spectres of *Iduu* shrine and survived. The skulls numbered more than the fingers of four men, a truly amazing feat for anyone, let alone a woman. Her ankles and arms were weighted with the thick ivory amulets that signalled her *Ozo* status in the twelve villages, a peer above all peers, a title reserved solely for old and wise men who have served their people and their gods well.

But Great Mother, Nnedi, was no ordinary woman. She was a bearded woman with hair on her chest, a man-woman with awesome powers of the occult and the mother of the most powerful medicine man, Oba. The assemblage awaited the verdict of mother and son with hushed breaths.

'My son, they beckon again,' Nnedi said, her voice as deep and husky as a man's. *'Ndichie*, the old ones, are calling home another son of our soil. Listen to their drums. It is fast and furious, a young man's beat,' she turned to the crowd of waiting men. 'Who amongst you have young men at the peak of their youth that are ailing with any sickness now?'

No one spoke. Everyone looked at his neighbour and looked away. The drums continued their frenzied beating.

'Who has young men that have travelled away from our village and are yet to return?' Again, Nnedi's voice boomed out in the night. This time, two arms were raised.

'Great Mother, my son journeyed to Awka village only two days gone to buy superior *Nzu,* white chalk and other herbs for our ancestor's shrine. He has yet to return. Is it for him that the drums beat? Is my son safe?' The question came through the tremulous voice of an old man in faded loincloths.

'Great Mother, my son left our village only this morning to Ogidi village to visit his father-in-law who they say is sick with the shakes. We expect him back tomorrow before the midday sun. Please tell me that the drums do not beat for him. He is my only son, my one eye that owes the debt to the blind man. His young wife is yet to swell with child. Please give us something to protect his life so that our family name is not wiped out of men's memory,' the second man was burly and tall with a full face of beard and the voice of a female. The villagers nicknamed him *Okwa*, the nightingale, on account of his high-pitched voice.

As he broke down in tears, the rest of the men joined the debate, some consoling the distraught fathers, others wondering aloud about factors that may predispose their sons to an early demise. Perhaps a snake bite even as they spoke? A sudden attack of witchcraft? A woman's poisoning hands? Or worse, a nocturnal attack by a malignant ghost or demon? Whose son would be next to join the ancestors before the cock crowed in the dawn?

Nnedi raised her right arm and again, silence descended in the *Obi*.

'Return to your homes and ease the minds of your womenfolk,' she commanded. 'There is nothing any of us can do to thwart the wishes of the gods and as you well know, once the ancestors beat their drums to welcome a new soul to their realm, there's little we can do except to wait and see for whom their drums beckons. It is sad that the rhythm of the drums is not the slow and steady beat that would herald the departure of one that has lived a ripe age,' she turned to the two worried fathers. 'Obika and Okwa, hold your hearts and wish no evil on your absent sons. They may yet return to you safe and alive. Come dawn, we shall know all. Go now. I need to confer with my son. *Kachifo*, may the night turn into day.'

Nnedi turned her back on the men, signifying an end to the meeting. The men returned the greeting as they filed out of the *Obi* in silence, each filled with their own demon thoughts of fear, anxiety and hopelessness. And the loud *Izaga* drums from *Iduu* shrine continued to beat their manic message of doom, filling the night with terror.

'My son, we have to be prepared in case we are required to visit *Iduu* shrine come morning,' Nnedi said, leading Oba to the fallen tree trunk that acted as a communal bench underneath The Great Shrine Tree. Oba nodded, his broad forehead furrowing in a deep frown. He rubbed the stump of his absent right ear with an abstract thumb.

'I would rather you don't go to *Iduu* tomorrow, Mama,' he said. 'If the need arises, then please let me handle it.'

'Why? Do you doubt your mother's powers?' Nnedi fixed a fierce right eye at him and despite himself, Oba felt a slight quiver in his heart. Of all *Amadioha's* creation, his mother was the only human that inspired fear in him - and a love so fierce it rivalled the love he felt for his son, Obinna. It frightened him to think of the time when she would no longer be there for him. Without her, without her wisdom, her powers, her knowledge and her unyielding love, he was nothing. Everything he knew about the occult and the gods, everything he knew about life and people was down to her.

'Great Mother, how can I doubt your powers? How can a mouse play with a tiger's tail? What am I but an ant beneath your mighty elephant's heel? I only ask because I want to learn, to perfect my skills and strengthen my heart with more encounters with the terrible entities of *Iduu.* I want to earn as many skulls as you have on your skin,' Oba lied. But the truth would only make his mother more stubborn.

Without doubt, Nnedi was the most powerful witchdoctor in all the twelve villages and beyond. Despite being heralded as the most powerful medicine-man alongside his mother, Oba knew where the real power lay. Everyone knew where the true power resided. But Nnedi was determined to secure his succession to the shrine and had been gradually delegating the bulk of her duties to him and stepping back from public affairs – with the exception of such unusual events as had taken place on the night, which required her superior wisdom.

Oba was frightened, frightened for his mother. The grey in her hair was now more than the ones the demons of *Iduu* had cursed her with. He doubted her ability to withstand another encounter with the terrible spectres of the shrine. A single encounter with those malignant forces was enough to induce insanity or death in an ordinary man. Nnedi had had over forty encounters with those awful ghouls and still spoke with her mind intact. But as everyone in the villages knew, each encounter had left its mark on her – lost sight in her left eye, a burn scar on her arm, a permanent limp to her left leg, premature greying of her hair, a missing right ear, a bite mark, with the perfect set of ghost-teeth indented permanently on her cheek. Even her voice had been stolen by a mischievous apparition in that shrine and replaced with its own deep timbre, depriving her eternally of the sweet lilting tones he remembered as a child.

He still shuddered at the remembrance of that awful day his mother had returned from yet another visit to *Iduu* and spoke with the unnatural voice of a man. The tremor in the entire village had taken weeks to subside. Tongues wagged and questions spilled – *who was Nnedi now? What evil demon had taken possession of her tongue? Had the entity also taken possession of her soul? Did it plan an evil attack on the villagers?* It had taken several moon cycles for the hysteria to subside. Even now, some people still ran inside their huts when they saw Nnedi about. That deep masculine voice on the lips of a woman still gave rise to a feeling of unease. But it helped to solidity his mother's authority. Even the most stubborn of men listened when she spoke and obeyed when she commanded. For all anyone knew, it could still be the demon speaking through her lips and who in their right minds would want to tangle with an evil spirit?

'My son, you need no further training in our art,' his mother's deep voice interrupted

Oba's musings. 'You are no ant beneath my elephant's heels. What you are is the right foot to my left foot, as sure-footed as I am in the ways of the shrine and the gods.' She placed a callused palm on his chest. 'I count two hands of skulls on your body. That is more than sufficient for your age. By the time you get to my age, *Amadioha* willing, you will no doubt accrue more skulls than I have. Be patient my son and don't be in a hurry to engage the spirits. Remember, when a child washes his hands thoroughly, he will be allowed to dine with his elders. Diligence always yields dividends.'

'I hear you, Great Mother and thank you. But I would still like to do this visit by myself should the need arise in the morning.' Oba was insistent.

For a while, Nnedi was silent, her fierce right eye staring into the distant unknown, unknown thoughts going through her mind. For the hundredth time, Oba wished he had his son, Obinna's gift. What wouldn't he give to be able to decipher the minds of men?

'As you wish,' Nnedi finally said with a deep sigh. 'I am an old woman after all. Perhaps it's time I left all these troubles to you. Truth be told, you really do not need my help anymore. You now know everything I know.'

'Rubbish Mama! Heavens forbid that you abandon our shrine's work. Where will I be without you? Where will our village be without your knowledge and powers, I ask you? Or have you forgotten that the flight of the eagle is always a source of envy to the kite? We are surrounded by enemies who would swallow us alive should you leave everything to me. So let's not hear another word about retiring, okay? The only retiring to be done tonight is to our beds, if our ancestors' drumming will allow us to catch a wink tonight.'

Oba helped his mother to her feet, even though she resisted his arm. *Stubborn old she-ram!* He smiled as he walked her back to her hut, built facing The Great Shrine Tree that dominated the *Obi*.

'*Kachifo!* May the night turn into day, great mother,' he saluted.

'And may the sun never die on your lifetime and your children's children's lifetimes, my son.'

Oba walked back to his hut, stooping outside to push aside the *Ubana* plants, a snake repellent foliage that grew wild around the entrance. He re-entered his hut, his movements stealthy like a night mouse. His sons' deep breathing assured him they had slept through the

228

ruckus that had taken place in the Obi. He retired to his dry-mud bed and lay on his back, staring into the brown palm-fronds that wove the thatching of his roof. He knew that it was useless to attempt sleeping. On such rare nights when the old ones drummed to welcome an impending soul into their realm, sleep became a luxury he could ill-afford. All everyone could do was wait…and watch their loved ones like a mother hen watches her chicks against a hawk.

It was the curse of the village, or perhaps, the blessing, that their ancestors always drummed a warning when a death was imminent in the village. The death always occurred before the break of dawn. It was a known oddity to the surrounding villages that the indigenes of his village only died at night, never in the day time.

Yet, there had been occasions when the eerie drumbeats had issued from the mouth of the shrine and no death had followed. There had equally been occasions when the drums had failed to beat and a citizen had disappeared, simply vanished like an object stolen by an expert robber. On such occasions, it fell on Oba or Nnedi to visit the oracle to seek the lost soul at *Iduu, The Water-mirror of Death.* Oba prayed that the morning would bring a definite conclusion, a confirmed death and a body to bury. No one prayed for the death of another but when the death was pre-ordained and spared another from a fate almost worse than death, then who would blame him for making the wish that would spare him another dreaded visit to the terrible shrine?

*****

The morning brought in the corpse...two corpses to be precise. It was neither of the travelling sons of Obika and Okwa. They were the bodies of the young wrestler, Ezugo, of the nimble feet and cunning eyes, together with Ngozi, the third wife of the village palm-wine tapper. Their bodies had been found in the bush, lying next to that terrible plant that blistered the skin, swelled the body and squeezed the life from the hearts of unwary men. The plant was well-known to every self-respecting son and daughter of the village. Only a fool, a stranger or in this case, two desperately randy cheats would allow their bodies to make contact with the deadly plant, which killed with the same speed as *Echieteka,* the viper.

Oba shook his head with weary resignation as he stared down at the swollen bodies of the doomed lovers. *What a waste!* At the end of the day, they had no chance once the ancestors' drums had beaten and they made contact with the killer plant. The only people that survived contact with the plant were witches and night-flyers, a sure proof of their evil powers. In fact, one of the skulls that adorned the shrine tree in his Obi belonged to that evil witch, Ajuluchukwu, notorious for killing the unborn babies in the stomachs of her rivals.

Oba recalled the day the entire village finally rose against the witch. They had chased her through the farms and wastelands till she stumbled and fell full-body against the deadly plant in her bid to escape the wrath of the villagers. She had been apprehended eventually and everyone had waited with hushed breaths for the inevitable blisters and swelling that followed contact with that lethal shrub. But the blasted woman remained as fresh and agile as a young antelope, her soul still primed for more evil.

The men had taken her into the bad forest and burnt the evil out of her before severing her head to ensure her restless spirit would never find her body to cause further mischief or achieve a complete reincarnation. Her bloodied and battered head had hung around his shrine tree, bound with powerful charms and invocations to prevent its resurrection, till the skin finally rotted away to reveal the smooth white skull that now adorned

The Great Shrine Tree, along with the skulls of other evil-doers. Incidents like that made his job worthwhile, secure in the knowledge that he was protecting his people from evil and harm.

*****

A few days later, Oba was awoken by another ruckus, this time, by his warring wives, Uzo and Ugodiya. The women were screeching like she-demons right outside his hut. As always, Oba cursed his luck, cursed the misfortune that had landed him with two wives. If only he had three or four wives like most men of his status! It would spare him the constant aggravation of two jealous women who had nothing better to do than to bicker away their lives. *How many thorns must a man bear beneath his heels before going crazy?* His chest heaved in a weary sigh. Every man knew there was peace in numbers. More wives meant more hands at the farm and less time for fights.

But the oracle had forbidden him that peace. It had also forbidden him the luxury of more sons. His power number was two, the creative number of nature, just as man came with woman, night came with day, the sky came with earth and good came with evil. To break the cycle in his life would result in the loss of his powers. The Oracle had spoken and he was but a servant to the oracle at the end of the day, bound to obey and serve. It was his lot to be yoked to the two women till either of them did away with the other. Oba secretly hoped that should that wonderful day come, it would be Uzo, his second wife that would emerge the victor. At least, Uzo had blessed him with his wonderful son, Obinna, unlike that termagant, Ugodiya, who was as lazy and stupid as the first son she had given him. As they say, the offspring of a Python will always resemble a snake.

Oba deliberately deafened his ears to the trouble taking place outside his hut. The women always started their fights right outside his doorway to see if they could drag him into their petty quarrels. But he always ensured they finished the fight outside their own huts when he'd had enough of their shenanigans and rushed at them with his machete. He debated if it was time to pull out his sharp blade but decided to let them carry on for a while longer till they wore themselves out. Women were like brainless chickens. You had to let them fight out the aggression in their bodies, vent the venom in their deadly tongues otherwise a man would have no peace in his house. Experience had taught him that too early an intervention with his machete only led to the continuation of the war in the farms or at the stream.

'Evil witch! I know you're feeding our husband some charms to keep him tied to your wrapper,' Oba heard the shrill accusation of his first wife, Ugodiya.

'You stupid woman! Have you forgotten who our husband is? How can I charm the most powerful medicine-man in the world without his knowledge? You just don't want to admit that he prefers me to you because your cooking is not fit for even the pigs in our pen.'

Good girl! Oba silently rooted for Uzo. *Smart woman!* He was glad Uzo had reminded the stupid wretch, Ugodiya, who she was married to. Imagine the fool woman saying that he, Oba, the oracle diviner, healer and killer of men, terror of spectres and demons, was charmed by a mere woman! At times like this, he wished his mother was like other mothers-in-law, involved in the domestic affairs of the family and keeping a tight rein on the womenfolk, who like every child, needed tight supervision and strict guidance. But Nnedi was who she was, a representative of the gods, with no time to waste on ignorant humans like his fighting wives.

Oba picked his machete and with a loud shout, rushed out of his hut. It was all for show as usual and he couldn't resist the soft chuckle that escaped his lips as he watched the two women rush on feet suddenly imbued with wings, into the safety of their huts. He stood outside his hut for a while, brandishing the sword and mouthing dire threats.

After a while, he heard the hushed and frightened voices of the wives calling out to each other, asking if he was still abroad with his weapon. And he knew it was time to retire. Their war was over…for the time being. They would soon emerge from their huts to gossip about his meanness and selfishness, briefly united as sisters in their mutual disappointment in him for failing to take sides in their fight. *Women! Pea-brained children that will never grow up! Amadioha! The woes of being a man!*

*****

Two weeks to the *Izaga* masquerade festival, his father's ghost paid him a visit. It happened on a rainy night. The skies thundered and the drops seeped through the thatched roof, dampening parts of the hut. Oba lay on his bed, waiting out the storm, thankful that the downpour had dispelled the stifling heat that had preceded its arrival. He checked that his sons were well covered and free from the leaks before returning to his bed.

He had just stretched out with his arms folded beneath his head, when a sudden light illuminated the hut, startling him. He turned his head and froze. The pores in his scalp pricked and the blood left his skin, chilling his bones to the marrow. His body began to shiver, violently, as the courage deserted his heart.

Standing in front of him was his father, Ide. Oba recognised him instantly. Despite the unearthly light that surrounded him, the ashy hue of his skin, the terrible despair in his black, black gaze, Oba knew it was none other than Ide, the father he had lost in his youth.

He stifled the shout in his mouth with a hand that trembled like the rest of his body. His palm was drenched in the same sweat that poured down his skin, chilling and warming his body in alternate bursts. He shut his eyes, shutting out the mirage. For surely, it was just a figment of his imagination, a false picture drawn by his tired mind. He lifted his lids, slowly, reluctantly.

Ide hadn't vanished. If anything, he was now nearer to the bed, his arm outstretched, seeking contact. Oba recoiled, terror pounding through his heart. He tried to talk bravery into his mind. *What kind of witchdoctor are you to cower at the sight of a ghost? Haven't you communed with the deities of the underworld? Haven't you spoken to multiple ghosts at the Iduu shrine?* But this was no unknown spectre with whom he geared himself for battle, protected by powerful charms and the blessings of his ancestors. This was his ancestor…his dead father. Who would protect him from his own blood should the ghost turn malevolent?

'Beware the great water, my son,' the voice that issued from the apparition was a dead monotone, heavy, as if dragged from the deepest recesses of hell. It was a voice of total despair and anguish. Oba suddenly felt all his terror evaporate, replaced by a feeling so powerful it hurt his heart. Intense pity. *Amadioha! What terror had driven his poor father to journey from their ancestors' realm to seek him out?*

'*Nna-anyi,* our father, I…I salute you!' Oba heard the tremor in his voice despite the disappearance of his fear. But it dented not his pride. It was impossible for a living soul to speak to the dead with a firm voice.

'Beware the great water, my son…the great water…beware…'

237

And with the same suddenness of its appearance, the ghost vanished. Right in front of his eyes, it just winked out as a shadow vanishes in sudden darkness. Oba jumped out of his bed and raced out of his hut. The pouring rain drenched his skin in seconds but he paid it scant heed. His feet took him to his mother's hut before he had time to get a hold on his mind and his male pride. But he needn't have worried. Nnedi was already awake and on her way out of her hut. They collided at her doorway.

'Mama…Ide… Ide just visited me,' he struggled to string his words together. He even forgot to chant the mandatory greeting that would protect his eyes from blindness. Such was his panic.

'I know…he came to my dreams too,' Nnedi said.

'I don't mean a dream. He appeared at my bedside. I saw him just as I'm seeing you now. I heard him just as I hear you now.'

'He spoke to you? What did he say?' Nnedi's voice pulsed with urgency, her body suddenly tense.

'Something about the great water. He said beware the great water.'

'What great water was he talking about? Does he mean *Omambala River* or *The Onitsha River*?'

'I have no idea, Mama. He disappeared before I could ask. One second he was there, standing beside my bed, looking down at me, his body glowing with this terrible light. And just as suddenly, he was gone. I tell you Mama, I have never seen such sadness in a person's eyes or heard such despair in anyone's voice, ever.' Oba felt the prickling of tears, allowing the drops to fall from his eyes. There was no shame in crying before his mother, the only human that had ever seen him cry. How many times had he cried each time she'd returned from the shrine with another bit of her missing, lost to the ghouls and demons of the shrine?

'Wipe your eyes, my son,' Nnedi led him towards the log bench beneath The Great Shrine Tree. She murmured a few silent words and suddenly, the rain ceased; but only around the shrine tree where they sat. The rest of the *Obi* and the village were still pelted by the hailstones that accompanied the midnight thunderstorm. Again Oba marvelled at his mother's skill at juju. No matter how many times he had witnessed her powers, it never ceased to astound him at the ease with which she commanded the forces of nature.

Unlike Nnedi, he still needed to *Igba-afa,* consult the oracles and perform invocations in order to access his own powers.

'All is well with your father,' Nnedi continued. 'He spoke to me in my dream as well. But for some reason, I cannot recall exactly what he said. But like you, I noticed the sadness of his aura and I knew something was very wrong. He has never paid me a visit since the day he returned to your ancestors. So, I knew this was no ordinary dream. In fact, I was on my way to confer with you when you arrived at my hut. Come, let us sit and talk it through while your wives are still asleep. Heaven knows when next we will have time to talk once they wake up and resume their bickering. Why you had to go and marry two such crazy women, I'll never know.'

Nnedi chuckled and Oba laughed out aloud, the tension broken.

'They would behave if you paid more attention to them like other mothers-in-law do,' he teased.

'Heavens forbid! They're your wives. You deal with them. I have enough grey hairs as it is without adding to them. Get them pregnant, I say. That'll keep them busy and they'll soon tire of their fights when they have to deal with their children's fights.' She paused briefly. 'Now we're on the matter, is there any reason why you haven't got your wives with more babies up till now?' Nnedi asked, turning a bright right eye to him. 'I know it's not my business to ask and I have kept my peace so far. But Obinna, your last son, is now almost seven years old. Surely, it's time the women filled your *Obi* with more children.'

Oba was silent for several seconds, thinking through his answer.

'Great Mother, we are both servants to the oracle,' he finally said. There was a finality in his voice which Nnedi recognised. She nodded her head several times, a sad smile twisting her scarred face.

'We are the servants of the oracle,' she repeated his words, her tone deliberate, heavy. 'May *Amadioha* keep your sons safe. May your name live forever in the lips of men!'

'*Ise!* So be it!' Oba chanted the obligatory response in a heartfelt voice.

'May evil keep its eyes away from your house!'

'*Ise!*

'May your days be long and your deeds be great!'

'*Ise!*'

'May your farms be fertile and your barn never empty of yam tubers!'

'*Ise!*'

'May whatever evil that dragged your father from his sleep into our home tonight be averted and thwarted!'

'*Ise!* So be it!'

For a few seconds, mother and son were silent, each pre-occupied with their private thoughts. Above them, the bright skulls hanging from ropes tied around the branches of The Great Shrine Tree clanged and rattled, stirred by the strong breeze that came with the rainy night. The smell of fermented palm-wine was strong, overpowering the other odours that would have come naturally from the decomposed foodstuff, chicken carcasses and fresh blood regularly offered to the gods of the tree and the dead ancestors buried around The Great Shrine Tree.

As one, Oba and Nnedi got up from the log bench and made their way towards the three raised graves underneath the tree. They paused in front of one of the graves, which was slightly bigger than the other two graves. Ide had been a very tall man in his lifetime, just like his son, Oba.

Like all the other graves, there was an ivory funnel protruding from the soil. Oba stooped to adjust the skewed funnel atop his father's grave.

'You need to refresh your father with palm-wine after his long journey tonight,' Nnedi murmured. Oba nodded.

'I'll do so before I retire. I think I still have a keg of palm-wine left over from yesterday's yield.'

'You can't feed your father stale palm-wine,' Nnedi admonished.

'It's only for tonight, till I get some fresh kegs tomorrow,' Oba replied. 'We can't leave Ide thirsty and patched till morning. As you said, he's had a long journey tonight and must be refreshed without delay. I'm sure he'll not mind that the palm-wine is a day old.'

Nnedi slowly nodded her agreement.

'Beware the great water…' she murmured to herself. 'The great water…' she tugged her one remaining ear in deep thought. 'Perhaps he will come back again and tell us what he means. Perhaps my dreams will come back to me…'

'Great Mother, with no disrespect, I am not waiting for either your dreams or Ide to come back before seeking answers. I plan to *Igba-afa* tonight, prepare my charms and fortify myself before going to *Iduu* shrine tomorrow to seek my father and our ancestors and find out the exact meaning of his message. We both know that whatever it is, signifies great danger to us,

243

otherwise Ide would never have made that arduous journey to warn us.'

Again, Nnedi nodded. 'Be careful, my son,' she said, placing a gentle hand on his shoulder. 'Watch out for deceitful spectres that will assume the image of your father to trick you. Always remember that your father had a particular loathing for chicken meat and it is one delicacy that the spirits can never resist. Make sure you take enough chicken meat with you to offer your father. By his reaction, you'll know his true spirit.'

Oba turned wondering eyes at Nnedi.

'Great lady! Wise mother! Peer without parallel! Where would I be without your superior wisdom?'

'In your ancestors' realm for sure, still awaiting your reincarnation,' she laughed.

Oba laughed with her, privately thanking the gods that brought him back to be raised by such an incredible mother as Nnedi. He prayed that in his next incarnation, he would return as Obinna's son. Heaven forbid that he ended up with the little lout, Uchenna, as his father in his next life. *Tufia! Amadioha forbid!* The mere thought of such a dire prospect caused an inward shudder to run through his body.

*****

Through the night, he dug deep into the earth to unearth his Lifestone from its secret place in the soft warm soil underneath The Great Shrine Tree. His *Chi*, his true soul and powers, resided in his personal Lifestone, the smooth triangular blood-drenched pebble embedded in the pulsating mass of red flesh wrapped in special herbs and leaves. The flesh was the *Obi-Dimpka*, the Forever Heart of a man, the heart that would never die as long as its guardian fed the Lifestone its daily diet of blood and libation and kept it safe. With the exception of his mother, no one else knew the location of his Lifestone.

Oba's *Obi-Dimpka* was originally the heart of a warrior killed in one of their numerous skirmishes with the neighbouring villages. His Lifestone kept the heart beating with the powerful charms and sacrifices he made. The stone fed on the spirit and energy of the Forever Heart, enabling him to access the secret powers of the occult and invoke the great deities at times of danger. With special incantations, he could call on the powers of his Lifestone to cloud the vision of enemies so that they ceased to see him. He could create hallucinatory images that drove his foes to insanity. He could even stay the rain in the clouds and bring drought to the farms of antagonists. Likewise, he could call on the rain to ruin a funeral, a wine-carrying wedding ceremony or a masquerade festival. His Lifestone warded off attacks by evil spirits and demons and rendered him nigh invincible when he clasped it in his hand. Every witchdoctor worthy of the title possessed their own Lifestone and Forever Heart. Oba was no different.

Oba arrived at the *Iduu* shrine before the crack of dawn. He made the early journey to avoid being seen in his full witchdoctor regalia by the early morning farmers. The white *Nzu* chalk running patterns across his face, the black charcoal circling his eyes, the grey ash dust coating his body, the multiple coral beads encircling his waist, the stringy dry raffia around his loins, the power-amulets weighting down his arms and ankles, the row of human skulls forming a bone-hat atop his head, the huge skin bag containing his Lifestone, charms, herbs, portions, bones and chicken meat - all those would terrify the wits out of the villagers. But they were an absolute necessity, indispensable in any confrontation with the spectres and demons that shared the shrine with *Ndichie,* the great ancestors.

As he approached the rushing stream that formed the dividing line between the human realm and the vast cave that housed the shrine, Oba turned his back to the cave. He started walking backwards, treading the shallow water with careful steps, shouting incantations and dropping the white bones that would lead him to safety afterwards. The bones were from enemies killed in the three days war they'd fought with Umuoji village some years gone, executed criminals that had wrought harm on their communities, slaves offered as sacrifices to appease the gods during the great famine that followed the locust plague.

The bones formed a silent white line from the riverbank to the mouth of the cave. The exit from the shrine was always hazardous, laden with terror and confusion. Without the bones, a man could lose his way back to the human realm when the bad spirits altered the landscape.

Oba knew he had reached the entrance of the shrine when the drumming started. Except this time, it wasn't the signature *Ijele* drums of his ancestors. The beat was a hollow sound, dull and heavy, echoing through his head, filled with dread and doom. There were other noises too…wails, shrieks, cackles, whistles and garbled voices cursing in various languages. He could pick out the dialect of his people in the garble and thought he recognised some voices amongst them. Occasionally, he heard that accursed name, Jesus, shouted by a desperate voice; Jesus, the dead god of the village outcasts and slaves, brought to them by the fool white-skinned demon that claimed he came off some big boat at *The River Niger* in Onitsha town. *Why would a person chose to ignore his ancestors and instead, worship a god whom they could see clearly nailed to death on a wooden cross?* But then, what could one expect from slaves and outcasts who were too lazy to farm, preferring instead to waste their days under the shade of a tree, learning how to speak the strange tongue of the white demon?

Suddenly, Oba was overcome with smoke, as a thick grey fog blanketed his vision, clogging his lungs and tearing his eyes. He grunted, a hard grin hiding the thudding in his heart. *It had started!*

His voice rose to a deafening pitch as he continued his backwards approach deeper into the cave, coughing and chanting spells. From long experience, he knew every turn, every twist, every dip and crack in that vast dark abode. With each step he took, he shook the rattles in his *Oji* and banged the metal staff on the hard soil of the cave. The *Oji*'s peculiar rattles scared away the minor demons that were sent as forerunners by the greater spirits to distract and confuse. Already, Oba could hear the wild jabbering and light patter of fleeing feet as the imps fled deeper into the shrine. He smiled grimly. *One down!*

He felt the temperature drop, a chill beyond the coldest Harmattan breeze filling the cave. In seconds, his skin was covered in goosebumps. Shivers rattled his body and teeth. The drums grew louder, pounding into his heart and his head, each heavy thud sounding like a death knoll.

From the dark fog, a cold hand reached out and touched his spine, softy. He felt the sudden swelling of his head, a shudder of repulsion. Every nerve in his body went raw as he tensed for the inevitable confrontation. It was almost time to turn around, to face the demons and gain entrance into his final destination – The Water Mirror of Death. That fleeting ghostly touch was the first sign, which was usually followed by…

….Obinna was lying on the floor, twelve feet away from him, a large knife protruding from his heart, his life-blood dampening the hard soil of the Cave.

'Papa…help me! I'm dying…' Obinna's beloved voice called out to him, his eyes dripping blood-tears, agony twisting the features of his sweet child's face. It was the sound Oba had dreamt about in his happiest fantasies, the voice of his favourite child used in speech. His mind told him that the miracle of his son's sudden recovery from dumbness was nothing more than a mirage, a trick of the shrine demons. Yet, the sight of the great knife in the boy's body pierced his heart, as if ten poisoned arrowheads had been fired into his own chest. His feet began to drag his heavy legs towards his son. His mind fought the impulse, fought to keep his body immobile. But his father's heart was stronger, his love too powerful to resist the cold reason of his mind.

Oba reached into his skin bag, his movements frantic, his breathing rapid, even as his feet drew closer to his dying son. He felt his knees buckle of their own accord, bringing him to the hard cold floor of the cave. He watched with horror as his left hand stretched, reaching out towards his son's wet cheeks. Heard the deafening shrieks of victory from the ghouls as they drew terrifyingly close to him…and felt the weight of relief as his right hand clasped the cold hardness of his Lifestone.

Instantly, his vision cleared. Obinna vanished. The ghouls shrieked in frustration and withdrew. He was on his knees, looking at an empty space. His heart was rushing and his breathing raspy. *It had been close...very close.* This time, they had fought him with the strongest weapon yet, his greatest weakness – his intense love for his son, Obinna. Without his Lifestone, no power on earth would have stayed his protective arms from cradling his injured son and forfeiting his own life in the process. The image-demon in the guise of his son would have taken possession of his body the second his hand made contact with Obinna.

In the past, they had shown him different images, impressions stolen from his thoughts and memories – an injured villager; a large bag of cowries, precious currency enough to build ten huts. He had always resisted the mirages, knowing them for what they were, thanks to the tutoring of his mother, who had learnt the lessons the hard way.

But this time, for the very first time ever, the spirits had read his emotions. They had pierced through the closed doors of his thoughts, his very being and accessed his soul. How that could happen was beyond his comprehension but it suddenly filled his heart with a blinding terror that threatened to drive him from the shrine. They were either getting too powerful or he was getting weaker. There was no other explanation he could come up with. Perhaps this new development had something to do with his father's spectral visit.

As he got to his feet once more, still dazed by the near miss, Oba heard the sound he had been seeking, the unmistakeable gush of flowing water. He had arrived at his destination.

Oba turned round to face the shrine. For several minutes, he stood motionless, stilling the tremors in his heart and body. His eyes remained shut as he chanted invocations. He called on the great ancestors, each by their true name, begging their intervention and protection from the spectres of the shrine. His hand held fast to his Lifestone as he dispersed herbs, powders, feathers and animal blood around him. His breathing laboured from the overpowering stench of blood and funk while his skin tingled from the cold mist coming from the great waterfall of *Iduu.*

Voices filled his ears, the sounds of the dead, their din drowning his words and threatening his sanity. He raised the volume of his voice, to make the great ancestors hear him through the cacophony of the dead. The more they increased their ruckus to thwart him, the louder he shouted, till his voice grew hoarse. But he dared not open his eyes and confront them till his ears picked out the serene voice of a great ancestor amidst the unholy din.

Just when he thought he could scream no more, that his voice would never break through their shrieks, he heard it; the wonderful familiar dialect of an *Ndichie*, an old one of the clan, come to answer his cries and guide him safely through the Water Mirror of Death, *Iduu.*

Oba opened his eyes... and froze. No matter how many times he made the visit to *Iduu*, no matter the number of occasions his eyes beheld that awesome sight, his heart never ceased to react with terror at each fresh sighting of the spectacular waterfall that was the passage-way to the underworld.

From a height beyond the sight of mortals, the waterfall covered the spherical vastness of the cave. His eyes could no longer see the jagged roof of the cave. What he saw was the night skies, an eternal darkness, a blackness so dense it seemed a solid matter. From the dark height fell the sparkling waterfall of *Iduu.* The water-curtain glowed with a blinding light that illuminated the entire cave. Its unearthly beauty brought a painful lump to his throat, filling him with awe and humility.

From nowhere, a sense of insignificance engulfed him, a sudden despair filling his heart. A violent trembling shook his body. The glittering water beckoned him into its safe haven, away from the burdens of life. Oba pulled on every will in his mind to resist the deadly call of *Iduu*. He shut his eyes and blocked his thoughts. The shrine was exerting its power on him, seeking the blood of another unwary human to feed its energy.

Several deep breaths later, he opened his eyes and saw them, just as he'd expected. *Some things never changed at Iduu*. In the mirror surface of the great water-curtain, he saw the spectres, the walking dead, wandering along an unseen road, peering through the waterfall, seeking a human face to plead their cause, to hear their anguish, vent their fury upon, send on an errand to their loved ones or merely observe in silent despair. Some of the spectres wore the faces of their death, others, the faces of their decomposition. Some had wasted away to skeletons while others metamorphosed to appalling ghouls, their features twisted, vile, evil. These were the ones that reached out to pull in unprepared humans into the fall and feed on their souls. Oba could see the skeletons and carcasses of both men and beast littering the hard wet floor of the shrine, victims of the soul-sucking ghouls. There were other decomposed bodies, skeletal remains, severed parts and skulls from sacrificial rituals to the deities of the shrine. Their blood, both stale and fresh, painted the cold surface of the cave, caking it with gore.

Instinctively, Oba stepped back, away from the thundering waterfall, his foot crunching a brittle bone. Frantically, his eyes sought his great ancestor, the *Ndichie*, whose soothing voice he had picked out from the cacophony of the dead.

He saw the ancestor…two of them…both of them his late father, Ide. The two ghosts were dressed in identical loincloths and wearing identical frowns. Both clasped identical metal staffs of an *Ozo,* a titled peer. Oba stared intently into their faces, trying to decipher the demon from the spirit. *Who was who? Which was his true father? Whose hand would he accept to lead him through The Water-mirror of Death and into the realm of the ancestors?*

The thoughts were only fleeting as his mind recalled Nnedi's words. Already, his hand was reaching into his skin-bag, seeking the chunky pieces of cooked chicken his wives had cooked on his orders. Even before he reached out an offering hand, the spectre to the left stretched out a greedy arm for the meat. The other ghost turned away, his face dressed in disgust, a deep frown cutting deep into his broad forehead. *Ide! His true father!*

Oba tossed the meat at the deceitful demon, who made a lunge for it. Other spectres fought it for the delicacy, shrieking, pulling, biting. In their distraction, Oba accepted the proffered arm of his father and was instantly sucked into the chilling gush of *Iduu.*

Darkness descended, filling his eyes. His mind died and the world of the living ended. He floated in a world of silent blackness, a neutral nothingness devoid of feelings, thought and dreams. There was no heat, no mind and no curiosity. He saw nothing. He heard nothing. He felt nothing. He desired nothing. He sought nothing and lacked nothing. He was just *a something,* waiting in eternal darkness... for nothing.

The light returned. With the same suddenness with which the darkness had descended, consciousness returned. Oba found himself walking along the wide sandy path that led to the ancestors' realm. He felt the walking movement of his legs. Yet his feet made no contact with the ground. By his side, his father float-walked along the path with the speed of a deer.

They were not alone. Around them swarmed the damned dead, attracted to his humanity like an ant to honey, seeking his light, his warmth, his essence. They sought his memories to replace their awful reality. Oba felt their probes, felt the insanity seeking entry to his besieged mind. His grip on his father's hand tightened and his hold on his Lifestone hardened. Ghostly hands reached for his face, made chilling contact, only to withdraw in agonised wails as his Lifestone repulsed them. The stone projected his thoughts to the spectres, promising dire retribution of the worst kind to any spirit – reincarnation as a chicken. It alerted them to his status as a witchdoctor, one so powerful he could walk the land of the dead while living; one so skilled he could return their damned souls to the land of the living as worthless chickens, food for man and spirit.

The ghosts kept their hands to themselves, but they stayed close, flitting around him, unable to resist the paradise promised by his humanity. It was a bliss they had once known and lost forever. Their evil deeds in their lifetime had ensured that they would never know the glory of reincarnation nor the peace of being a *Ndichie*, a great ancestor, residing in dignity in the realm of the dead, watching over their living kin and whiling away their days in peaceful contemplation amongst their peers.

By his side, his father walked in silence, his face set towards the endless road. Oba allowed the wonder of their union to enfold him. *He, Oba, was once again in the realm of the dead and this time, he was walking with his father!*

'Ide…Great Father, killer of lions and men, warrior-heart, Great Spirit and ancestor, I salute you,' Oba hailed, hearing the hollow ring of his voice as if spoken from a distance. He waited to be acknowledged by the spirit – that was, if the spirit accepted his salute. *One can never be sure how the minds of The Old Ones worked.*

'My son,' his father's voice was as a whisper in the wind. 'My heart is heavy by your presence here. Yet, I give thanks to *Amadioha* that you come in the flesh and not in spirit. Long may you live, my son. Long may your light shine. Short may the lives of your enemies be. May the sun never set in your lifetime.'

'*Ise!* So be it!' Oba mouthed the usual response automatically, distracted by the tremor he heard in his father's voice. He'd caught fear, a muted kind of terror behind The Old One's words. 'Great Father, tell me, what ails your mind? What is it that disturbs your sleep and has brought you up to our world to my bedside?'

His father turned to him and Oba felt his heart skip a beat. Tears, blood tears, fell from his father's eyes.

'You will look into The Soul-Pond and see what our eyes have seen. It is a sight that has filled your ancestors with anguish. It is a fate that we pray will never befall you nor the entire Idemmili clans. Long may your light shine, my son. Short may the lives of our enemies be.'

The ghost would not utter another word till they arrived at the dusky world of the great ancestors. Oba knew they had reached their destination when the spectres that had dogged their trail vanished into the unknown beyond.

A feeling of incredible joy filled his heart as his eyes took in the serene home of his ancestors, their final resting place, the utopia he hoped to share with them when his time came to join them. Oba felt a tight knot form behind his throat. Ancestor after ancestor glided over to meet him, embrace him, clasp his arms in camaraderie. They hailed him with intoxicating names – peerless witchdoctor, fearless heart, conqueror of worlds, faithful guardian of his people.

The accolades poured from spirits who had themselves received similar praise for great feats in their former lives. Oba felt a sense of humility as he'd never felt in his lifetime. His smiles were laced with tears as he returned praise with praise, hugs with hugs, calling out the ancestors he recognised by name, awed by the sight of The Old Ones all gathered in a single abode.

Soon, the greetings were done and Oba noticed grave looks replace their earlier cheer. As if with one mind, the ancestors glided towards a cluster of trees, the only plant life Oba had seen since entering the barren world of the dead. As they drew closer to the trees, he noticed several Old Ones gathered around a small body of water, peering into the spherical pond with intensity. The Old Ones around him led Oba to the pond and pointed at the clear still water.

Oba leaned forward to look. He screamed. His body began to shudder and a weakness took over his limbs. He would have slumped had the ancestors not held him up. His mind grappled with the abysmal images he had seen in The Soul-Pond.

He had seen himself, his corpse, lying beneath a large body of water, bloated and roped up with thick metal chains. He was not alone. Around him, scattered beneath the great river were several young men from his clan. He recognised most of them, knew them by name and kinship. Like him, they were all chained with that appalling black metal, just like his corpse. What stunned him the most was the condition of their bodies. They all bore horrific injuries on their bodies and faces, wounds which were inflicted by brutal human hands and weapons rather than any water life-form – lacerations and multiple swellings, evidence of beatings, whippings and trauma.

Oba dragged himself back to The Soul-Pond, his knees trembling like a new-born piglet's. He needed to see more inside his ancestors' mirror of the future. It was the water-mirror that showed them who would be joining them from the clans, the mirror that instigated their drumming to welcome the new soul and guide it safely to their realm.

Again, the shock of seeing his own swollen and battered corpse brought the shivers to his spine but he forced himself to look. He had to know who all the dead were, the name of the great river that housed their corpses and the cause of their injuries and death.

None of the ancestors could answer his questions. No one knew the name or location of the great river nor the cause of their captivity and death. The Soul-Pond only revealed the dead faces, not the secret behind their demise.

'That was why we had to get your father to you,' one of the Old Ones said, his voice heavy. 'We tried to send messages through dreams but no one seemed able to remember the dreams. It was as if a thick fog blanketed their memories, as if Queen Ill-fortune herself intervened to ensure nothing would avert the course of her will. It took all of our collective energies to get your father to you. We must not let our clan die. You are our greatest witchdoctor, you and your peerless mother. We beseech you, use all your powers, everything you can call upon to avert this evil on our people.'

As Oba left the realm of the ancestors several hours later, he wondered if it was already too late to save his people. The earlier confrontation with the spectres of the shrine now showed that it was his powers that had weakened and not the growth of their own powers. They had easily read his deepest emotions, his love for his son, Obinna. Only a man near to the gates of death would yield his soul so easily to the inhabitants of the underworld. He had a bad feeling he was counting his days on earth and if that was the case, then what in *Amadioha*'s earth can a dead man do for the living?

*****

Obinna welcomed him back with a tight hug, holding onto his waist with a fierceness that did not surprise Oba. The child was after all an *Nshi-shi,* a Thought-Smeller, one of the blessed few that could smell the good and evil in men's hearts.

'It is alright, my son. Your father is just fine. Come now, I have some peanuts for you,' Oba reached into his skin-bag and withdrew the small package of nuts wrapped in palm-fronds. The child shook his head, great tears pouring from his eyes. Oba dropped the bag and lifted the boy onto his laps. He held him close, rocking him, soothing him with soft words. At times like these, it broke his heart that his beloved son could not speak, could not say all the things he had read in the minds of men that brought sorrow to his heart. At times, the child seemed to carry the weight of the world on his small shoulders, blessed or cursed as he was, to smell the darkest secrets of men.

Oba had tried to cloak his mind when he saw the child running towards him as he returned from his terrifying journey to *Iduu* shrine. Yet, the child had smelled something through his skin. It had always been that way with Obinna from the first time he exhibited his powerful gift when he was no more than a toddler. Oba remembered the stunned look on everyone's face when the child had stumbled his way over to a visitor and started sniffing the man's legs as a he-dog sniffs his mate. Even before the adults could admonish the child for the disrespect shown a visitor, Obinna started waving his little hands under his nose in the gesture of one that had smelled a foul thing. Even when the visitor later turned out to be a woman-violator, one who mounted defenceless women with force, Oba had failed to link his son's strange behaviour with his uncanny gift. It had taken several more incidents for people to realise the meanings behind Obinna's strange actions. Oba could not count the number of times the child's warning had saved him and the clans from disaster. None-the-less, it hurt his soul that he could not bear the burden of the inner-sight for his young, dumb son.

Exactly a week following his visit to the shrine, Obinna waved his hand under his nose when his step-mother, Ugodiya, came into Oba's hut to deliver his breakfast. It was the first time ever that the child had used that peculiar gesture on anyone in the immediate family. Oba was stunned, Ugodiya, furious.

'Evil child! How dare you accuse me of evil?' she screamed. 'Oba, tell your dumb son to mind his manners or I will give him a thrashing he'll never forget, idiot boy,' she stormed out of his hut before Oba could respond. Not that one could ever get in any word edgewise when Ugodiya was at full steam. The woman could scream for the whole Idemmili villages and more.

For three more days, Obinna continued to wave his hands under his nose whenever Ugodiya came within his vicinity, running away from her, his eyes filled with terror. Oba was puzzled and worried. He questioned Ugodiya extensively – did she hit the lad? Did she shout at him? Did she single him out unfairly in favour of her own son, Uchenna? Her vehement denials had the ring of truth to them yet something about her, something bad, even evil, haunted his son.

On the fourth night, they came for him.

Oba was awoken by sounds of commotion, screams, wails and a deafening noise that sounded like thunder. Except it was not raining and no lightning brightened the dark skies. The noise seemed to be coming from beyond his *Obi*, right into the wider clans. It sounded like war, as if men fought men to the kill. The family mongrel was barking like it was the end of the world. Instinctively, his hand reached for his

Lifestone above the *Ngige* woven shelf, even as he screamed to his sons to wake up.

His hand came out empty. A baffled look clouded his face. He searched again, this time more frantically. He reached for his skin-bag. Maybe, by some inexplicable way, the stone had found its way into his skin-bag. It was not beyond reason to expect the Lifestone to move by itself. It had drank enough blood after all. Every Igbo son knew that anything, inanimate or living, which is fed a daily diet of blood and human worship, will assume supernatural powers. His Lifestone was no different.

It took him several stunned minutes to realise that his Lifestone was gone for good; that his soul-protector and source of power had vanished into the night. He didn't have time to dwell on the implications. The noises drew closer to his *Obi*. Obinna was standing beside him, silent as always, but not Uchenna.

'Where's your brother?' Oba asked, leading the boy from the hut. He saw Nnedi rushing towards him, her hand clasping her skin-bag.

'Give me the boy. We must protect him at all costs,' Nnedi said, her face a mixture of fury and fear.

'Where is Uchenna?' Oba repeated the question. 'He wasn't on his mat when I woke up.'

'He's with his mother and good riddance. I saw then sneaking away before the troubles started. Arm yourself my son. I hear them coming for you. I have sent out a fog as thick as the clouds above. It will only delay them for a while, enough time for you to consult with the oracle and invoke your powers. Let your Lifestone guide you. I must preserve the child,' his mother hugged him tightly before dragging Obinna away. The boy's mouth opened in a silent shriek, anguish and terror in his wide eyes. Oba had to prise the child's arms away from his waist, watching as his mother ran towards the thick bushes with him. He saw Uzo, his second wife running towards him, the same look of terror in her eyes.

'Go after your son,' he said to her. She shook her head.

'I will stay with you, our husband.'

'Obey your husband, woman. Go after your son and take good care of him till the men finish their work.'

For several seconds, Uzo stood her ground, mutiny on her face. Oba wanted to hold her, hug her, thank her for her loyalty. But he knew he must not show weakness with a woman, even his favourite wife and the mother of his beloved son.

'Do you dare disobey your husband?' he made his voice a thunder, seeing the fear replace the stubbornness in her face. She turned and ran towards the bush that his mother had disappeared into.

Oba made his way towards The Great Shrine Tree to *Gba-afa,* consult the oracles. With his Lifestone gone, he had to find out how to defend his people from the evil he could hear all around him. Already, the air was choked with smoke from both Nnedi's spells and burning huts. The skies lit up with the blaze of torched roofs and farms. Screams of pain filled the air and the infernal thunderous blasts he could not identify. Heavy footsteps thundered towards his *Obi,* accompanied by that booming sound that mimicked thunder. He knew they were coming for him, whoever they were. It could be the devils from Umuoji village, come to avenge their defeat at the border war a few years gone. His Lifestone and Juju had facilitated his people's victory in that war, filling their enemies' vision with terrifying hallucinations, shrouding his people in an impenetrable mist that enabled them to kill in invisibility.

Now, his Lifestone was gone. He was almost powerless, he the greatest witchdoctor in the twelve villages and beyond. His only hope lay in preparing enough herbs and charms to access the spirits of the shrine tree and get their powers to defend his people. But time was against him. The brown hamlet dog ran wild around him, barking furiously. Oba patted his head gently, his action calming the animal. It trotted alongside him, wagging its tail, ignoring the ruckus going on.

Oba knelt before the great tree, staring up at its vast branches. He lifted his arms over his head and began to chant the secret invocations. He called on all the gods of The Great Shrine Tree, each by their true names. He wrung the neck of the nearest strung chicken and allowed its blood and feathers to quench the thirst of the gods. He spread the secret herbs and powders, human bones and elephants' tusks ground into fine white dust. He completed the secret ritual of *Igba-afa* and then he waited in silence, his body still, his mind linked to the spirits of the tree.

He heard it…*finally*. Just when he thought he would never get an answer; when he heard his enemies' footsteps closing fast behind him, he heard the sweet melodious voice from beneath The Great Shrine Tree. The voice was female, pure in its clarity, like the sweet spring that flowed over the smooth pebbles of the village stream. It insinuated itself into his head, filling him with dizziness, awe and joy.

'Omambala River will bring you back, my son,' the words rang inside his head, clear and strong. 'Do not fear; your bones shall rise again. The river will bring you home.'

Then he heard them, his enemies; heard their loud voices filled with hate. He stood up and turned to face them and shock ran through his entire body.

White demons! Two of them, holding long weapons from which they issued the thunder-sounds he'd heard through the night. But they were not alone. They were with several men of his own skin, men whose tribal marks defined as strangers from the Yoruba tribes. The strangers all welded long sharp machetes. Behind them were a trail of villagers all from his clan, young boys and grown men, chained together with the evil metal he had seen in The Soul-Pond. He knew each of them even without looking at their terrified faces. He had seen them in that appalling water-mirror of his ancestors. They shouted out his name, screamed curses at their captors and begged him to save them.

It had begun. The beginning of the end.

'That is him. That is the one we seek, their great medicine-man, Oba.'

Something about the voice jarred Oba's shocked senses. He peered into the crowd and saw him. *Obianuju, his brother-in-law and the witchdoctor of the white demons' deity.* It was he that tried to get the other villagers to worship the white demons' dead god, the one that was nailed to a wooden cross. Oba was married to the man's worthless sister, Ugodiya. His brother-in-law had never hidden his hatred of Oba's powers and had tried to frustrate his marriage to his sister. Thankfully, his late father-in-law had been more enlightened than his deluded son and had blessed Oba's marriage to Ugodiya, a marriage he had since rued from the day the wretched woman entered his *Obi* with her lazy and quarrelsome disposition.

Sudden enlightenment filled Oba's mind – Obinna's strange reactions to his stepmother, his missing Lifestone, Ugodiya's escape with her son even before the attacks – he had been betrayed from his innermost circle. As his people say, a man's greatest enemy is the one that shares his mat with him.

'Obianuju! Viper of the night! I hear your voice!' Oba shouted, anger raging through every vein in his body.

'I hear you too and see your useless face,' Obianuju screamed back. 'Where then is your so-called powers now, eh? My sister is well rid of you tonight. Her son is your first son and will take his rightful place in your *Obi,* long denied him by that whore and her dumb demon-son,' Obianuju's voice was scathing, triumphant. 'Your people are finished. We have your clansmen in chains. You will join them to travel the great River Omambala to the white man's kingdom. Our people will take over your lands, your farms and your huts and bring in the worship of the one true God, Jesus, to this backward village. There is nothing you can do about it. We have your Lifestone. Your powers are finished. You are finished.'

Suddenly, a cry pierced through Obianuju's rant. Oba turned to see his second wife, Uzo, hurtling towards them, fury and hatred veiling her face. She threw herself at him, clasping him as tightly as her son had done. Great tears poured from her eyes.

'Do you know who you're speaking to?' she screamed at the gathering. 'This is Oba, the greatest witchdoctor in the entire world. He will curse you and your descendants with eternal misfortune if you don't go away right….'

A hard blow by Obianuju's machete felled her to the ground. Oba saw the severed head of

272

the wife he had loved the best roll a short distance from the body which was still twitching on the sandy soil of his *Obi*. The sight killed something in his soul and inflamed him as nothing else had ever done. A red mist clouded his vision, bringing a tight lump to his throat. He lifted his machete to kill the traitor.

The white demons shouted out in strange tongues and several hands felled him to his knees, dragging him to the ground. The enslaved villagers wailed in hopeless rage at the manhandling of their greatest son. Oba forced his rage to subside. He was fighting a futile battle. He was outnumbered. Fate was against him, but only for the moment. The event was already marked in his life-calendar and nothing would stop its progress.

But all was not lost. The Great Goddess had spoken. He will return to his *Obi* one day. No matter how long it took, or where the great river Omambala takes them, they would all return to the clan one day. He heard the words ring over and over in his head even as the cold metal chains bound his ankles, his arms and his neck.

'Omambala River will bring you back, my son. Do not fear; your bones shall rise again. The river will bring you home.'

*****

(Part Two)

Obinna steeled himself as he drew closer to the banks of Omambala River for his weekly ablutions. He could hear the deep boisterous voices of the other bathers at the male section of the river bank, their voices filled with easy camaraderie. The squeals and giggles coming from the women's section intermingled with the voices of their children.

The sounds filled him with sudden self-loathing. He was a man, a grown man, a man already pledged in marriage to a woman. His age-grade were successful farmers, fathers and warriors, fully-fledged members of the community. Yet here he was, quaking inside like a boy at his first masquerade initiation ritual at the prospect of bathing in the river like everyone in the village did. He wanted to skirt around the low cliffs and avoid the dreaded chore but he knew better. It was shameful enough that he had reduced his bathing days to just once a week, without compounding things by shirking that activity altogether. After all, what decent Igbo son would shun the daily ablutions at Omambala

River, an activity that was more a social event than a sanitation ritual?

He was aware the villagers regarded him as a weird freak due to his aversion to bathing coupled with his other abnormalities. The men accepted his strangeness with amused contempt while the women found his pleasant features and gangly physique endearing despite his speech impediment and unnatural skills. They constantly fussed over him, bringing him food, weaving mats for him and rooting for him at the regular moonlight wrestling matches in the village square. Each time he mated with a woman, he read their amazed thoughts regarding the cleanliness of his body considering his known aversion to bathing. What no one realised, save his grandmother, Nnedi, was that he cleaned himself rigorously every day inside the dark privacy of his hut. Nnedi was the only person that knew his secret and the terrors that kept him away from the river bank.

He was eight years old, barely twelve moons after the abduction of his father, when he first encountered the river ghouls. Since then, they had tormented his life with relentless zeal. Twice, they attempted to invade his sleep in his childhood; two nights in a row they'd broken into his dreams, sending him fleeing from his mat with silent screams, to the safety of his grandmother's arms. Nnedi had woven several powerful charms which he wore around his neck in sleep. The charms kept them away from his dreams but nothing could keep them away from the river.

Many times, Obinna wished he could speak, give his grandmother the terrifying details of his river encounters rather than just the bare facts he could sign-speak. But he was cursed by the gods, doubly cursed. His grandmother said he was blessed, that his ability to see the pictures in the minds of men and prophesy their timeline on earth was a great gift. He begged to differ. He was sick of seeing the evil in the hearts of men, weary of seeing the terrifying dark misty shadow that hovered over those whose deaths were imminent. Who in their right mind would see that as a blessing, coupled with being without a voice? He would give everything for the chance to hear his voice in speech; just for once, to hear the pitch, the tone, the words he heard only in his mind. One day of speech was all he needed to tell his grandmother everything, every little detail of his river tormentors.

Nnedi said the supernatural attack was sent to him by his step uncle, Obianuju, the evil traitor that had taken over his father's *Obi* after that dreadful raid in the village almost sixteen years gone. Obinna still remembered the events of that terrible night as if they'd happened just a few moons ago. What he didn't recall, Nnedi made sure he knew. He must never forget the terrible acts of betrayal by his stepmother, Ugodiya, in connivance with her brother, Obianuju, the charlatan witchdoctor of the white demons' dead god. *Ugodiya and Obianuju.* The names played ceaselessly in his mind, the twin faces of treachery and evil.

The frightening flight through the thick bushes teaming with snakes and poisonous plants was something Obinna would take to his grave. His grandmother's charms had kept them safe in that deadly bush till daybreak, when they returned to their *Obi* and almost lost their lives in the process. Ugodiya had crowed as she pointed out the freshly dug mound that held the body of his mother. She'd told him two more graves were waiting to receive his and Nnedi's bodies as soon as her brother cut off their heads.

Obianuju, had rushed at his grandmother with his machete, screaming vile curses and dire threats. Without Nnedi's powder charms, which froze him to the spot like a wooden statue, his eyes glazed, lips drooling like the village idiot's, Obinna had no doubt they would have been killed that fateful morning. He had read the evil in his stepmother, smelt the corruption reeking in her soul, seeping through her pores. He'd heard the malice she bore for him and his mother in her thoughts and smelt her hatred for his father and grandmother.

He had tried to warn his father about Ugodiya in the only way he knew how to in those days. To his credit, Oba had taken his warning seriously, enough to question his stepmother vigorously. But Obinna knew he could not have averted the disaster that followed without the power of speech. The gods had doubly cursed him with the second eye and the lost tongue.

They had made their escape that same morning following his father's abduction, to Ojoto, a village not too far from their own. The chief of Ojoto owed Nnedi a debt of gratitude for providing the charmed potion that enabled his last wife to bear two sons after his first three wives only produced daughters. The chief gave them a hut and farmland to cultivate and offered them his protection. He was also happy to access Obinna's skills to his advantage, especially as his gift gradually evolved into full mind-reading without contact or sniffing.

Thanks to his grandmother's charms, their farm was fertile and their yam barns filled to overflow. Obinna had added a second hut, a large hut, one big enough to house his future wife, Nnenna, the chief's daughter. Yet, the burning bitterness he felt towards his stepmother and her brother clawed his heart, day and night. He yearned for the day he would avenge his parents' death and reclaim his citizenship again. As much as he was grateful to the chief, Ojoto was not his village or the ancestral ground of his *Chi*. But what could he alone do? His grandmother was fast aging and her powers were waning. It was as if she lost the desire to live and practice her art with the abduction of his father and their forced exile in Ojoto. *If only he didn't possess a woman's heart. If only he was more like his father, Oba, brave, fearless and wise.*

Obinna's steps slowed, almost to tortoise pace as he began the slow descent to the river bank for his wash. The smell of the river was everywhere, a smell that was a combination of black soap, palm kernel oil, roasting fish, damp sand and the unique rank odour of Omambala River. A handful of fishing rafts littered the banks of the river. He spied some fishermen out in their rafts piling their trade. Several women roasted freshly caught fish in open fires in the neutral zone, offering the treat to the menfolk while the children fought over the fish-heads.

The men saw Obinna as he hesitated at the descent of the male section. Some of them called out to him, inviting him to join in the fun. They were all naked, black wet bodies glistening beneath the intense afternoon sun like polished ebony. The river looked vast, its calm murkiness disturbed only by the ripples caused by the bathing men. The air was humid and still. Obinna sensed a waiting quality in its breeze-less heat. His nostrils twitched as they picked out the smell he had come to dread, the other smell of a different river, a terrifying river full of unspeakable horrors.

They were close. He could sense them in the waters of Omambala River, seeking his scent amongst the many male bodies in the river bank. *Why him? Why couldn't anyone else see them, hear them?* He thought it had something to do with his impediment. They knew his tongue could never tell what his eyes had seen, could never reveal their malignant presence in the village bathing waters. People would only laugh at him if he tried to explain, make more fun of his weirdness. Only Nnedi knew the truth but there was no one else like his grandmother in the village, not even his betrothed, Nnenna, a girl with the beauty of the mermaid and the brains of a sheep.

Obinna fiddled with his coral necklace, his grandmother's protective charms, rubbing the smooth white beads with trembling fingers. He dragged his reluctant feet towards the sandy bank, offering a row of white teeth to the bathing men, hiding his terror behind the brilliance of his smile. The quake in his heart grew stronger as he pulled off his loincloth, stilling the strong urge to cover his nakedness with his hands. It wasn't as if he were less endowed than the other men. Yet, they strutted around with ease, flaunting their organs with the pride of peacocks while he cringed inside like a chicken, embarrassed by his nudity and cowered by their confidence. Perhaps it was a good thing his father did not live to see the pathetic, cowardly, freak he had turned into. He kept the smile plastered on his face as he made his way into the shallow section of the river. He placed both feet into the tepid water and stooped to splash his face.

Everything changed, in an instant, just as he'd known it would. In the space of a breath, Omambala River disappeared, swallowed up by the other bigger, unknown river that was wrapped in a shroud of grey, the colour of a stormy cloud. The tepid warmth of Omambala was replaced by the chilly freezing waters of the strange river. The smell of dead fish was over-powering, coupled with other odours alien to him. The silence was absolute, like a gravesite in the middle of the night. It was as if the world had ceased to exist, as if all life had become extinct. An overwhelming feeling of insignificance fell on him. And despair, a dark mind-cloud, as deep as the vast cold river.

The deadly water grew around him, rising to his waist, pulling him deeper, closer...*to them*. His heart raced and his body felt like a new-born abandoned to the hailstones of a violent thunderstorm. He shivered with cold and terror. The river rose higher, right to his chest, seeking its ultimate goal – his head, his breath, his life. A ripple stirred the surface of the waters and a deep gulf suddenly opened before him.

Obinna saw them, rising from the misty bottomless depths, the walking skeletons, the chained ghouls of the river. They rose in a terrifying mass of white, rattling bones dragging creaking chains, wormy algae crawling from empty dark sockets. Grinning skulls called out to him, their terrible voices reverberating in his head. Bony arms reached out to him, beckoning closer. The black rusty chains dragged behind them, holding them back, like a metal leash on a wild dog. They howled in frustration, fighting the chains, skeletal arms flaying wildly, skulls shaking, struggling to free the evil bands on their necks. Their legs dragged, knees bent, bare ribcages pushed forward, like men climbing a mountain, fighting the impossible. Their visage was awful in their helpless rage, a fury that grew the more they tried and failed to grab him.

Obinna felt the dreaded dizziness engulf him, the fuzziness that weakened his resolve and urged him towards their chained embrace. He shut his eyes and did what he had always done in his previous encounters with them. He went into the secret place in his mind, the blank side of his mind, the dark hole, devoid of all life. It was a void without colour, without words, without pictures and without emotions. He wrapped himself in the black cocoon and waited, quietly, patiently, till his heart stilled, his breathing calmed and his frozen limbs thawed.

The river loosened its hold on him and Obinna stumbled to freedom, collapsing on the wet sandy shore. He opened his eyes. He was once again on the noisy sunny beach of Omambala River, hearing the wonderful voices of the jeering men, their human laughter, their ordinary mortal words – 'There goes the dumb freak again, terrified of getting his body wet,' they mocked. Some sprinkled him with fine white sand while others splashed water on him in jest. Their laughter rang out in merriment.

Obinna laughed with them, his eyes and mouth stretched wide in his silent desperate laugh, the manic laughter of a drowning man who realises the futility of existence at the dying seconds of his life. He laughed with them as they laughed at him, laughed at himself even as his heart cried. Finally, he pulled himself from the sand and donned his loincloth.

It was over, for the time-being. He had survived another battle with the ghastly ghouls of Omambala River. *But for how much longer?* The thought insinuated itself into his tired mind. He knew it was only a matter of time before they got him. There was only so long his luck would hold, only so hard his will could fight. The thought filled him with a terror that threatened to steal his sanity. What was the use in knowing the death-date of everyone else when he couldn't see the time of his own demise, the exact day the ghouls would finally draw him into the cold grey depths of that terrible river of death?

*****

The Python came into his bed three nights later, exactly seven days preceding his marriage to Nnenna. He had been in sleep, dreaming. What he dreamed about he couldn't tell. All he knew as

284

that he was choking in his sleep, dying. A heavy feeling settled on his chest, weighting him down to an eternal sleep-death.

Obinna jerked awake to find the python curled on his chest, pinning him to his mat. His hand encountered the firm smooth skin of the great reptile. He froze, instinctively withdrawing his hand, feeling the sudden shiver run through his body. He held his breath and tried to still every movement in his body. He immediately knew what had occurred. He would be a fool or a stranger to the twelve villages not to realise what was going on. *A Great Spirit had paid him an unexpected visit!* For some unfathomable reason, he had been singled out for the incredible honour of receiving a deity.

Obinna's thoughts ran riot as he tried to come to terms with the phenomenon; for it was indeed a rare and amazing event for a Great Spirit to visit a mortal in the physical form of the revered Python. He stilled his body and went into the other secret place of his mind, the bright side of his mind, the picture place, the place of light and sound. He allowed his thoughts to flow into the Python's.

'Great Spirit! He that moves in realms too mysterious for mortals to fathom! Great Deity, I greet you, I welcome you!' he sent his thoughts to the deity. He could not keep the shakes from his heart and felt its heavy thudding beneath the crushing weight of the great reptile. He felt the Python move, adjust its curled length, increasing its comfort and his discomfort. 'May your visit portend only good for my family. May your presence avert hazards in our huts. May my body that receives your great weight be filled with the spirit of your wisdom, your strength and longevity.'

Obinna kept still after his salutations, labouring beneath the deadly weight of the Python. He had sent his thoughts to the Great Spirit and could only await its next move. He had smelt no evil intent in the deity, which appeared ready to spend eternity on his chest.

The Python slowly lifted its head from its curled weight and looked at him. Their eyes connected and held, the Python and the man, spirit and mortal. Obinna felt the sudden swelling of his head, a chilling of his flesh and a sprinkle of goosebumps on his body. The Python's head was massive, the size of a cooking pot. Its stripped eyes glittered a deadly green and gold and its forked tongue flickered incessantly in the moon-lit dimness of the hut. The sight sent the terrors into Obinna's heart. The Python's gaze was terrifying to hold. Obinna forced himself to keep his lids unclosed. The deity would only speak to open eyes and open hearts. Holding the piercing gaze of the Python was a feat that would freeze the hearts of normal men but Obinna knew his heart would cope with the task, somewhat. He had the curse of the gods. He had smelt no evil in the deity.

Then the Python struck. Its great head grew, expanded, mouth stretched to an endless gulf. It swallowed him whole, sucking him into its length, dragging him through a sticky molasses of hell and into….

…..into a realm of incredible light and splendour, a dazzling kaleidoscope of colours, a wondrous and awesome world of unbearable, impossible beauty. There was water everywhere, warm water, clear water, sparkling water like stars, glowing with light and hues. Obinna was wrapped in warmth, the cocoon warmth of a mother's womb. The lights filled his body, shooting into his pores like lightning, travelling though his veins like fire. He heard a voice, a female voice, sweet, melodious, pure. It called him by name, sang his name like a victory song.

Then everything changed, with the speed of a blink. He was back again in the unhallowed grave of the chained skeletons, the dusky world of chilly water, sea-life and white bones. Except this time, they were no longer skeletons. This time, he could see them for who they were, the men they had been before the water dragged them to its cold depths. He could hear the words in their howls, the sounds that had sent the chills to his bones in his previous encounters with them – 'Bring us home,' they howled, arms out-stretched, black faces desperate. 'Bring us home.'

Obinna began to howl. Great silent sobs wracked his body as he stared into the beloved face of his father, Oba. He recognised other faces amongst the dead; kinsmen from his clan, people he had thought were still alive in the village, people he had hated and resented for years for turning their backs on him and doing nothing to restore him to his father's *Obi.*

And all this while - all this time - they had been dead, lying underground in the cold water grave of his visions in Omambala River, calling to him, begging to be brought home to their huts and clan. He had failed them. He had ignored their pleas. He had not seen their true faces nor known their voices. He, Obinna, who should have known better, who had the so-called special gift. He, who had been loved the best by Oba and should have recognised his father even in death.

Obinna floated over to his father, who struggled with the heavy black chains weighting him down to the sea-bed. He flowed into Oba's outstretched arms, his tears merging with the cold salty water of the sea. His father's tears joined his own. They clung to each other, father and son, held fast amidst the chains and fish. He sniffed his father's skin, seeking the familiar scent of his happy childhood, the smell of strength, courage, goodness and an all-encompassing love that was his father's unique scent. But all he smelt was fish, the unfamiliar smells of the great strange river, nothing from Oba's soul, no pictures from his father's mind or heart. The dead have no soul-scent. Fresh sorrow engulfed him as his tears flowed with renewed force.

'Obinna, his father's heart, my good son…at last!' He heard the familiar voice of his father, the distinct raspy voice he'd thought he would never hear again. 'You finally know us. How long have we waited in this unhallowed grave for this day to arrive! But it is now over. You have come to fulfil the promise made to us by the great spirit of Omambala River, The Great Goddess *Abgomma Orimiri*. Finally, we shall return to our people and our land.' Oba held him close, his tears running unchecked in his fierce face, tears Obinna had never seen and would never have believed possible had he not witnessed it. He stroke the empty space of Oba's right ear, remembrance and nostalgia swelling his senses.

Then he was engulfed in other arms, the joyful, yet, desperate arms of his kinsmen. They clung to him as a man would grip a clay-pot of water in the drought season. Everyone was talking at the same time, each desperate to know about their village, their hamlet, their children, their farms, their parents, their wives. Once again, Obinna felt the burden of his dumbness weigh heavy on his shoulders. He could only shake his head and use his arms and fingers as best he could. There was nothing with which to draw on the sea-bed and his thoughts could not be read by the desperate ghosts.

Somehow he managed to make himself understood – only to an extent. He told them about their old village, snippets of news he'd gathered from strangers over his sixteen years of exile in *Ojoto*; about the stronghold of the white-demon's dead god, enforced on the villagers by their guns and their witchdoctor, Obianuju, his step uncle. He'd heard that the young men cared for nothing, that the farms lay abandoned, that numerous wooden crosses hung outside huts, that confusion pervaded his old fatherland. The ghosts raged at his news, fury and sorrow raising their voices in howls. Their chains rattled loudly and the sound brought back the terror of his encounters to Obinna. He frowned down at the chains, turning puzzled eyes to Oba.

'The white demons and their slaves did this to us,' Oba said. 'Your stepmother and her brother sold us out. They got your brother, Uchenna, to steal my Lifestone. My powers were destroyed and I could not protect our people from the evil that befell us that night. But The Great Spirit of Omambala told me that our bones shall rise again, that she will bring us back to our people.' Oba paused, a faraway look in his eyes. 'The white demons put these chains on us but they forgot who they were dealing with. We are *Igbo* sons. We have never been slaves, not to men, not to the gods and not even to our revered ancestors. We will only serve where our hearts lead us, but will never be bound in servitude. Even with their great chains, we killed the white demons and escaped from their ship when it arrived at their lands. Then we all heard her, the Great Goddess of Omambala River. We all heard her call, telling us to walk into the River, that the great River will bring us home. We did, didn't we, kinsmen?'

All the gathered ghosts nodded, their eyes filled with tears at the remembrance.

'Who can ever forget the voice of The Great Spirit, that pure melodious voice of ancient wisdom?' Oba continued. 'We heard and we obeyed, all of us, every single member of our clan as you can see for yourself. Others, not of our people, opted to stay on the shores of the white demons rather than trust in the powers of our great goddess. But not your father, not your kinsmen,' Obinna saw the old fierce pride flash in his father's eyes, a feeling echoed in the mien of the other ghosts. He felt his heart expand, fill up with pride, humbled to be in the presence of such great men, proud to be of their clan, to call them *Umunna*, kinsmen.

'We have waited for the goddess to bring us home. For uncountable moons, we have waited, seeking, hoping. You have the gift, the sight. My blood flows in your veins. I called to you but you were a child, not old enough to do a man's work. Now, the time has come. The day of our return has arrived. The feast of *Alusi Onwu,* the great deity of death, will take place in a few nights. I have been keeping score. You are too young to know its implications but it is the one night in every generation when the dead can roam the land of the living again, when the deities can bring to life the ones they chose, when the bones of the dead can rise again to life,' Oba paused as the chained ghosts cheered, hope and light sparkling in their eyes, like little children awaiting a moonlight fable.

Obinna felt his eyes prick, tears clouding his vision. His heart swelled up in intense pity for them. His father's raspy voice reclaimed his attention. 'I was the greatest witchdoctor in the twelve villages and beyond. I can bring our kinsmen home again from this unhallowed grave. The Great Spirit of the River has given us the sign. We have seen her light, recognised her unmistakeable colours through the dense mist of this accursed river. But first, you must retrieve my Lifestone from your stepmother. Without my Lifestone, I cannot call on the powers and deities that will aid and hasten our return to our land. My mother will know what to do. Go back. Tell Nnedi you have seen her son. Tell her you have seen her kinsmen. Tell her we are safe. Tell her we are coming home.'

The Python turned its head away and broke eye contact with him. Obinna blinked. He was back on his straw mat, drenched in sweat, alive, breathing. He felt the cold skin of the great Python as it pulled itself away from his chest, crawling towards the open doorway of his hut. As the tail dropped off his stomach, Obinna leapt to his feet, stumbling back against the red mud wall of his hut. The fear came out of him in cold waves. His breathing was ragged, like a woman that had barely escaped the whips of the fearsome masquerade, *Ijele*. He gasped for air through open mouth that cried out in a silent wail.

Emotions coursed through his body – terror, awe, panic, confusion. He mind recollected everything with the vivid clarity of the village spring. And with recollection came a sudden sense of urgency, a resolute determination that filled him with jubilation. *He had been shown the past and the future. He, Obinna, the mute freak, had been chosen to fulfil the wishes of the gods.*

He stumbled across to his grandmother's hut on legs that felt weighted with wet mud, heavy and powerless. Nnedi calmed him with a gourd of palm-wine, not minding the lateness of the hour. She watched his face and read his emotions as he recounted his vision. She read the truth in his eyes and his floor markings. Her eyes lit with joy such as Obinna had never witnessed in all their time together. Her raptured gaze held his as he recounted his encounter with his father and dead kinsmen. The floor of her hut was covered in drawings, pebbles, broomsticks, *Nzu* chalk and everything Obinna could use to tell his story. Several times in the narration, his grandmother slapped her knees with glee, shouting out her son's name with a voice loud enough to awaken the entire hamlet.

'My good son, his father's heart, blessed of the gods!' her voice was loud, ecstatic, cloaked in pride and joy. 'You have been chosen by the Great Spirit, *Agbomma Orimiri,* the water goddess, to do wondrous things for our people. Oba lives! My son lives. I see an end to our troubles at last. Soon, the lion will topple the usurping hyena, the eagle will destroy the envious kite, the shark will reclaim his realm from the catfish and blood will prove the thicker of water. All is well…all is well.'

Obinna burrowed into his grandmother's withered neck, sniffing the goodness in her soul. Nnedi's skin was the only skin he now sniffed in his adulthood since his gift evolved. Her skin reflected back love, warmth, kindness and everything good to his troubled soul.

Suddenly, he recoiled, stunned by an unfamiliar emotion he smelt in her pores – hatred, pure undiluted hatred that almost felled him by its intensity. He pressed his nostrils deeper into her skin, keeping his eyes shut, allowing the picture place in his mind to open up and draw in Nnedi's thoughts. He knew she wouldn't mind if he read her mind, just this once.

Then he smiled, a hard cold smile that was alien to his usual calm pleasantness. His soul recognised Nnedi's hatred, identified with it. He too would gladly pitchfork, burn, butcher and destroy the evil duo of his stepmother, Ugodiya and her brother, Obianuju. As for his half-brother, Uchenna, knowing what he now knew about their father's stolen Lifestone, he felt nothing but pity and contempt for the weak and greedy boy he recalled from their childhood. Only *Amadioha* knew how Uchenna was faring now with no one to guide and mould him except his evil mother and treacherous uncle.

'Go back to sleep my son and prepare yourself for your task,' Nnedi's soothing voice interrupted his thoughts. 'I know I will not catch a bat's wink tonight with the news you have just given me. Great changes are coming our way. Wrongs will be made right soon. Be prepared my good son. Be prepared.'

The following night, Nnedi took him into the bush. He carried her skin-bag of herbs, powders, potions, two live chickens for the sacrifice and other paraphernalia of her trade. As they walked in the deep gloom, she murmured incessantly to herself, her voice strong and light like a young bride's. Together, they entered the thick bush surrounding the village masquerade shrine. Once at the bush, he built a strong fire and sliced the necks of the chickens, allowing their blood to flow into the boiling brew his grandmother had prepared. It took them the best of the night to complete the potion but once it was done, Obinna knew the time had come for his journey to his ancestral home, his father's *Obi*, a place he had not seen since the terrible day his grandmother saved him from the deadly machete of his step-uncle, Obianuju.

His heart beat with both fear and excitement. There was anticipation at the thought of seeing his village and his clansmen again after such a long time, even though he knew they wouldn't see him - couldn't see him - not with Nnedi's magic charm of invisibility. There was also fear at the thought of what he might have to do should his stepmother fail to hand over his father's Lifestone. He had never taken the life of another human being and the idea filled him with dread even as his heart was filled with loathing for the woman.

In the end, the task had proved easier than he had anticipated. The long walk to his father's village had been uneventful. Nnedi's invisibility charm which he wore round his waist and neck worked its magic. He was seen by numerous people but their minds failed to register his presence. The charm's power lay in its ability to cloud people's minds, but not their vision. Obinna read several thoughts as the people crossed his path, thoughts about farms, husbands, children, food, rain, palm-wine, everything but him. In one sad case, he also saw the terrible black mist hovering around a beautiful young woman, her exposed firm breasts covered in colourful artwork. He quickly averted his eyes from the shadow. *Poor doomed girl*! *Amadioha* willing, she would be well-received by her ancestors in the other world and enjoy a better reincarnation that would let her live to a ripe old age.

The first person he saw when he stepped foot in his father's old *Obi* for the first time in sixteen years, was his half-brother, Uchenna. Obinna instantly recognised the overweight, blotched-skinned and drunk man as the light-skinned chubby glutton he'd once played with as a boy. The opaque milkiness of Uchenna's pupils evidenced a life wasted on palm-wine and indolence. Obinna watched his brother stumble towards a broad tree stump that stood at the centre of the *Obi* like a mammoth circular table. A faint memory stirred in his mind, a recollection of something great, gigantic, powerful. *The Great Shrine Tree!*

He stared in stunned horror at the area where the tree had once stood, a towering guardian of the hamlet. The broad stump now serving as Uchenna's stool was the sole remnant of that mighty tree. Sudden tears flooded his eyes. An intense feeling of loss overwhelmed him, a loss that was all-encompassing, choking; the loss of his father, his mother, his happy childhood, his home and village, even his speech. The destruction of the great tree, for some inexplicable reason, symbolised everything he had lost in his life and with it came a burning fury at the people he held responsible – Ugodiya and Obianuju. He knew he would have killed them both without the slightest hesitation had they been in the *Obi* and he would have made sure they knew him, saw him for who he was without the foggy mind created by the invisibility charm.

Obinna allowed the rage to subside, stilling the rush in his heart and the trembling in his limbs. He had more important work to do, a monumental task entrusted to him by the gods and his dead kinsmen. Despite his defects, his unworthiness, he had been chosen to bring home the lost heroes of their clan. He would not let them down now. He would not allow the useless duo of Ugodiya and Obianuju to distract him from the important task of retrieving his father's Lifestone.

Obinna drew closer to his brother, where he lay sprawled on the massive tree stump. For several seconds, he stood before Uchenna, watching his lips move in the incoherent ramblings of the stupidly drunk. Their eyes met but he knew there was no recognition or awareness of his presence in Uchenna's befuddled mind. He went into the picture place of his mind, the place that collected the words, the thoughts and feelings of men. He entered Uchenna's mind. And recoiled.

Tufia! Abomination! Evil beyond belief! His poor father! That his *Obi* should degenerate to this. What Obinna saw in his brother's mind was the incestuous affair between his step-mother, Ugodiya and her own brother, Obianuju. Uchenna's alcohol-fuzzled mind sent out pictures and thoughts in random sequence. Obinna saw the images his brother had seen, pictures of Ugodiya and her brother tangled in unholy passion in the bushes, inside Oba's hut and even on the floor in front of the white demons' dead god, who was staring down at them from his nailed position on the wooden cross. The image confirmed the falseness of that god to Obinna. No witchdoctor worthy of the title, would dare disrespect their god's shrine in such a manner without getting struck down by lightning or *Echieteka* the viper. The fact that Obianuju would defile the shrine of his deity without repercussions only emphasised how vital it was to bring back Oba without delay. The true gods of his people would once more be served and honoured as in the past, before Obianuju brought in the false god of the white demons to their village.

More images flooded his mind from his brother's thoughts. He saw Uchenna holding something in his palm, staring at the object with intense concentration. He read confusion, regret and nostalgia in Uchenna's thoughts, coupled with self-pity, anger and fear. The object his brother held was his father's Lifestone. He remembered the triangular smoothness of that stone from his childhood. Even without its blood coating, Obinna felt the power emanating from the Lifestone held in his brother's hand.

He picked another image from the confused plethora of pictures in Uchenna's mind. He saw Uchenna replacing the stone inside Ugodiya's hut, underneath her grinding stone. Uchenna's hatred of his mother and fear of his uncle coloured the other mundane images he picked up. Obinna felt sudden pity for the overweight, pathetic drunk he beheld, coupled with anger at his weakness. Uchenna was the *Okpala*, the first son of a great man, the one that should defend their father's honour and expose the abomination going on between his mother and his uncle. He felt the rage begin to build again in his heart for his loathsome step-mother and step-uncle. Again, he pushed it back, deep inside his stomach. The day would come when he would let it rise, give it free rein to do its violent pleasure on those evil duo.

Obinna entered Ugodiya's hut, which was as cluttered and dirty as the woman that owned it, a shameless woman who left her grinding stone unwashed. Slowly, carefully, he withdrew the Lifestone from underneath the heavy granite. For several seconds, he fought the wild racing of his heart as he felt the cold hardness of the Lifestone in his palm. He stared at its unique triangular shape, overwhelmed by a feeling of reverence and awe. *Oba's Lifestone!*

His heart throbbed with joy as he left the family's old *Obi* with the prized Lifestone tucked away inside his loincloth; but not before he'd knocked down the large wooden cross adorning the entrance of his father's old hut, now occupied by his detested step-uncle, Obianuju. Obinna broke the cross into several pieces, the act giving him a feeling that was sharp and sweet, like a man discovering that the beauty who spurned his love remained an unhappy spinster. He would have liked it better if the cross had been Obianuju's bones.

Back at his adopted village, his grandmother welcomed him with tears and smiles. He read the relief in her eyes and realised she must have doubted the efficacy of her own charms. Age and sorrow had drained the bulk of her powers but not all. Obinna was thankful he hadn't read her fears before his journey to his father's village. Her fears would have stoked his cowardice. His grandmother's mind was the one sanctuary he rarely invaded. He didn't need to. They kept nothing from each other. *Till now*. He could not bring himself to tell Nnedi the evil he had read in his half-brother's mind, the defilement of his father's honour and the destruction of The Great Shrine Tree. The truth would destroy the old woman and he needed her to live and witness the triumphant return of her only son. He now held the Lifestone, the secret to Oba's soul. All it needed was its proper home to flourish, a new *Obi-Dimkpa,* the Forever Heart of a man. And fresh blood; blood strong enough to resurrect its dormant powers, blood that shared the same bloodline with Oba - human blood, his blood.

The following night, he accompanied Nnedi to *Ajo-ofia*, the bad bush, to collect the heart of a recent corpse, a young woman who they said took her own life after being forcefully mounted by a man on her way back from the market. Nnedi said it was not the ideal home for the Lifestone, which worked best with a man's heart. Nonetheless, it was a human heart, a fresh human heart. Obinna sensed her fears about the new heart, her worries that the accursed death of the owner might affect the powers of the Lifestone. But time was against them and they had to make do with what was available.

It was easy to locate the newest grave amongst the numerous mounds of the accursed dead at *Ajo-ofia*. The disturbed earth marked the spot and the soil was soft beneath Obinna's hoe. In no time, he struck the soft flesh of the corpse, buried only in a raffia-mat coffin.

Obinna's heart leapt into his mouth when the light from their wick lamp revealed the colourful patterns on the young woman's breasts, breasts still firm in death as they had been when their paths briefly crossed on his way to his father's village the day before. His hands trembled violently and he could not get himself to cut into the flesh and extract her heart.

Nnedi did the job with cold and ruthless efficiency, wrapping the bloody heart inside the special herbs she'd prepared for it. It was left to Obinna to re-bury the young woman. He dug deep into the shallow grave, mutely asking her forgiveness as he covered her desecrated corpse with the soft, warm soil of the unhallowed grounds. It was the first time he had witnessed the darker side of his grandmother's art. He prayed it would be the last. He had no right to call his brother a coward when he'd left an old woman to execute a chore he was too terrified to do.

They made their slow way back to Nnedi's hut. Once inside, his grandmother wasted no time in performing the secret rituals to awaken the Lifestone. Her blade was sharp on Obinna's flesh, cutting deep and sure. He stifled his grunt of pain, feeling the warm spurt of blood leave his veins for the Lifestone, now safely embedded in the dead woman's heart. A hissing sound emanated from the stone as it soaked up his blood like dry soil to rainfall.

The heart jerked. Then stopped. Nnedi chanted and waited. Several seconds passed but the heart remained dead. Nnedi squeezed more blood from Obinna's throbbing veins. The stone sizzled louder. Again, the heart leaped, stronger, longer. Soon, it settled into the steady beat of a functional *Obi-Dimkpa*, pulsating with life, fully animated by the powers of the awakened Lifestone.

Nnedi hooted with joy, her voice deafening in the small gloomy hut. Obinna's smile mirrored her joy. Their mission was complete. All that remained was for him to return the Lifestone to its rightful owner, Oba, in his unhallowed watery grave.

Obinna felt the sudden rapid beating of his heart, a mixture of exhilaration and terror. This journey would not be like the last. It would not be a python-induced vision. This time, he would enter the murky waters of Omambala River bearing the Lifestone. This time, he would not escape into the secret place in his mind when they came for him; the blank place, the safe place. This time, he would let them get him.

The next morning, he awoke fresh and prepared for his traditional marriage to his betrothed, Nnenna, the chief's daughter. He welcomed the visiting kinsmen from his late mother's clan who had come to represent his blood family at the occasion. Had his father and clansmen lived, they would have been the ones to proudly accompany him into the chief's presence and negotiate a favourable bride price for him.

Nnedi turned up in her most colourful body paint and beads, her face wreathed in unfamiliar smiles. Obinna dressed in his best loincloth, oiling his skin liberally with the fresh palm-kernel oil supplied by Nnedi, till it glowed like a polished Benin bronze mask. He performed all the marriage rites with his usual calm and pleasant demeanour. He accepted the gourd of palm-wine from his new bride and drank it down in one long gulp and when it was time to dance, he performed the act with gusto, acknowledging the cheers with shinning eyes and waving hands. He broke Kola-nuts with the elders at the appropriate time and presented gifts to the female relatives of his bride as was the norm. Finally, the bride price was successfully negotiated and refreshments were served in abundance.

Later that night, Obinna proved his manhood to his new bride multiple times, taking pride in her passionate response, knowing that the art of pleasuring women was the one area of his life in which he excelled. His dumbness ceased to matter and his normal diffidence vanished when a woman was under his naked body.

As the rooster crowed in the dawn, Obinna left his tired bride still asleep on their mat and made the short walk to his grandmother's hut. Nnedi was already up, her face still covered in the happy smile she'd worn the previous day at his wedding.

'My good son!' she held him close, pressing his head into her still impressive bosom. 'His father's heart! Blessed of the gods! May the sun never set in your house.'

Obinna inhaled deeply, allowing the love and goodness to flow into him, sooth him, calm and prepare him for the daunting task that awaited him at the end of the day. Already he could hear the wild drumming of the village masquerade groups heralding the feast of *Alusi Onwu,* the night the dead arose to roam the lands of the living, the night his dead kinsmen would rise to life from their watery grave.

'Come, my good son,' Nnedi led him to a corner of her hut where the wick lamp cast its dull light on the mud walls. She pulled up a short stool and motioned him to the floor. He assumed his usual cross-legged position on the polished hard mud flooring and waited. He watched with a wry smile as Nnedi piled the brown tobacco powder into her nostrils, inhaling deeply before releasing a loud sneeze accompanied by a louder fart. He waved his hands under his nose with exaggerated motions, his eyes lit up in a mischievous smile.

'Silly boy!' Nnedi laughed. 'At least this is better than the foulness you smell in people's thoughts, eh?' she coated her gums with the brown snuff to numb her toothache before replacing the remnant under her stool. 'So, you did well by your bride, eh?' her eyes twinkled. Obinna nodded, looking away, cloaking his embarrassment with a desperate smile. Sometimes, he wished his grandmother was less blunt, more like the other old women in the village. 'Good. She should give us strong sons soon. But now, your real work begins. The night of *Alusi Onwu* draws close. Soon you will head out to Omambala River.'

Nnedi paused, a faraway look in her one good eye. Several seconds of silence passed. Obinna waited patiently. One never knew when the old were communicating with the spirits, seeing as they were close to becoming spirits themselves. In Nnedi's case, she could well be in communication with the deities. He saw awareness return to her pupil, a sort of confused consciousness, soon replaced by resolute clarity. She took his hand in her own, her grip as hard as a man's.

'Always remember that the gods are with you. The Great Goddess, *Agbomma Orimiri*, has sent you on this important errand. You go into her kingdom, Omambala River, with her blessing. Fear not. Let your heart be strong. Your father awaits you. Your kinsmen depend on you to bring them home. Remember, you will not be alone, my good son. We will go together to the river tonight and we will come back together, all of us. We will all come back together,' the old woman's voice trembled with strong emotions, tears filling her eyes, dimming the burning light in her one good eye. Obinna swallowed the tight lump lodged in his neck, holding tight to her hands. He stroked the withered skin, offering comfort, yet seeking her strength. Nnedi's love and strength would guide him through the terrible ordeal that awaited him at the river of death.

The village drums were still beating when Obinna left for Omambala River at the full moon, accompanied by his grandmother. All day, the festival of *Alusi Onwu* had brought in celebrations to the twelve villages and beyond. Village squares heaved with people dressed in their best paints, feathers, raffias, loincloths and beads. Open fires blazed over massive pots brimming with delicacies from goat-head casserole to fish pepper-soup. Happy voices were raised in songs and chants, women and children's voices, and even the occasional man. And in the open squares, beneath the blazing sun, the masquerade drums brought the dance to even the laziest feet.

In each hamlet, the women worked with frenzied vigour, cleaning, scrubbing and decorating the various *Obi* and huts. The men tended the graves of the ancestors with special care, pouring endless gourdes of palm-wine into open funnels at the graves sites. They were only too aware that after the daytime festivities, the night of *Alusi Onwu* would descend upon them, the night when the spirits of their loved ones could either be resurrected for good or for a poignant brief visit with their living relatives. Nobody wanted to be caught unawares in an unclean hut and empty pots by their returned dead.

Obinna celebrated the Feast of *Alusi Onwu* with his new bride in silent panic. Nonetheless, he stole several passionate encounters with Nnenna in-between the cooking and cleaning. He endured the good-natured teasing of the hamlet women with his habitual shy smile, cloaking the dread inside. His heart beat with the silent terror that had accompanied him like a dark shroud since the night the Python deity paid him its terrifying visit. He watched the setting sun with apprehensive eyes, aware that in a few hours, he would make his rendezvous with the river ghouls and return his father's Lifestone to him. He was uncertain of his own fate. The Great Goddess had not shown

311

him that part of his destiny. And he, who could see the life-calendar of other people, could not see his own black mist of death. All he could do in the meantime was to fill his new bride with as many seeds of reincarnation as he could, in the hope of fertilising her womb with his replacement should he fall at that unhallowed watery grave of his kinsmen. Nnedi must have something to hold onto should his mission fail.

*****

They were waiting for him just as he knew they would. They rose from the deep misty gulf in their chained skeletal mass, reaching out to him, bony arms outstretched. Empty sockets dripping dead seaweed, bore into his terrified eyes. Obinna felt the familiar terror rise in waves of cold shivers, numbing his limbs. He tried to see through the white howling bones, to recognise his father's features amongst the skinless ghouls. But all he saw was horror; all he felt was terror. The fear froze his breath and raced his heart. It urged him to flee, to escape into the secret place in his mind, the safe place, the blank place. The impulse to shut his eyes was overpowering, the desperate need to shut out the chained nightmare struggling against their heavy rusty chains.

He resisted. Yet, he turned away from them, briefly, seeking his grandmother's comforting presence at the sandy beach of Omambala River. Nnedi was nowhere to be found and the landscape was again an alien one. All he saw was a vast body of water the colour of a stormy sky. There was no escape. Already, he felt the sudden chilling temperature of the strange river, a cold that seeped through his pores, freezing his limbs to numb lifelessness. The foul alien smell was everywhere, the smell of dead fish and rotten corpses, the smell of decay and despair. Their howls grew louder, their movements frenzied.

Obinna wanted to shout, to speak to them. 'I have your Lifestone, father,' the words shrieked inside his head, seeking audible release. He cursed yet again the evil of his dead tongue. The water started to rise. This time, its progress was rapid, like a lion ripping into its prey before it could escape. In seconds, it had risen higher than it had ever done in his previous encounters, covering his chest and neck. He was running out of time. Soon, he would cease to breathe and drown.

It was then that he heard the voice, a sweet melodious voice that surrounded him, seeming to call from the river, the air, the deepest part of his mind. *'Give him the Lifestone,'* the voice said, the words like a song, lulling him like a snake's hypnotic sway. *'Give him the Lifestone.'*

Obinna obeyed. He stretched out his hand to the skeletons, the hand clutching the Lifestone. He prayed they would accept the gift and let him go. He was a shameless coward regardless of his best intentions. He knew that they were his kinsmen; that beneath the terrifying white bones lay his father, Oba. Yet, his coward's heart only sought escape. Even with The Great Goddess's help, all he wanted was out. He didn't care. He had a lifetime to loathe himself if he managed to get out of the river alive.

A sudden silence descended. The ghouls stilled their voices and halted their straining against the chains. They stared at the Lifestone in Obinna's palm, a hushed expectancy in the air. They were motionless, silent, waiting. All except one; the biggest skeleton in the centre of the bony mass. *Oba!* It pushed its way through the tight mass, rattling bones and chains. The rusty heavy chains hauled it back, causing a loud howl of frustration to bust from its gaping jaw.

Obinna lunged forward. He forgot his fear and reached out to his father. In that second, the water went over his head and he began to choke. The river filled his nose and his open mouth,

314

hurting his throat and heart. His legs kicked and his hands flayed, his actions desperate, panic-fuelled. He saw the Lifestone leave his hand and float down the grey depths of the river. A bony claw caught it before it hit the river-bed. A manic howl erupted amongst the chained ghouls. It sounded like cheering to Obinna but he couldn't be sure. The roaring in his ears was deafening and everything had ceased to matter. A sudden calm settled over him and he stopped his struggles against the river. The desperate need to escape vanished, leaving in its wake a strange peace, like a man that drinks soured palm-wine yet enjoys the best sleep of his life.

Obinna floated closer to the ghouls, till he settled right in their midst. They surrounded him, their bones digging into his flesh, leaving no pain. *They were so beautiful, so awesome in their terrible deadness.* He reached out to them and felt his shoulders gripped by strong claws. He turned to see the large skeleton, the one that now held the Lifestone, staring down at him. It stretched forth its right arm and Obinna felt a searing pain in his chest, a deep piercing. It felt like a burn but also like a knife. He looked down and saw the Lifestone embedded in his heart, moving, burrowing deep like a beetle. It glowed like burning charcoal, pulsating against his exposed flesh.

The Skeleton gripping him began to glow, just like the Lifestone, a brilliant bony statue in the twilight watery grave. Obinna knew who it was…who he was. The knowledge gave him no feeling, no joy nor sadness. He was in a place beyond emotions. A growing darkness was crowding his mind, solid, impenetrable. He allowed it to build, to broaden. It was a good darkness.

'Don't be afraid, my son,' the darkness said, right inside his head. 'We're going home soon.'

Obinna nodded; at least, he thought he did. He couldn't be sure. He just wanted to sleep and never wake up. The darkness was good, safe, all strength and all love. He yielded to its warmth and gave in to the sleep.

*****

Oba opened his eyes. To life. The first thing he saw was the sky, the brilliant star-speckled moonlit skies of the human realm. An indescribable bliss flooded his body. *He was home! Home! The Great Goddess had kept her word!* He touched his thighs, his stomach. His

316

hand connected with his manhood. It throbbed, warm and firm. A human body, padded with flesh and hair, instead of the skeletal bones he was accustomed to. *He did it! By the Great Goddess and all the deities, he'd achieved the near-impossible. He had returned in the body of his son, the living body of his son, Obinna.*

Oba felt a stirring inside, a sluggish awakening, like an elephant turning over in deep sleep. Obinna's low moan was loud in his head. *It's alright my son, his father's true heart. Sleep still. I am with you. Soon it will all be over. Just a little while longer.* Oba's voice was soundless, its message a tender comfort to his son's distressed spirit. Obinna sighed softly. Soon, a gradual calm descended within. The boy slept. Once again, Oba was alone inside the body of his son.

Then he saw her, his mother, staring down at him, her eyes filled with unfamiliar tears, her face older, dearer.

'Great Mother!' his voice sounded rusty, like the sound of the vile chains that had held him down in that cold alien river-bed. 'May these eyes that behold you never go blind,' his tears joined her own, pouring freely, unchecked, without shame.

Through the mist of his tears, he saw the awe in her good eye, the wonder and joy.

'My son! Oba! Great Witchdoctor! Brave heart! You speak! You speak! You have returned! You have come back to me! May The Great Goddess be praised!' Nnedi's voice broke, trembled into choking sobs. Oba felt her shudders through the arms that still cradled him on the sandy beach of Omambala River. He inhaled deeply, slowly, savouring the unique scents of Omambala. *He would know that wonderful river anywhere.*

He felt the cool breeze raise the dust, tickling his nostrils. The sneeze built up, strong, irresistible, culminating in a mighty shout. Oba gave a loud laugh. It felt so good, so incredibly good to once again enjoy that simple human act.

Nnedi stroked his face, the wonder still in her eyes.

'Great Mother, take me back to my *Obi*. There is little time and so much to do before this night is over,' he raised himself from the ground, stooping to help his mother to her feet. It hurt his heart to see her so weakened, so old. He had been gone for too long.

'The boy…where is Obinna?' Nnedi's voice was taut, hushed, like a new mother in dread of awakening her troublesome baby.

'Do not worry. Obinna is fine. He lives; he sleeps. Soon, he will awaken. We shall all

318

awaken. Our bones shall rise again, soon. Very soon,' he stared into the brown murky waters of Omambala River, a cold, hard smile on his face. His hand raised in an unconscious motion to his right ear, rubbing the missing lobe in an abstract manner. Surprise flooded his face when he connected with an ear. He gave a sheepish grin as he caught Nnedi's stunned gaze.

'Now I truly believe,' she said, her hand mimicking his earlier gesture, rubbing her own missing lobe. 'My son, you are truly back. Even your voice…your laughter. The Great Goddess has brought you back. You have conquered death. The sun shall never set in your house again. *Nnoọ*…welcome home, my son,' again, she held him close, dampening his chest with her warm tears. He hugged her back, tight and long, unable to get enough of her, of life, human warmth and love. His feet dug deep into the sand, real sand, *home sand*. His eyes took in the thick foliage, the green vegetation, the wild African plants, the familiar sights of home. And again, his heart sang a joyous tune that had the same refrain. *Home! Home!*

Together, they made the short walk back to Nnedi's hut. They were not alone as they travelled the night. The dusty route heaved with people, the living and the dead. Oba recognised some fleshless ones amongst the mass they encountered. Their movements were hurried, like people desperate to catch the market before it closed. Like him, they only had till dawn to roam amongst the living, commune with their relatives, get their vengeance or leave a message. That one night of *Alusi Onwu,* the deity of death, was all they had and Oba intended to make the best use of it. He would return to The Great Shrine Tree, consult with the oracle and deities, make the appropriate sacrifices and brew the charms that would bring home the spirits of his chained kinsmen for good. He was the only one with the powers to raise their bones from that accursed watery grave. With the young, strong body of his son, he would achieve the impossible before the rooster crowed in the dawn. *Obinna!* His second and true son. The two of them working together. *Two!* His fate number, for good or evil. This time, he knew it would be for good.

The first person Oba met on entering the hamlet was Nnenna. She flung herself at him, her eyes wide with fear.

'*Dim,* my husband Obinna, where have you been? I've searched all evening for you. Have you forgotten what night this is?' her voice was hushed, almost a whisper. The dead were abroad and the living must keep their voices low, especially the womenfolk.

'I am well. Calm yourself woman,' Oba saw her eyes widen. A second later, her mouth let out a terrified scream. He had forgotten to hide his voice. Obinna was a born mute.

Nnenna's screams awoke the hamlet. In seconds, they were surrounded. People stared in stunned disbelief at Obinna, the mute boy-man who now spoke in a deep raspy voice of a fully-fledged man, a man of power, of authority. The miracles of *Alusi Onwu* night would never cease to astound. He was the living manifestation of the awesome powers of the great deity of death. Even his bearing, his walk, his posture, were those of a man of stature. That was the night the legend of *Alusi Onwu* was reborn in the twelve villages and beyond, the night that faith in the deities was re-affirmed. *Who, but a mad man, can doubt the evidence of their own eyes and ears?*

Oba was hugged by many, his arms clasped by the men, cheered and feted by the womenfolk, including Nnenna, whose initial fear had now turned to pride and joy. He was led into his hut by the eager bride, even as he tried to break free and complete his mission with haste. Again, he felt the sleeping one stir within, reluctantly, lacklustre. Oba urged Obinna to consciousness, unwilling to lie with the young bride. But Nnenna was eager, insistent, and the boy would not wake up. So, Oba coupled with her while his son slept, savoured once more the musky scent of a woman.

In the aftermath of release, he wept for his dead wife, Uzo, she of the faithful heart, struck down so brutally by the hands of treachery. The thought resurrected his hate. Two people, two treacherous vermin, needed to be removed from *Amadioha's* earth before the cock crowed in the dawn. He would not start his consultations with the oracle till he had dispatched Obianuju and Ugodiya to their ancestors' hell. He had sworn vengeance to Uzo's headless corpse on that fateful night of bloody treachery and by the great deity, *Alusi Onwu,* he would give her that vengeance tonight.

He left Nnenna without a word. She was so tired by his insatiable possession that he doubted she would notice his absence. Not that it mattered one way or the other to him. He found Nnedi waiting for him outside her hut, her face, cloaked in anxiety. The hamlet had retired and the wide courtyard was still.

'Great Mother, it is time I left for my *Obi*,' he held her hands, feeling their trembling, their sweatiness. 'There is much to be done before the night awakens to dawn. The journey will be too much for you. Await my return…our return. Soon, everything will be alright.'

Nnedi hugged him close, holding him as if she would never let go.

'Great witchdoctor! My son! Go well. The great goddess is with you. Go and fulfil your destiny,' she paused briefly. 'Promise me one thing,' she said, her voice fierce, hard. 'Promise me you will dispatch those two worms to their unsanctified graves tonight. Obianuju and Ugodiya. Feed them the soil of the grave. Bring back our honour to us.'

'*Eze-Nwanyi!* King-woman! Do you need to ask an old man to fart? Go; rest now. Tonight, justice will be done.'

The stars still covered the skies when he finally entered the familiar, yet, strange grounds of his old *Obi*. Oba stood at the entrance of his hamlet inhaling deeply. He was overwhelmed by joy so intense that hot tears flooded his eyes. For a brief second, he awaited the excited barks of his brown mongrel, the familiar rattling of the skulls hanging on The Great Shrine Tree.

Then Oba noticed the barren space where his shrine tree once stood. For several minutes, he stared in stunned disbelief at the broad stump of the felled tree. Sudden rage, like boiling lava filled his heart, coursing through his blood. His grip on his Lifestone tightened as he fought for control. *A rash head never achieved a victory in battle*. They had felled The Great Shrine Tree, desecrated the graves of his ancestors, defiled the abode of his *Chi* and destroyed his honour. Obianuju and Ugodiya, his two nemesis, the unlucky two of his fate number. Tonight, he would feed them the worms of the grave.

His feet took him to his old hut. His eyes widened at the sight of a massive cross hung over the entrance, the cross of the white-demons' dead god. *The white demons!* The memory of his time on their slave ship flooded his mind, filling him with bitter bile. The chains, the floggings, humiliations, starvation, abuse; grown men and women crowded at the belly of the ship like dead fish at the bottom of a fisherman's boat. *Him, Oba, the greatest witchdoctor in the twelve villages and beyond, reduced to no more than an animal by the white demons. But he'd had his revenge! By Amadioha and all the deities, he'd had his vengeance on them.*

In the end, even the captives from the unknown villages had listened to his words, his promises of victory, freedom. They listened and they believed. Rising against the white demons had been easy when the time came. In their belief in their guns, they had not expected the fight left in the spirits of the battered men and women aboard their death-ship, the final fight of the desperate, of people who had nothing more to lose. He himself had personally dispatched two of the white demons to their ancestors. Others had jumped ship, drowning in the same river they had tossed the dead captives into like rotten fish.

With a loud oath, Oba reached up and pulled down the cross hanging on the entrance of his *Obi* and smashed it to pieces. The sound awakened the occupants of the hut, just as he'd hoped. The brown raffia mat over the entrance of his hut was pushed aside and a man emerged, an old man. Oba stared hard at the features of the man. He wasn't as young as the last time they'd met but he would recognise those piggy eyes anywhere, the lax lower lips and overall smarminess of features. *Obianuju!*

For a second, Oba was transported to a different time, a different scene. He saw the sharp machete, the gloating features, Uzo's severed head, her twitching body still clasping his knees, soaking his legs and the ground with her life's blood, which gushed like a red river from her severed neck. The red mist descended.

'Young man, who the hell are you and what are you doing in my *Obi* at this unholy hour of the night?' Obianuju glared at him, arms akimbo. Then he saw the desecration of his cross, the wooden pieces of the relic lying on the ground. His features clouded in fury, an ugly look in his eyes. 'So! It was you that broke the cross the last time, eh? You dare destroy our Lord's cross, you wretched pagan?'

Oba had heard enough. With a loud curse, he grasped Obianuju by both arms, pulling him close till their faces almost touched.

'Viper of the night! I find you again,' his voice was low, hard. 'Take a good look at me. Take a long look and start praying to every deity you know. I have returned to reclaim my *Obi* and my honour,' he saw the terror fill Obianuju's eyes, coupled with disbelief. 'Yes, it is me, Oba, the greatest witchdoctor in the twelve villages and beyond.'

'Jesus! No… it's… it's not possible,' Obianuju stuttered, his voice hoarse. He strained to break free from Oba's painful grip. 'It can't be true…no one returns from the white man's land. This is not you…a young man. This is just a trick, a sick joke to frighten an old man. Shame on you, young man, shame,' Obianuju's voice grew stronger, braver.

326

'Foolish man!' Oba gave a harsh laugh. 'Stupid man. Do you not recognise my voice, even in this body? Have you forgotten who you're dealing with? Did you think that anyone or anything could hold me down, even death? Did you truly believe that you, your worthless sister or your dead god were strong enough to destroy me?' Oba thrust his blood-coated Lifestone into Obianuju's petrified face. The man recoiled, his eyes wide with terror. 'Fool man! Do you know what tonight is or have you completely forgotten the customs of your own people?' Oba did not hide the sneer in his voice. 'Let me remind you then. It is the night of *Alusi Onwu*…yes, the night the dead return to the living and the living return to the grave-worms. I am back and you are leaving. Goodbye vile viper!'

Oba plunged his knife into the stomach of his arch enemy. Over and over again, his hand stabbed, slashed, shoved, until Obianuju's blood flowed as freely as Uzo's blood had once done, till his screams choked into blood-filled gurgles, till finally, he became silent. Oba stood, staring down at the dead man, a cold smile on his face. His breath came in short bursts and the sweat poured down his face. He raised his hand to wipe it off, leaving a bloodied trail on his cheek.

He saw a woman stumble from his hut, perhaps, Obianuju's wife. There was something familiar about her, something in the discontented lines on her face. *Ugodiya! What was she doing in her brother's hut at that time off the night?* She stared at him, a blank look on her face. Then she saw the prone and bloodied body of her brother on the ground. Her scream pierced the night as she fell to her knees, cradling Obianuju's head, her words, her touch, those of a lover, not a sister.

In a flash, Oba understood. It was as if the sun had flooded a dark hut with light. All those years back; something had always seemed wrong between those two. Obianuju's hatred and resistance to his marriage to Ugodiya had been beyond reason. Yet, he had been too blind to see the evil, the abomination that was right under his nose.

With another shout, Oba pulled up the keening woman, his grip strong on her arms.

'Vile and disgusting apology to womanhood! I finally see you for what you are. Take a good look at me. Listen to my voice. Your brother…your lover…,' he spat on the floor, his face screwed up in disgust. 'Obianuju knew who I was before I killed him,' he pushed his Lifestone into her face, just as he'd done with Obianuju. He saw the same recognition and terror fill her eyes.

328

'I am back. I inhabit the body of my son, Obinna, the same boy you called a dumb freak. As you can see, I speak through his lips. I speak for both of us and my mother when I tell you to go join your worthless brother and his useless dead god.'

This time, he only needed one stab, straight into her withered chest, to accomplish his goal. She slumped to the ground next to her brother, her staring eyes still harbouring the horror of her dying seconds. He stared down at the two bloody corpses. A deep peace descended on him, a feeling of completion. It weakened his limbs, clouding his vision. All of a sudden, he felt dizzy, tired. All he wanted to do was to sleep, just like the sleeping one within; sleep for eternity and never wake up.

Suddenly, he heard footsteps behind him, followed by shouts and screams. He turned round to see a crowd of people descending on him. He saw their intention in their eyes, heard it in their angry voices. He raised his Lifestone to weave its magic. But his arms were weak, as if weighted with heavy rocks.

'I am Oba! I have returned! Listen to me. I am your witchdoctor, taken by the white demons a long time ago. But I am back…I have…' A heavy blow knocked him to the ground. A foot kicked him in the stomach. He groaned, doubled up in pain. He looked up and saw a face amongst the crowd. It was the only light-skinned face in the sea of dark, furious faces.

'Uchenna! Don't you know your father? Don't you recognise your father's voice?' Oba's voice pierced through the shouts. The kicking stopped and the punches stalled. All eyes turned to Uchenna. There was uncertainty on their faces. 'Uchenna…it is me, Oba, your father. Help me.'

He saw a startled look in Uchenna's face. Recognition flared in his eyes, a displaced awareness. His face turned ugly.

'Obinna… I know you, you useless mute. So now you speak, eh? And you think you will come and take over my birth-right?' Uchenna turned to the mob. 'This is my half-brother. He has always hated me for being the *Okpara,* the first son. Now, he has killed my mother and my uncle. You can see his dastardly handiwork for yourselves. Kill him! Kill the bastard!' Uchenna's voice was pitched like a woman's, hatred contorting his features, spittle flying from his fleshy lips, lips Oba suddenly realised were identical to Obianuju's own.

The sorrow in his heart almost drowned out his will to live. He saw Uchenna's fists join the other fists raining down on his head, the podgy soft hands he had raised as his own, the son

330

he now knew was never his. He tasted the warm saltiness of his blood, coated with snot. Another hard fist struck the back of his head. Then another…and another. His Lifestone fell from his hand, rolling a few feet away. He made a frantic lunge for it, pushing through the angry crowd with a sudden surge of adrenalin. He stooped to grab it and a foot connected with his head. He reeled, a wave of dizziness washing over him.

The sleeping one awoke with a terrible shriek. Oba felt his son's panic and tried to sooth him. But Obinna resisted, seeking repossession of his body, his ebbing life. Oba tried to focus, to fight the weakness and harness his old skills. He called on the powers of his Lifestone to cloud the vision of his attackers, fill their minds with madness. But several more feet joined the punching fists and his body was beginning to throb with a pain that eclipsed a lion's maul. Obinna's screams were relentless and his powers gone. *It had been too long…so long. The body he had was not fully ready to harbour his spirit and for some reason, his Lifestone was no longer as strong as it used to be. But he didn't come back to die like this. The goddess didn't bring him back from the accursed river to die a chicken's death. He had a mission to fulfil. His kinsmen depended on him to bring them home.*

Oba started to crawl towards the stump of The Great Shrine Tree. The vicious feet rained on him, joined by stones and sticks. He felt the warm red liquid pour from his nose, his mouth, soaking the dry ground of what had once been his *Obi*. Still he crawled, inch by tortured inch, edging closer. Their voices filled his head, righteous voices, the vengeful voices of Obianuju's faithful acolytes, worshippers of the dead god on the wooden cross, together with his false son. Their shouts fought for space with Obinna's terrified screams inside his head.

He dragged his battered body forward, nearer, closer to the tree. The dust clouded his vision and choked his nostrils, the dust and his gushing blood. Through his haze he saw The Great Shrine Tree beckon. Like a waiting bride, it called out to him. No longer a sad stump, it towered, tall and majestic as he remembered, shimmering with white skulls and feathers, its crawling roots bloated on blood and flesh. He stretched his hand to it, pushed his Lifestone into the soil underneath its roots with trembling fingers. *They were there, the deities, his ancestors, The Great Goddess. They were all there. They would not desert him now.*

He pushed the pain away, forced the angry voices into a black hole. And listened. He slumped on the roots of the tree, placed his head on their hard bulk and waited. The darkness came in waves, dragging him in and out of hot showers of pain. His son's tortured cries had died down, leaving a silent dead place in his head. Deep sadness filled his heart.

'I'm sorry my son...so sorry. This isn't the end I'd planned for you. But fear not. I am with you. We are together....as we will be for eternity. This is not the end. Just the beginning. Obinna ... his father's true heart...my true son.'

And just as he knew it would be, as he'd hoped would happen, he heard it. From the depths of The Great Shrine Tree, it called out to him; the sweet melodious voice of eternal hope.

*****

Epilogue

In the twelve villages and beyond, the villagers continue to celebrate the feast of *Alusi Onwu* to the present day. And every time that epic event occurs, they recall with gusto the legend of the return of Oba, the greatest witchdoctor in the twelve villages and beyond. They say that he walked abroad on the night of *Alusi Onwu* several generations ago, to exact a terrible vengeance on the people that had betrayed him and stolen his *Obi*.

They recount the incredible story of the birth of twin boys by a young woman named Nnenna, the young bride of the mute, Obinna, son of the great witchdoctor, Oba. The tragic mother had died giving birth to the twins, leaving the aged great-grandmother, Nnedi, to raise them. They say Nnedi defied death for several years till the boys reached the age of Masquerade initiation. No person in living memory had lived as long as Nnedi did.

The strange peculiarities surrounding the twin boys were another source of great discuss amongst the villagers. They say that one of the twins, the one with a missing right ear, was born mute. Despite his impediment, he could make the most powerful charms, charms of such potency as have never been known in the twelve village and beyond. He healed the sick with his charms and some even say he had the power to bring back the dead had he so wished. Such was the strength of his charms.

The other twin, the speaking one, had the gift of the second sight. He foretold the coming of the great drought and the plague of the locusts. He was also a drawer and a sculptor, creating such works of art that astounded even the white men.

They say the white rulers collected most of his charcoal artwork and took them back to their lands. Yet, the one piece of art he refused to give to the white men, the one that is hidden in the secret shrine of *Alusi Onwu* till the present time, is the haunting drawing of the chained skeletons, straining against their thick rusty chains underneath a vast river, the colour of a stormy cloud.

*****

Lightning Source UK Ltd.
Milton Keynes UK
UKHW021027280919
350638UK00013B/262/P